Friends of the Family

FRIENDS OF THE FAMILY

A NOVEL BY

Lynn Freed

STORY LINE PRESS
ASHLAND, OREGON

This novel is a work of fiction. Names, characters, places and incidents are either the product of the author's imagination or are used fictitiously. Any resemblance to actual events or locales or persons, living or dead, is entirely coincidental.

First published by The New American Library, Inc.
Paperback reprint 2000

Published by Story Line Press
Three Oaks Farm
PO Box 1240
Ashland, OR 97520-0055
www.storylinepress.com

Cover Painting, "Garden Scene, 1919" by Thomas Hart Benton
Book Design by Lysa McDowell

Library of Congress Cataloging-in-Publication Data

Freed, Lynn.
[Heart change]
Friends of the family : a novel / by Lynn Freed.
p.cm.
Previously published as: Heart change.
ISBN 1-885266-95-2 (pbk. : alk. paper)
1. Women physicians—Fiction. 2. Mothers and daughters—Fiction. 3. San Francisco (Calif.)—Fiction. 4. Music teachers—Fiction. I. Title.

PR9369.3.F68 H43 2000
823'.914—dc21 00-061219

To Anne and Jessica

1

The year had moved so quickly since the last school picnic that Marion, standing still for a moment in the fall sun, had to close her eyes against the spin. She was thirty-six. This past year had constituted one thirty-sixth of her life; the previous year, one thirty-fifth. The years ahead would be even smaller until, at the end, like planets spinning out of sight, they would vanish exponentially. It was odd. The days still equaled days and the weeks, weeks. They measured up equally against each other and against the days and weeks of her past. August was still August and May, May. In fact, Monday to Friday now seemed to pass more slowly than when she, like Sarah, had been a girl at school. But it was the years that had changed their currency, seemed cheaper and quicker and worth less. Marion tossed her head and opened her eyes. She disliked self-pity even in its subtlest disguise. She prided herself on her common sense and on the fact that she, unlike other women she knew, got on with things, coped, resisted nostalgia. She wrapped up the sandwiches and then went down to the basement for a bottle of good red wine and the picnic basket.

The Roths had lived for eleven years, in a large square house on a good street ten minutes from work and twenty minutes from school. Marion liked neat solutions. Even the house seemed tailored to their needs. She and Jonathan each had a study and Sarah used the small breakfast room, which must have been tacked onto the house thirty years before, for practicing. Sarah had played the cello for six years, since she was eight, and was considered competent by Sumiko Nishimoto, her teacher. But Sarah, despite Sumiko's scrupulous assessment, was privately determined to become a cellist of renown and closed herself and her cello into the breakfast room for longer and longer periods each day. On a Sunday, like today, she would begin practicing after breakfast and continue all day, stopping only for lunch.

Marion heard the dull tremor of Sarah's scales as she ran up the stairs from the basement with the basket and the wine. She stopped at the door of the breakfast room. They were late for the picnic again this year. Last year they had arrived so conspicuously late that she'd felt, almost tangibly, the animosity of the half-drunk, half-blond mothers towards *her*, the professional, a woman who always had an excuse. They had been discussing horses and riding schools when she edged her way into the circle with a fresh glass of wine.

"Does Sarah ride?" asked Kathy Mason, mother of Mallory. Sarah hated.Mallory.

"No, oh no," replied Marion with a false laugh. "She can barely ride a bicycle. Sarah plays the cello, you know." And immediately she regretted saying it, regretted the false laugh, the apologetic shrinking of her shoulders, the gulp of wine she took afterwards. They all turned, smiled, and then went on about horses. She moved away to find Jonathan. When she saw him sitting alone with the Sunday *Times* under a tree, she stalked up and hissed, "Next year we'll be here on time."

"What? Oh, why?" he asked, keeping a finger on his place.

"Because I can't stand horses or horsey people," she said and spun around to go for more wine.

And now here they were again, one year later. Jonathan was still out jogging, Sarah sawing through her endless scales, and she, Marion, must bear the brunt of their indifference. Holding the basket, she stood outside the breakfast room door and stared through the glass and the diaphanous curtain on the other side at the solid image of Sarah, knees planted apart, head swaying heavily through the last of her exercises. Marion put her hand on the door handle but stopped before she turned it, fighting down a nameless irritation which seemed lately to be visiting her more and more often. She had to fight it down because to give it vent was to open herself to the forces of mad irrationality. It was, she thought, and then unthought immediately, almost a revulsion for her own kind.

The music stopped and she heard Sarah laying the instrument carefully in its case, then the bow. Snap, the case was shut. Quickly Marion turned the handle and opened the door to face her, almost startling the girl.

"What is it, Mother?" she asked, standing up, incurious, with her arms hanging awkwardly at her sides, blinking through her spectacles. Marion stared at her daughter, whose resistance seemed to her, just then, invincible. Her formality and politeness allowed Marion no approach. Ever since she had been a child, Sarah had retreated at the slightest indication of hostility and aggression. Like Jonathan, she had no confidence in catharsis, in "emotional displays," as he put it. And then, after she began the cello with Sumiko, she had gradually adopted Sumiko's formal silences, her matter-of-fact statements of the truth. It's a powerful shield, thought Marion, a little envious.

"Aren't you going to change?" she asked.

"No, why?" replied Sarah, still staring.

"I think a long skirt is inappropriate for a picnic, don't you?"

"No, I like it."

Marion looked at her daughter and softened. How absurd, she thought, to caution this child on style. Her defiance of appropriate dress was part of her shield and who was she to remove such fragile defenses? Marion took her all in. Sarah, at fourteen, was a head taller than she and twenty pounds heavier. She could have been a Rubens model, carrying most of her weight as she did between shoulders and thighs in a full-breasted, high-wasted, unfashionable body. But the luxurious sensuality of her breasts and hips tapered off almost comically into long and willowy legs and arms. They could be the legs of a model, thought Marion, imagining the shapely thighs and calves under the long muslin skirt. Sarah herself found the fullness of her woman's figure and the expanse of her legs and arms a mortification. She always kept her legs slightly apart and parallel when standing or sitting, giving the impression that she was about to speak, or leave, or do something. Her hands were comfortable only when she played the cello. The rest of the time she either swung them self-consciously or clasped some object between them—a spoon or a hairbrush—and stroked or tortured it until Marion exploded.

Right now Sarah fiddled with a wisp of hair which had escaped her bun. She wore her hair swept back self-consciously, like a ballerina, emphasizing her small head.

"Sarah, won't you have your hair cut? You'd look so lovely in a softer style."

For a moment Sarah's eyes sparked. "I like it like this," she said.

They stood there for a few seconds, embarrassed. Then they both heard Jonathan's key in the front door, and Marion remembered the origin of her irritation.

"We are late for the picnic again this year. Do you realize it's almost one o'clock?"

Sarah edged past her in silence towards the hall.

"Hi, Daddy," she said.

"If you don't want to go, that's just fine with me," Marion went on, "but I hate being late."

She heard the door slam and imagined Jonathan's shrug of resignation in response to the woman-gone-wild. She heard him flop onto the rug, filling the hall with the smell of his sweat and the rhythms of his panting. He lay down and stretched himself out, staring at the ceiling, exhilarated as always by the pain of overexercise.

"Wowee!" she heard, and then, "Owie kazowie!"

Marion stepped into the hall, swallowing her habitual complaint that he was sweating-up the rug. She hated the smell of his sweat on that rug or even in the laundry basket, but he refused to take her complaints seriously. In fact, he seemed to find her distaste provocative, for he very often came after her in his running togs, inviting her into his shower by way of compensation. Today, clearly, that was not possible, so he stretched out his arms to her and said, "Give me two minutes to rest and I'll go shower. We'll be there before dessert this year, I promise."

Marion clung onto the basket and sidestepped him, keeping her ankles out of reach. She went into the kitchen and packed the basket, listening as Jonathan finally picked himself up and went to shower. She heard the water rushing against the glass doors; she heard him drop the soap and curse. She heard Sarah close her bedroom door, heard her open and close closets and drawers, heard her humming a few phrases of her Bach suite over and over. She heard the Sunday traffic and the neighborhood children outside. Marion stood in the kitchen listening to her house, her street, her world. It is not, she thought, a symphony.

They arrived at the picnic, held annually on the school's hockey field, just as coffee was being served from a huge portable urn.

"Marion Roth!" called a woman in a high peep from about twenty yards away. And over she came towards them, trying to keep her heels from sinking into the turf. She was dressed for a matinee or a luncheon in skirt and blouse and stockings.

"I thought this was a picnic?" asked Jonathan, suddenly insecure in the face of silk and tweed.

"It is!" said Marion. "Dede's the class rep this year and takes her role seriously. Anyway, I doubt that she owns a pair of pants."

"Marion!" Dede came up, out of breath. "We thought you were at the hospital or something. How *neat* that you could come!"

"We're always late, Dede. Actually I switched my schedule so that I wouldn't be on call today, but, you know, what with Jonathan's jogging and Sarah's practicing . . ." She tried to catch Jonathan's eye, but he was intent on adjusting his sunglasses to the correct angle.

"And *here* is Sarah!" said Dede, trying to catch the girl's hand. Sarah clung to the tablecloth she was carrying and twisted both hands into it. "How are you, my dear?"

"Oh, fine, thank you, Mrs. Benton."

"Well," said Dede, giggling, "there's still some vino in the old jug, so come on over." She started back and the Roths straggled behind. As they approached the group, everyone turned, some waving. They smiled back.

Marion chose a spot near a group of fathers and told Sarah to spread the cloth there. Then she opened her own bottle of good claret and poured two glasses, turning her face to the sun and smiling again.

It really was a lovely day, the time of the year Marion liked best. The sun was still warm, but the grass was cool, the shade cold. She laid out the sandwiches, the cheese, the antipasto, and the glasses of wine and sat back, relaxing for the first time that day. Something in the season, in the smells of grass and sun and wine, relaxed her. Perhaps it was the ripeness of the year, discernible even in the middle of the city in places like this where the earth was open to the sky for a few acres. She felt part of the fullness, part of the slanting of the earth away from the sun.

As the wine reached her elbows and knees, Marion looked around her. She saw Sarah standing amongst a group of teachers and girls smiling and nodding. Jonathan had settled himself in the shade next to the fence. She saw a group of mothers swaying and laughing, tall and thin. And she felt suddenly benign towards them all, even the women as they stood discussing ballroom-dancing classes and the junior prom. Marion wondered how they could ever have depressed her. Really, she wondered, what are they, what were they ever to me, that they had the power to spoil my day?

Marion closed her eyes and lay back on the grass with her hands under her head. The sun and the wine had set her cheeks on fire and warmed her breasts. She could almost feel the glow through her skin and into her bones when suddenly she was lying in shadow. Looking up, she saw Sarah standing in front of the sun, hovering really, grasping her skirt on either side. And there was someone behind her in the sun's shadow—a man.

"Mother," Sarah said in a low voice. "Mother, this is Mr. López."

"How do you do, Dr. Roth?" said the young man, bowing slightly. "I have been wanting to meet you."

Marion tried to scramble to her feet, but her legs buckled under her and her head spun from the wine and the sun.

"Good Lord!" she muttered.

"Here, let me help you." He deftly hoisted her up, releasing her as soon as she was steady.

"Well," said Marion, ignoring Sarah's warning, pleading stare and intoxicated still by her own sense of well-being, "well, Mr. López, thank you! You saved me from an ignominious fall from power."

López laughed and when he did, she saw with wonder the sweetness of his smile. He was, in fact, beautiful. Everything in his face and body was in perfect balance. He was small, about her own size, and, she guessed, about ten years younger. There was a grace about him that suggested a dancer or, because of his size, a gymnast. But he was too little conscious of his body to be a gymnast. He presented himself casually. It was almost as if he'd never taken account of his smooth caramel skin, his jet-black hair, his onyx eyes, and full, sensual mouth. Sarah had never mentioned his beauty. Marion wondered whether he was gay.

"Ah, Mr. López," she said, "Sarah has mentioned you so often. What a pleasure it has been for her to have a teacher of your caliber."

López bowed again and smiled, looking her directly in the eye.

No, she decided, he's not gay.

"Would you like a glass of wine? It's not the house vintage."

"I would love one, thank you." He settled himself casually beside the table cloth. Sarah shifted from foot to foot.

"Sarah, would you like some juice? A sandwich? I'm sorry, darling, but if these noble ladies saw me offering you wine it would be all over."

"Oh, Mother! You know I hate wine."

"Well, then, Sarah," said López, holding his glass up to the sun, "you have a treat in store for you when you grow up."

Sarah still stood above them, staring through the extended wine glass. She seemed to sway slightly, as if under its spell.

"I'll go get Daddy." She spun around and strode off across the field.

"He's under that tree over there, with the paper," Marion shouted. "My husband," she said, turning to López, "would read the *Times* while Rome burned."

"Well, Sarah must look like your Nero," he said, smiling still, "because I see none of you in her."

Marion was succumbing to the effects of her second glass of wine and to this young man's smile, so full of charm and sweetness that it made her giddy.

"Sarah looks like him," she said. "And, in many ways, I guess, she is like him."

"She is a very ambitious student. Is your husband ambitious too?"

"Ah, yes. They are both ambitious. Ambition, you know, is the stuff of power."

López sat up and looked at Marion with frank interest. "You speak often of power," he said. "That is the second time you have mentioned the word in five minutes. What do you mean by it?"

Marion smiled. "I mean success," she said. "Power is control. It is independence. It is owing nothing to anyone."

López looked down into his wine. He twirled the stem this way, that way, so that the inside of the glass was coated with a fine purple film. Looking down into the vortex of the glass, he seemed to be struggling for words. Marion saw him struggle and wanted to help him as she would a patient or a child, but she was not practiced in phrases. She could not lay them on as one would a salve or a liniment.

Finally, he smiled. "We have very different views on power," he said, preparing to leave.

"Why?" asked Marion quickly. "What do you mean by power?"

His eyes flew around her face, her mouth, the angle of her chin, with the uncertainty of a foot testing a stone in the river. Then he clasped one knee in both hands and stared at her soberly over the top of it.

"I mean the power of a poem," he said. "Or a symphony. Even a blade of grass." He picked one blade from the ground and chewed on the sweet base of it, looking at her as he curled his lips back into another smile. "And you—you are powerful. You have the power of a beautiful woman. That, you know, is more potent for me than any amount of money."

The flattery worked on Marion like the pull of a long-forgotten muscle. She felt the thud and twinge in her groin, the heat, the rush of blood, as would a dancer long returned upon dancing again. No, she thought, he doesn't need my help in finding words. She pulled up a blade too and nibbled at it in response, smiling back at him, wishing for God knows what. Then she blushed and looked away.

Jonathan and Sarah were strolling across the field towards them. López had seen them too and was standing up to greet them, but he stopped on his haunches, balancing himself with the tips of all ten fingers.

"To my way of thinking, Dr. Roth, control and success can keep the soul in poverty, and that poverty is not powerful. Really, we do talk of different powers."

Marion didn't get up when Jonathan and Sarah arrived. She lay back and observed the trio, especially the sweet young Latin. Sarah and Jonathan towered above him. Jonathan was asking about financing for the arts, José's musical background, Stradivarius cellos, while Sarah folded and unfolded her arms, never saying a word. In contrast to the loose angles of their bodies, their disproportion and untidiness, López was shaped like a god. He stood and smiled and spoke with the bearing of a natural superior, such that even Jonathan seemed to defer to him, did not interrupt as he usually did. And yet, Marion, lying there, the pulse still beating in her groin, felt wiser than he, omnipotent in her worldliness. Somehow, she felt herself in command. Her thoughts wandered to the clinic and her office, to her manageable life. This is power, she thought, the power to control one's own life, the power to remain oneself, unaltered by grass and symphonies and other people's beauty. His argument is really special pleading, she thought. In his position, as music teacher in this place, I'd also make a case for poetry and blades of grass, God knows. But he can't change the way things are. Feeling is cheap in this world. That's not where the power lies.

Marion stretched out on her back and stared up at the sky. It was a dark, bright blue and almost cloudless. A few gulls, attracted by the barbecue smoke, swooped in from the bay and glided high above. Marion imagined a camera suspended up there panning the whole field of picnickers and then, on noticing her, zooming in for a closer look. She wanted to see herself as a stranger on the screen, both actress and audience. She closed her eyes. Patterns of red and yellow remained on her eyelids until she saw a strange figure emerge amongst them. It was a woman walking along a beach at the water's edge. She seemed not really to be walking, but to be levitating just above the ground, moving effortlessly like a silent hovercraft amidst the dunes and scrub. As she moved she kept angling towards the water and looking down as if to catch her own reflection. The sea churned and boiled, but she could snatch glimpses of herself between the waves. She smiled and her reflection smiled back. The mirrored face filled the screen. It was marvelous, full of wisdom, full of possibilities. As it smiled out of the waves at the figure on the land, it seemed to ebb and flow with the swell of the sea from youth to old age and back again. And yet, somehow, it was youthful in its old age and antique in its youthfulness.

Marion wanted to call out from the audience, "That is me! That is my face!" But her mouth wouldn't move, her voice dried up in her throat. As the camera retreated, she saw the figure bend closer to the water until she could breathe the mist above the waves. Marion could taste the salt on her own lips and she opened her eyes.

"It's not really my field you know," Jonathan was saying with a laugh. "But Marion here handles that sort of thing at the clinic."

They all turned to look at Marion who was just then returning to her own body. She focused slowly on them.

"Have a good nap?" asked Jonathan.

"Mmm."

"Well, José here— I may call you José, may I not?" he asked, turning to López. López smiled in acquiescence. "He has cello elbow or violin shoulder or something and I suggested he get the whole thing taken care of at the clinic." Jonathan turned back to López. "They cover all the bases you know—X rays, physiotherapy, the works—and they won't fleece you in the process."

"That's very kind of you," said López, bowing again. "Where is your clinic, Dr. Roth?"

"Oh, call her Marion," said Jonathan in a jolly voice. "I'm sure she'd prefer that, wouldn't you, honey?"

"Absolutely," said Marion. "Do you have a clinic card on you, Jon?"

Jonathan nodded and wriggled his wallet out of his jeans.

"We're open after eight A.M., Monday to Saturday," said Marion. "Call any time."

"Good, thank you. I'll call for an appointment on Monday. Do I ask for you?"

"Well, two of us do general medicine. You'd see one of us first and then, if necessary go through the others." She looked at him and added, "I work mornings till two and Fridays all day."

"Fridays are best for me, as a matter of fact, because I'm free after eleven. Your hours, however, sound better than mine."

"Oh, she has the good life," Jonathan said, stretching and grunting approvingly. "Practices her craft in the mornings and has four afternoons free to sail, swim, crochet, cook, what-have-you."

Marion began to pack up the picnic. "You've forgotten my night and weekend call, and I've never crocheted in my life. As for sailing and swimming, I can't remember the last time I took the boat out. I don't even know if I'd remember how, on my own."

"I have never been sailing," José said quickly. "It seems so unrelaxing."

"Oh, no, no, no!" shouted Jonathan, wild to have found a neophyte. "It is a wonderful contest—man and nature, man and the sea. Ever read Hemingway?"

"Yes," replied López. "But I don't like him. I prefer Conrad. Conrad's descriptions of the ocean are not at all relaxing."

"Well, I wouldn't know about Conrad," said Jonathan, "but all I can say is that sailing gives a man a sense of power—a sort of control."

Marion and José stared at each other. She felt unclothed, like some savage viewed for the first time by Puritans wearing cloth and leather. She was ashamed. She did not want Jonathan aligning himself with her so unintentionally. He sounded wrong. It sounded wrong.

"Perhaps what you mean," she said, turning to Jonathan, "is that sailing makes one feel alone *with* nature—the sea, the wind, and so forth."

"No, that is *not* what I meant. I mean that it makes one feel in control—or out of control for that matter. It is a contest for power."

"Well," said José, "I must go. I shall call the clinic on Monday Dr.—Marion. And it was a pleasure to meet Sarah's parents. Goodbye, Sarah, see you at rehearsal tomorrow."

Sarah flushed and took a few steps backwards. "Yes. Goodbye, Mr. López."

"Well," said Jonathan, sitting down, "he seems like a nice guy. Bit delicate, but at least he doesn't seem to be a fag."

"Oh, Daddy! I wish you wouldn't talk like that!"

Marion noticed her daughter's quivering lip and scarlet cheeks and wished, as she had so often wished before, that Sarah had a good friend to talk to. She could not understand the girl's solitary proclivities. Sarah had never had a special friend and seemed not to want one. And there seemed to be no hope of any intimacy between them, between mother and daughter. Sarah resisted even the most tentative of Marion's overtures. So what was the point of trying?

Marion looked around at the other girls on the field. They stood bunched in groups, awkwardly adolescent.

"Sarah, wouldn't you like to ask one of those girls over to the house today?"

"No."

"Who's that girl over there? The one talking to Muffy Larson?"

"She's the new girl. She's in the orchestra."

"What about her?"

"No!"

Marion gave up. She struggled to her feet, slapped the grass off her jeans, and looked around.

"Come, Sarah," she said. "Let's walk to the others over there. I need to say my piece and then we can go."

"Do I have to?"

Marion took Sarah's elbow in reply and they walked across the field together, a strange and mismatched pair. Marion, with spine straight and hips swinging slightly, chatted uneasily at Sarah, who strained under her grip and said not a word in reply. As they approached the main group of parents, Marion saw José on the edge, looking at her. He stood back and listened with interest as she penetrated the crowd and spoke with this one and that one in loud, forced platitudes. His observation disconcerted her. Every time she looked up, he was just where he had been, listening intently. And then she was irritated with herself for her awkwardness. What did it matter to her what this music teacher thought of her smooth social clichés? Why should she be embarrassed to be classed with these women? She tried to interject a note of iconoclasm into her patter, but it came out three-legged and hopeless. She knew she must sound drunk, although in fact, she was by now completely sober. The crowd was beginning to loosen and dissolve around her. But Marion persisted in a satire of the P.E. teacher for Sandy Van Wick, even though she could hear Sandy's weak laugh and feel her pulling away with the others. And then, suddenly, she was left alone in the middle of a sentence with Sarah silent at her side as the other parents moved off in groups, laughing and talking. Marion turned quickly to leave. José must have left already. She scanned the field to its edges.

"I'm here, behind you. See you Friday." Marion turned. There he was lacing up his shoe and smiling at her from below, his eyes soft and very black in the fading sunlight. Marion's own eyes flashed in anger even as she bared her teeth in a smile and said good-bye. She had always responded this way to being caught out. She hated, as much as any man did, the exposure of her soft and naked throat.

When they were all in the car, Marion's irritation was stronger than it had been that morning.

"Never again!" she snapped for the fourth time. "I will not go through that again. Next year you two can go without me."

"Oh, come on, now," said Jonathan, laying a hand on her thigh.

"It wasn't all that bad. Dede and company left you alone, and you seemed to be having quite a conversation with that López guy."

Marion shrugged. "There's something sneaky about him," she said. "Ugh."

"That's not true!" Sarah shrieked from behind. "Why do you have to say those things about people, Mother? Why can't you keep your opinions to yourself?"

"Good Lord!" said Marion, turning around. "The first words you say to me all day and you sound like a shrew."

"You're the shrew! You're the shrew!" screamed Sarah, bursting into wild sobs.

"Look what you've done now," Jonathan said, as he pulled into the garage and turned off the motor. Sarah jumped out of the car and clattered up the stairs. Marion continued to sit where she was while Jonathan took the picnic things out of the trunk. After a while he came around to her window and looked in. "Coming up?" he asked. "Or should I bring dinner down to you?"

Marion ignored him and unbuckled her seat belt but remained where she was, staring straight ahead. She heard Jonathan close the garage and go upstairs, calling for Sarah in singsong, childish tones. The chilly basement gloom seemed to close in around her as if to shut her off, shut her into her own sensations. She shivered. Jonathan and Sarah were two floors above, and most of the children on the street were having dinner. She was quite alone. She heard the random ticking of the car as it cooled off, and she wrapped her arms around her shivering body. She felt suddenly insufficient. There seemed to be no rhythm, no harmony, to her solitary world. The power which she had felt earlier in the full flush of the wine seemed like hubris now in the face of this strange discord in her heart. There seemed to be nothing to look forward to in her life, no upward spiral, no far-off goal. She hung her head and closed her eyes, trying again to conjure up the hovering figure on the beach. But she couldn't. All she saw now was black space with nothing in it. Then she thought of José López and his sweet smile, his words, the angle of his hips. Where was he in all this? What was it about him that had sparked her discontent?

2

Friday morning came like early spring. There had been no spaces since Sunday for Marion to feel the passing of the week. On Monday and Wednesday nights she had been called out three times each. And on Tuesday she had bought a new Volvo. Her old one had suddenly irritated her with its gasping and lurching and she had driven it directly to the dealer, wondering why she hadn't done so months ago. Then on Thursday she and Beth had taken the boat out for the first time since the spring and sailed it around Arcata. They had felt like girls again, at school, with Marion leading Beth away from her scholarly devotions. Last Sunday seemed like last year. And Marion had had no time or desire to bring it closer.

Marion parked the new car in her usual spot at the clinic, taking care to leave space on either side for her neighbors. She loved new things, particularly new machines and utensils. They promised a new start, another chance, something to change things for the better. A new electric kettle, a fine espresso machine, would give her pleasure for weeks. She felt luxurious in their efficiency and in the quality of their service. And there was something more, something about just having them, that made her feel happy, even complacent, like a hen on her eggs. But once the shine was dulled by use, or an element needed repair or replacement, then Marion relaxed and forgot about them. They became again kettles or coffeemakers. This car, however, would be new for months with its fresh red shine and its clean vinyl smell. Marion walked away from it and into the clinic feeling very fortunate.

She walked through the waiting room to her office, took off her sweater, put on her white coat, and then sat at her desk to examine her appointment list. Fridays were always chaotic, but it was the sort of chaos that Marion adored. She loved to wade through her long list of patients, dispatching them for this test and that test, taking histories, pitting herself against the mysteries of vague ailments and new syndromes. On Fridays Marion felt like a real doctor, making order out of chaos.

Marion took her appointment list with her while she went to the front office to get herself some coffee. She stood at the machine, stirring absentmindedly while she thought about her burgeoning group of women patients. Women sought Marion out. They passed her name around and she found a new one on her list almost every week. Jonathan was amused. As a gynecologist, he considered himself an expert on women's preferences and offered all sorts of dark theories on suppressed homosexuality, with Marion representing the strong mother, the older sister. Marion rolled her eyes. She couldn't stand Jonathan in this of all modes. He was obnoxiously self-assured in his role of woman-knower, with pelvis thrust forward, hands in his pockets jangling change. She thought of her mother who scorned such crass pronouncements and had always stiffened in the face of lay psychologizing. Dr. Gertrude Klauber, Psychoanalyst. *She* never made pronouncements on human behavior. And Marion had inherited her mother's distaste for posturing, her respect for the dull sheen of quality. Marion tossed her head, took a sip of coffee, and shook out her appointment list.

And there it was, nestled among the Goldbergs, Uptons, Harpers: "2 P.M.: Mr. J. López. (New patient)" Some coffee slopped out of her cup and onto the floor and she bent to wipe it up with a tissue, spilling more. She had forgotten him until now. She had overlooked his name twice when she scanned the list earlier. How, she wondered, how was it possible?

It is a question of tone, she thought when she was back in her office and behind her desk. It is a question of what tone to adopt with him. I am the doctor, he is the teacher of my child. I'm embarrassed to be doctor and not parent, to have him here in my other world. But she gave herself no comfort with this analysis and pushed away the list while she went through her mail. She had five minutes till her first appointment. She reached for her phone to buzz Ben McCarthy, her counterpart in the clinic.

But Ben was at her door just then, peeping in to see if she was busy.

"Hi! I won't disturb you if you're on the phone," he said.

"I was calling you. Come in."

Ben sat down quickly and put his coffee cup on her desk. He was a neat Boy Scout of a man, clean and trim, without any apparent vices. Marion smiled at him affectionately. These morning chats were sweet and brief and easily digested, like cookies with her coffee. Ben had been in love with her ever since she joined the clinic, and she found his devotion comforting. It was safe and distant and unspoken, with none of the lust and urgency that made office affairs disastrous. He had no idea, in fact, that she knew. They usually discussed their families.

"You never mentioned that picnic you were dreading," he said. "How was it?"

"Godawful."

Ben blushed. He was married to a minister's daughter and it always excited him to hear Marion blaspheme. "How so?"

"Oh, those horsey mamas and colorless children and—" Here Marion sighed extravagantly. "Oh, I don't know, Ben. I just don't fit in."

"That's because you're special," he said, smiling openly. "You're a free spirit, as they say. For heaven's sake, don't change that." He blushed again.

A nurse came to the door to announce her first patient and Ben stood up to leave. "Have a nice weekend," he said.

Marion grimaced. "For God's sake, Ben, won't you drop that phrase? It's a curse. Look what it brought me last weekend."

"Sorry, sorry, sorry." He laughed and closed the door.

Marion worked efficiently through her long list of patients, never forgetting to check her watch each time she saw a new one. She was running behind and skipped lunch to make up the difference. There were two more patients before 2 P.M., and she found herself looking in the mirror, looking at the list, and looking at the clock like a teenager waiting for the doorbell. She was angry with herself. It was absurd. And then the nurse came to the door and announced, "Mr. López."

Marion stood up and smiled. "José," she said. "Come in and sit down."

She could hear herself as Dr. Roth, not as the mother of Sarah. It sounded fine. She opened José's clinic form in front of her and sat down, flapping through the pages. When she looked up, he was sitting with his legs crossed, examining her certificates on the walls. She returned to the forms. "Be with you in a minute," she said and went on flapping through the pages. On the second page she saw "Marital Status: Divorced. Children: One son, 5 yrs."

Marion put the forms down and stared at José. He was intent on her residency certificate.

"You have a five-year-old, José?" she asked incredulously. "How old are you, for heaven's sake?"

José looked at her, surprised in his turn. "Oh, didn't I put it down? I'm twenty-nine, almost thirty."

"Oh, oh yes, I see." Marion blushed and laughed uneasily. "That was not a professional question. I was just surprised."

"Why?" he asked, smiling that sweet smile she remembered now from Sunday.

"I thought that you were about twenty-two. You certainly don't look over twenty-five. And then, you don't seem like a father."

"And do you seem like a mother?"

José crossed his arms and laughed. He seemed quite relaxed, quite self-assured, and either didn't notice her discomfort or had the politeness to pretend not to. Marion was grateful.

"I was married very young," he said. "To another student at the conservatoire. A singer. She lives in Paris now and Étienne lives with her parents. I only see him once a year, but he will soon be old enough to come to me for the summers. I go back to my family in Mexico City, you know, every summer."

Marion stared at him. She longed to ask him a dozen questions unrelated to his health. Who was his ex-wife? Was she as beautiful as he? Which conservatoire? What kind of a family did he come from? Rich? Middle-class?

Instead, she took a careful medical history and then asked for the symptoms of his complaint. As he told her of his shoulder and back pain, as he touched his shoulder and his back, she noticed his hands. They were liquid, supple, delicate. They made her want to touch them and turn them over. She realized suddenly that she would be examining him within minutes, doctor and patient. She buzzed for the nurse.

"Will you show Mr. López to the examining room, please? I'll be through in a few minutes."

When the door closed, Marion rested her forehead on the palms of her hands. She did not enjoy this tumult in her heart and stomach and she refused to give it legitimacy by a close examination. The afternoon sun was now turning her small office into a sauna and she jumped up quickly to open a window and let in the cool air. Papers blew about on her desk and her hair was lifted around her hot neck. I need a vacation, she thought. I need a change. She stood up, hung her stethoscope around her neck, and walked through to the examining room.

When she opened the door, she saw José draped in a white clinic gown, fiddling with the loudspeaker above the examining table. He was standing on the steel frame of the table, stretching up so that the gown fell away from his body and exposed his smooth muscular thigh. He didn't notice Marion standing at the door looking at him. Finally, he jumped back onto the table exasperated, muttering something in Spanish.

"What on earth are you doing?" Marion asked, laughing.

He looked up fiercely and growled towards the speaker which was now sputtering out a Mantovani version of "Deep Purple."

"That Muzak is sent from hell to torment me," he said, resting his chin on one knee and looking up at her. "It comes to me in my nightmares."

Marion laughed and leaned back against the door. "I don't even hear it. I suppose they play it to calm the patients."

"Calm! It makes me into a wild man."

Marion bent over and flipped a switch. The music stopped.

"See?" she said. "No need to have a tantrum."

José smiled and she smiled back.

"Now," she said, "let's have a look at you. Please sit up facing the window."

Marion stepped over to the table and gently parted the clinic gown over his shoulders. He looked down into his lap silently as she laid her hands on his neck. She could feel his muscles working under the smooth skin as she prodded and manipulated. The room was hot, as hot as her office, and his skin was slightly moist under her fingers. She moved her hands across his back in automatic, familiar patterns while she asked him questions in a voice that seemed to come from under the ocean.

She rested her hands on his shoulders for a moment, "Please lie down now."

He lay back and closed his eyes while she rolled the gown down to his waist. She looked at him waiting for him to open his eyes, but he kept them closed and lay there waiting. She noticed his hands stretching and relaxing and picked one up, turning the palm up towards her face. It was perfect, as he was perfect, without a crack or a callus. She wanted to kiss it, as if it would take life from her and give life back, but she just held it there, staring into the smooth flesh. She knew she should release his hand and get on with her job, but she couldn't even think of what it was she was supposed to be doing. At a great distance she heard footsteps and voices and children crying. But in this room there was just the heat and the silence that bound her. She looked down again at José and saw that he was looking at her.

"What future do you see for me?" he asked softly. Marion released his hand immediately, feeling the blood beating up into her temples. She quickly manipulated his arm and shoulder, asking where this hurt, how that felt. He didn't answer. Finally, she stepped back and wiped her hand across her forehead.

"God, it's hot in here," she said. She stumbled across the room to open the tiny window but, as she did so, she felt him grab her arm and return her to where she had stood. He swung his legs down and sat up on the table to face her. Marion swayed slightly on her feet. She tried to imagine how long they'd been there, what the time was, the day of the week, which year. There were no clues. All she knew for certain was that she could hear him breathing, could feel his grip around her wrist, and could not make a sound.

"You are beautiful," he said, never moving his eyes from hers. "Why do you not listen to your heart? I hear it knocking behind closed doors."

Marion stepped back and withdrew her hand. She grasped the lapel of her white coat and felt the plastic badge there. Perspiration ran in rivulets between her breasts, down and around the contours of her body. Her eyes focused on a shelf of bottles and syringes and then moved along the wall to the clock. It was 2:45. Sarah would be on her way home. They were all going to Beth's for dinner that night. Ben was next door talking in his low monotone. She had to wash her hair. And the car was outside. She could smell it, see the new keys, the leather and brass key ring. She had four more patients to see and, oh, God, her head was gliding. There was a knock at the door.

"Dr. Roth?"

"Yes." Marion opened the door. She heard José pull up his gown and stand up.

"Mrs. Blantyre is on the phone."

"Oh, yes. I'll be there in a minute." Marion turned to José. He was looking out of the window at the cement wall of the building next door.

"Take two aspirins four times a day for a week, and let me know how you are feeling next Friday. Bursitis sometimes just needs rest and can take weeks, or months, to heal. Is it a waste of time telling you not to use your right arm for a few weeks?"

"A complete waste," he answered, not turning around.

"Well, anyway, let me know. Forgive me," she said, flipping the Muzak switch back on. "The next patient may need calming."

Marion tossed her head and walked back to her office. She closed the door and sat down to talk to Mrs. Blantyre. Then she stretched out her arms and legs and arched her body up towards the ceiling, collapsing again into her chair. She felt incomplete, ashamed, inadequate, everything she despised in herself and others. He was gorgeous, yes, but she'd met many gorgeous men before without being reduced to this state. It was as if he saw in her what she didn't want to have anyone see, but then she couldn't imagine what it was that she was hiding. Her heart "knocking behind closed doors" for God's sake. What could he mean? There was definitely a sexual attraction there, of course. Marion knew the signs by now. And he clearly felt it too, although, she wondered, why her? He must have had dozens of women; younger, trendy women. Maybe he made a habit of hypnotizing women with his charm and then telling them to listen to their hearts. Good god, what an idiot she must have looked, staring into his palm. Marion blushed again. She would hand him over to Ben when he came back. There was no other way of dealing with this. It was absurd and inappropriate. If he weren't Sarah's teacher, it would be simpler, but she'd have to see him at every concert, at every school function. Marion would simply have to ignore what had happened today and hope that he would too. Next time she saw him, she'd discuss Sarah's training and progress. He would get the message. He was no fool.

When Marion got home that evening she was exhausted and cross. She even thought of sending Jonathan and Sarah to Beth's and staying home herself, but she knew that Jonathan would object loudly and refuse to go without her. And she hated to disappoint Beth. Beth and Jonathan worked together in the same OB-GYN group. It was Marion who changed the tone of these evenings they spent together from shop to fun. But she didn't feel much fun and she wasn't at all in the mood for Alex and his bearded psychiatric pronouncements. In fact, Marion was beginning to feel cramped by the medical confines of their world. She had always embraced the fraternity as a blessed alternative to the society of Mary Ellis Moore and the corporate structure. She had felt lucky, envied. But now she began to wonder, as she hooked on her earrings and fluffed out her hair, whether there wasn't a whole world left out. She didn't like José pointing out her heart and its knocking. She objected to his assumption that there was anything lacking in her life. If Marion was to be criticized, she wanted to choose the critic and the criticism. She had always, in fact, been criticized for her strengths, not for her deficits. And if her heart had been knocking, she had certainly never heard it.

But now, somehow, José's criticism tuned her into her own heart's echoes and dull thuds. It made her strengths seem weaker, cheaper by their irrelevance. She looked at herself in the mirror and wondered what would reaffirm her power.

Jonathan returned from his job exhilarated. He sang loudly in the shower while Marion was dressing and then loped through to the bedroom, trailing water behind him. He stood behind Marion, looking at her in the mirror, with his hands on her shoulders.

"You look gorgeous tonight."

"Thank you."

"What's the time?"

"There's no time," she said, getting up quickly and throwing things into her purse. Jonathan lay back on the bed groaning.

"For God's sake, you're wet! You're wetting the bed!" Marion shouted.

"I need a diaper," he said, raising his two hairy legs in the air and kicking.

Marion stood at the door and looked at him with disgust. She looked at his large, hairy torso, his soggy genitals flopping between his thighs like rotten fruit, his long bony legs, and she tried to remember what it was that she used to find exciting about this man. It was lost. Gone. Like rain in the desert. There were not even any twinges any more. Only a large reserve of irritation. But this kind of regressive horseplay was more than irritating. It made her stomach turn. She opened the door and called Sarah.

"Are you nearly ready?"

"I'll be ready in five or ten minutes."

"Well, hurry up. We're due there in five minutes."

"Why don't you go ahead then, and Daddy and I will follow?"

Marion stood at the top of the stairs for a moment, challenged.

"I think that's an excellent suggestion," she said and trotted down to her car.

When Marion arrived at Beth's, she flopped down in the kitchen while Beth, with methodical precision, washed and dried lettuce.

"Where are Jonathan and Sarah?"

"Coming. They're late, and I took Sarah's suggestion and came on ahead. That child is beginning to irritate me beyond words. Can I have a drink?"

"Of course. Help yourself."

Marion filled the ice bucket, dropped two cubes into a glass, cut herself a slice of lemon, and poured out some Campari. She felt at home in Beth's house, like a worldly cousin or older sister. It was Marion who had found the house for Beth and Alex, the decorator, the school for their retarded boy. She felt somehow responsible for Beth, as if she stood between Beth and the world. It always surprised her, gratified her in a way, when Jonathan told her of Beth's competence and popularity with her patients. Beth had a reticence, a sort of solid reserve, that seemed to work against popularity. And yet she, like Marion, had her name passed from friend to friend. Beth had to be coaxed to take an afternoon off these days despite the fact that she too worked part-time.

It was strange. In many ways Marion felt much further removed from Sarah than she did from Beth—Beth who was as different from Marion as a friend could be. Sweet Beth. Sensible Beth. Their friendship had always been an anomaly—Marion, the social chameleon with a genius for the give and take of intimacy, knowing, as if by instinct, which side to show to whom; and Beth, unchanging, herself in all company, ignored behind the bright beams of Marion's social graces.

But it was Beth, in fact, who had led Marion towards medicine. Beth had made her choice in grade school. She had always known she wanted to be a doctor, even when they had played doctor and patient together with Marion's nurse kit. Everyone knew. It had become a commonplace.

It was Marion who couldn't choose. She had planned a succession of wonderful futures for herself as an actress or a pianist, and then as a lawyer, an anthropologist, or a scientist. But she liked to keep things open. She could never eliminate a possibility without sensing the limitation of her own power to choose. And she couldn't find in herself that purity of enthusiasm for some one thing, that self-fueling flame, that had seemed to fire the heroines of the past.

People had always expected success from Marion Klauber. Just success. Unspecified. And Marion was indeed a winner of prizes, a high scorer in a world of tests and measures. She understood that she had not the independence of spirit to turn away from received success, to spin her own webs of wonder. She needed an established standard within which to excel. She also required that her standard be higher and more special than the general. Marion had carefully excluded herself from the assumptions that other women made about their futures. She scorned the traditional female fields of teaching and social work. But somehow she had always counted on someone to point out an established path for her to follow. That someone, in the end, had turned out to be Beth.

Marion watched Beth as she moved across her kitchen, opening and shutting, stirring, wiping, washing each knife or bowl as soon as she had used it. No wonder she was such a hopeless cook. She followed the rules too precisely. She wasn't much of a surgeon either, according to Jonathan. But she was an excellent diagnostician. He himself compensated for his mediocre diagnostic skills with his fine talent for surgery. And Beth, who as a student had assisted him whenever she could, whenever he invited her, was reverential in her praise. They worked well together, Beth and Jonathan. Their talents were exactly complementary.

Beth stopped in front of Marion, wiping her hands on her apron. Her body had thickened over the last five years into a solid rectangle, and her face was fuller, flabbier than before, strangely nondescript. It was a face which, despite the years Marion had known it, could not be conjured into memory at will. Perhaps this was because Beth's obvious features were not tangible. Her intelligence and kindness and modesty showed up more in her expression, in the sweet warmth of her small blue eyes, than in the distribution of skin and bone.

"Why is Sarah irritating you?" Beth asked. Marion seldom complained about Sarah to Beth, in deference to Beth's own much greater problems with Alfred.

"Oh, hell, Beth, she's so damned solid, sort of secretive. She's like Bigfoot mooching through the house guarding her secrets. She hasn't got a single friend. She doesn't talk on the phone like any normal teenager. All she lives for is that damned cello and I haven't got the heart to tell her she's never going to make it."

"But, Marion, she's always been like that. She's different. You've got a nerve to complain about that. Imagine having a teenybopper?"

"It sounds fine right now," said Marion, finishing her Campari and pouring another one. She reached into the cupboard and pulled out some Ritz crackers while she talked.

"And," Beth added, "it's not your place to tell her she's never going to make anything."

Marion stared into the cracker box while she fished out the last broken pieces. "It's not just that though. You're right, she has always been different. But lately she's become sort of touchy, almost hysterical. Anything I say sets her off. I mean, I criticized the music teacher at school the other day, called him sneaky or something, and she burst into tears."

"Maybe she's got a crush on him."

"Don't be nuts. How can you imagine that? She's never looked at a male. The sight of Jonathan's jockey shorts makes her blush."

"Well, she may be starting now."

"No, that's not it," said Marion, wishing she hadn't started this conversation. "It's got something to do with me. She's too controlled with me in some ways, with her tight little bitchy suggestions. And then, over nothing at all, she gets hysterical."

"It still sounds like a variation on normal teenage behavior to me. Do you want to speak to Alex before they arrive? He's in his study."

"No, no. He'll give me all that mother-daughter shit. No, thanks. I love Alex dearly, but he should stick to his anal-retentives. Do you remember when he had me making mudpies with Sarah? Jesus!"

"OK. But have you discussed this with Jonathan?" Beth had stopped her preparations and was sitting opposite Marion at the counter.

"Jonathan! You've got to be joking! He is the classic avoider and denier. First, he'll avoid all discussion on an unpleasant topic. Then he'll deny there's anything wrong. Oh, and then he'll blame me if it's unavoidable and undeniable."

Beth laughed. She loved Marion, and she envied her her energy, her anger, her misanthropic self-interest.

"Well," she said, "perhaps you should talk to her then. You never know."

"Ha!" said Marion. "You don't know what it's like to be the only compulsive articulator in a family like mine."

"I can't imagine two like you in one family anyway."

The doorbell rang and Marion heard Beth greet Jonathan. She heard Jonathan kiss Beth and recommend the wine he'd brought, delivering a short homily on the vineyard and the vintage. Marion couldn't imagine how Beth stood his patronization here or at the office. But she seemed unaffected by it, and so did Alex. They both accepted comments and advice gratefully, as though they were ingenues to the good life. Perhaps the fact that Alfred was so badly retarded made them pull together; perhaps he didn't stress their marriage as a normal child would. Marion watched Sarah come into the kitchen to greet Beth. Sarah liked Beth. They seemed comfortable with each other's silences.

"How are you, my dear?" Beth asked.

"Fine, thanks." Sarah smiled and began shaking salt out of a salt shaker into her hand.

"You look fine. And what a lovely skirt," said Beth.

"Mother hates it."

"I do not hate it. I just think it's inappropriate for school picnics."

"Well," said Beth, "let's see. Will you take this and this to the table, Sarah? Come, let's all sit down."

The dinner was dull. Marion felt dull and had no desire to liven everyone else up. Jonathan kidded Alex as usual about nuts and loonies, and Beth spoke to Sarah, who said very little in reply. Marion watched the two of them. Beth was talking about her schooldays, her mother, her dog. It was all very dull. But Sarah seemed to love it. She had a sweet, satisfied smile on her face as Beth described, for at least the fourth time that Marion could remember, the day her dog chewed through the living room rug.

Marion drank two glasses of Jonathan's claret and then allowed herself at last to go over the day's events. José came immediately into clear focus against the backdrop of Beth's murmuring and the clinking of the dishes. She saw him on the examining table looking up at her. She saw his shoulders, and his thighs under the clinic gown. And then she heard his voice and the softly rounded syllables when he called her beautiful. How could I have doubted him? she wondered. I should have bent down and kissed him right there. Why did I give that chance up? For this? In a state of exquisite regret, Marion looked up at Jonathan and he caught her eye.

"Are you OK, honey?" he asked. "You're flushed."

"Oh, I'm fine, thanks," Marion mumbled.

"Isn't she gorgeous since she cut her hair?" Jonathan asked the assembled company. He looked around for congratulations. Alex and Beth agreed loudly. Sarah looked down into her empty plate.

"Oh, for God's sake!" said Marion with such venom that even Jonathan tightened. He looked at her and then at Beth.

"Fridays!" he said quickly. "She plays doctor and finds out what it's like in the real world."

"Oh, come on, you two," said Beth. "Who's for a cordial?"

"No, no, no!" shouted Jonathan, swinging back in his chair. "Cognac after that meal. Courvoisier by preference."

"Will you do it then? Sarah and I will clear the table."

Sarah scraped her chair back and knocked it over with a crash.

"Jeezuss!" hissed Marion. "I can't take much more of this."

Quickly, Sarah replaced the chair and ran into the kitchen. Marion heard Beth's soft voice once or twice over Sarah's muffled sniffs. Alex led Jonathan into the living room where they spoke in low voices. Marion knew she was being discussed in both places. She even knew what they were saying. And she didn't care. All she wanted was to turn time back, to be back in the examining room with José, to tell him that he too was beautiful, to have the courage to face her own desires, to open her heart to him. She felt absurd and inappropriate and she really didn't care.

Marion slipped quietly out of the dining room and across the hall. She heard Alex intoning, between puffs on his pipe. "Stress" . . . "competitive stress" . . . "generational conflict." Jonathan was silent. He stole a few glances at the newspaper that lay on the couch next to him. Alex noticed her at the door and stopped his monologue.

"What's new in the news?" she asked Jonathan. He pushed the paper away quickly.

"Wowee, it's ten o'clock. I think you would benefit from a good night's sleep, my beauty," he said with a wink to Alex.

"Well, you may be right," said Marion, yawning without need. "I have my car here and I can just slip off without disturbing the rest of you." She walked over to Jonathan and kissed him lightly on the forehead. Then she kissed Alex.

"Thank you for dinner. I'm sorry I'm so bombed out."

"Oh, that's just fine. Get some sleep."

Marion walked through to the kitchen where Beth and Sarah were loading the dishwasher.

"Bethy, I'm going to slip out. I'm dead beat."

Beth shot a triumphant glance at Sarah. "Good! Unplug the phone. I don't expect to hear from you till noon. Can't we sail tomorrow afternoon instead?"

"Sure. OK, Sarah?"

"Oh, no—uh—I have rehearsal. It's OK, though. I didn't want to sail anyway."

"What time is your rehearsal?" Marion asked.

"Two."

"Well, we'll drop you on the way and pick you up at five. OK?"

"Thank you."

Marion leaned over and hugged Beth. "Thank you for a lovely dinner. Do you know what a gem you are?"

"Yes. Yes. Go home!"

Marion drove home through the cool night streets of the city thinking of tomorrow, two o'clock, five o'clock. The night air blew in around her hot head. She missed her turn-off and had to backtrack along one-way streets. The house loomed up out of the darkness. It looked enormous and unfamiliar, like some gothic fortress. Marion drove into the garage, closed the door, and ran up the stairs two at a time, as if she were pursued by muggers and rapists. She switched on every light she passed and checked the doors and windows. She threw off her clothes and washed quickly. The she swallowed a Valium and slipped under the covers. She wanted to be asleep by the time Jonathan came home.

3

Sarah was sitting on the short wall at the base of the school steps when Jonathan, Marion, Beth, and Alex drove in to pick her up. They were late, but Sarah never seemed to mind being kept waiting after rehearsals. She either sat alone or hung around in the music room, listening to José coaching the other students. She was considered a star in this orchestra, though she accepted the billing without any sense of real triumph. She wanted to deserve top billing on a broader canvas than was given by the Mary Ellis Moore school orchestra. But she was drawn out of herself by José, who consulted her as an equal on phrasing or interpretation and any number of orchestra matters. He even phoned her at home sometimes. She had begun to feel important to him.

The school garden was in full bloom. Red and orange geraniums blazed out of the flower beds in the setting sun. The walls were covered in pink bougainvillea and all the flowers—red and orange and pink—tossed and shook together in the sharp wind. The school seemed festive and inviting, a lovely place to spend a Saturday afternoon.

Marion envied Sarah this scene, especially when she remembered the cement and wire fencing of her own school in New York. But, of course, Sarah would know nothing of that. Even at fourteen, she seemed to know gratitude only in the abstract. It was natural for her to take the flowers and the sun for granted. And yet Marion couldn't help the twinges of resentment, irrational and without any foundation in her own childhood, that made her wish to see this child disconcerted. She wished someone would come along and tell Sarah that all the work in the world would not turn her into a Rostropovich. She just couldn't stand being party to the myth about Sarah's success.

And then Marion saw Sarah sitting there on the wall, happy, the sun dancing and glinting off the brasses on her cello case, and she was sorry. She suddenly wanted to take the girl in her arms and tell her she'd be in Carnegie Hall one day. She wanted to cry. She wanted to beg forgiveness for what she'd felt and never said.

Sarah stood up as they approached, and waved back towards the school door. Marion got out to let Sarah sit between Jonathan and her in the front seat and glanced as she did towards the school. José was standing on the other side of the glass door, talking casually to a few students. Marion hesitated.

"Well, come on, let's go!" said Jonathan. "It's five-thirty. Come on, Marion!"

"Oh, hang on a minute. Do you mind? I just have to give José a message about a change in his next appointment. It's easier than chasing him round on the phone. OK?"

"OK. But hurry."

Marion skipped up the stairs, tossing her hair back out of her eyes. She stepped quickly up to the door and pulled it open. There was no one there. She looked up and down the hall. No one. She hesitated again and then marched in the direction of the music room. She heard her footsteps echoing down the hall and smelled the familiar school cleaning fluid on vinyl flooring. Thank God I'm not fourteen, she thought, opening a few doors and looking in on the still life of deserted class rooms. The music room was empty. She stopped for a moment to look around, and then she heard a door open behind her.

"Dr. Roth?"

"José!"

"Uh—can I help you?"

"I was looking for you in the music room," she said, standing there like Sarah, not knowing what to do with her hands.

He looked tired, even irritated. And she felt like a schoolgirl with a bad grade asking for a favor.

"Please," she said in a high small voice. "Please forgive me for yesterday. It's just that I didn't know what to think."

"How can you 'know what to think'? You think what you think. That is all. It's fine. I made a mistake. It is I who should be sorry."

He didn't look sorry and Marion couldn't remember ever having felt so humiliated. Yet even in her humiliation she told herself that she had to say something. She had to have him back.

"José, I want to see you. I want to explain a few things to you, but not in the clinic. Don't you see that I'm a doctor there? It's inappropriate." Marion immediately bit her lip.

"Yes, you're right, it was as you say *inappropriate*. But, Dr. Roth, life is not always appropriate, or convenient, or discreet, or all the other bourgeois clichés that you pretend to despise. I saw you, I watched you at the picnic and again in your office, with fire in your heart for me. And I returned to you fire for fire. Yes, it is dangerous, it is inappropriate as you say, but it is the truth. You turn away from the truth. Well," he said, stepping back into the classroom, "we're both the losers, hey?"

The door closed on its spring and left Marion standing where she was, staring down the empty hall. She stepped up and pulled it open again. José was packing his things into a briefcase. He didn't look up.

"OK," she said, "I tend to play it safe. But I came in here, didn't I? I came to find you. I apologized. At least you could have the graciousness to accept."

"I did—I do—accept." He went on sorting music and notes. She stood still, fighting down her anger. Finally he looked up at her and smiled.

"You are spoiled. You are used to getting your own way. We have lots of girls like you here."

Marion opened her mouth to object, but José went on.

"No, no. I like it. I like to see fire, even if it's the anger in your eyes."

The car honked in the distance and suddenly Marion remembered the others. "I must go," she said. "They're waiting."

José came up to her and laid a hand on each shoulder, smiling at her like some mentor, some uncle. Marion stared back at him defiantly.

"Will you come to my place one afternoon this week, say Wednesday?"

Marion blushed, and blushed again, knowing that he saw.

"What time?" she asked.

"About three. I live in Sausalito. Here," he said, scribbling on the back of some staff paper. "Here's my address."

Marion folded the paper neatly corner to corner and slid it into her jeans pocket.

"Wednesday," she said, "at three." She took his hand and brushed her lips across his palm. Then she fled the room and the school and ran down the steps to the car.

"Where in hell have you been?" asked Jonathan.

"Oh, sorry! I couldn't find the damned classroom. And then I went into one and couldn't get out. What a maze that place is. It's unbelievably badly planned."

Marion babbled on as they rolled off down the driveway. José was right. She should act on impulse. She felt the wad of paper in her pocket and sat back like a sultan, smiling. Then she leaned over and tapped Sarah on the knee. Sarah stiffened and looked at her blankly.

"Mr. López thinks highly of you. I'm very pleased."

Sarah blushed.

"You know," said Marion, "we didn't phone Grandpa last night. We should phone as soon as we get home. He loves to hear your playing complimented. He also wants to hear a tape of the Bach."

"I know. But it's not ready."

"So what?" said Marion. "Settle down and do it tonight."

"I'm baby-sitting Alfred."

Beth leaned forward, over Marion's shoulder. "We're going to the psychiatric banquet. I told you."

"Oh, yes, yes. I forgot."

They dropped Alex and Beth and then drove home. The sun had already set and the house was cold. Marion darted upstairs and ran a hot bath for herself. While the water was running, she took out José's address and slipped it between the shelf lining and the shelf in her closet. She felt wonderful, decadent, triumphant, like some great heroine of nineteenth-century fiction. This assignation made everything seem brighter and more tolerable, even Jonathan. Marion eased herself into her steaming bath and rested her head against the cool porcelain tub. She watched the steam rise off the water and curl up to the ceiling. Her arms and feet floated up towards the surface of the water. She held up her fingers and toes, then her legs and arms for inspection. They were smooth and healthy, still brown from the summer. She stood up and balanced on the edge of the tub to see herself in the medicine cabinet mirror. Through the steam haze she saw the soft contours of her own body. She saw her breasts in profile, her ample hips, her small waist. Marion lifted her arms to make herself look thinner and twisted her body, throwing her head back. She didn't feel thirty-six. She felt ageless. She felt desired. She felt wild with desire herself. And yet there was an urgency, almost a threat, in what she felt that she'd never felt as a girl. She wanted to wait for nothing, for no one. Even Wednesday seemed dangerously far away.

Jonathan stood in the bathroom door as Marion stepped back down into the tub.

"Oh, hi! Please close the door, it's cold."

"What were you doing?" he asked, closing the door and locking it.

"Admiring myself."

"Boy, did you look sexy there!" Jonathan was climbing out of his clothes and preparing to get into the bath with her. He threw his things onto the floor, looking meaningfully at Marion as he did so. Marion watched his back as he stood at the toilet before getting in. She stared at his back, his blemishes, his black body hair, his pink buttocks, and she closed her eyes to wipe out the image. She tried to replace it with José's face and hands and black eyes. She lay back as Jonathan climbed in and began to fondle her breasts and imagined José with her in the ocean, on the grass. She could feel his hot breath, wet, near her ear, hear his voice. He was begging her to release him as he mounted her. He was panting, clutching at her like an animal in the water, in the dark. She raised her legs wide to receive him, to give him the release he begged for. And while she did, she released herself, her body arching and buckling under the power of its deliverance. Then she lay back and let the waves wash over her. Her head spun and dipped. Worlds passed by, planets with their moons. Marion was released from gravity, floating out into her own constellation. And yet she felt a weight on her chest, a rock of lead restraining her flight. She couldn't breathe. Her chest and throat were in a vise. Suddenly she opened her eyes in panic. Jonathan lay over her in the bathtub, sprawled end to end.

"Move!" she wheezed. "I can't breathe. Please!"

They had met in Marion's first week of medical school and she slept with him three nights later. For Marion it was a revelation.

It wasn't as if she was inexperienced. She had slept with a few of her college boyfriends before, without much anticipation or regret. But somehow sex had always seemed ridiculous to Marion. She found male passion a bore, quite distasteful, in fact, the distorted face above her own and all that animal thrusting. She had wondered what the fuss was about.

But Jonathan was different. He knew his subject. That first night he seduced her with consummate care. He talked and joked softly while he kissed and touched her, stroked her with patience and skill. And, for the first time in her life, Marion was carried beyond comment. She was silenced by the craving of her own body for release. She was beyond words, beyond self-consciousness, and she responded to him with the untutored passion that feeds male fantasy.

Marion lay back afterwards still unable to talk. She looked at him as he lit a cigarette, as he put on his robe and went to get some champagne, as he poured it into two glasses and brought one to her, kissing her gently before he gave it to her. For the first time in her life, she knew the intoxication of the mind by the body and she never wanted it to end. She drank the champagne in a few gulps and then sank back luxuriously into his down pillows.

"Why?" she asked. "Why me?"

"Because I've watched you. You're brilliant, you're witty, you're God damn gorgeous. I want you, Marion Klauber, and I'm used to getting what I want."

It was true. As the only Roth son, and the youngest of four children, Jonathan was indeed used to having his own way. He also had a sort of noisy charm that, combined with a clearheaded ambition and hard work, compensated for his lack of natural academic ability. He was not a prize winner. He lowered his goals, in fact, to his own level of comfortable academic mediocrity and looked at those who did achieve with frank admiration. Marion Klauber was one of them. She was irresistible. She had the self-possession and lightheartedness of a woman who needed no man to complete her life. He had known that he could have her if he worked it right. It had just been a question of how and how soon.

And it couldn't have been easier. Their affair settled into a cozy form of symbiosis. Jonathan was proud of her. He worshiped her, deferred to her superiority, molded himself to her moods and needs. His conquest of a superior woman, in fact, elevated his own self-esteem. He felt comfortable with strong women, released from the bondage of male dominance.

Marion herself played duchess, exerting, inclining, rewarding. She loved the freedom he gave her to control their liaison. She loved making love. And she loved, above all, the comfort and relaxation of a mate just sufficiently inferior to insure her perpetual supremacy.

Then, one day, Marion found out she was pregnant. And the compound began to curdle.

By Wednesday, Marion was in that strange half-world of fear and deceit that makes even the familiar exciting. She couldn't eat or sleep, and yet she was smiling, iridescent. She made a point of sweetening her time with Jonathan. She humored him, didn't complain about the football on Monday night. She offered to pick up some music and new strings downtown for Sarah. But she also forgot things. One day she forgot her briefcase and had to keep three patients waiting while she went home to get it. She forgot her Tuesday lunch date with Beth. And she forgot to pick up the music and strings for Sarah. My God, thought Marion, I am ridiculous. I never forget. But she enjoyed chastising herself. It served to remind her of herself, of the person she had been until just now.

Driving across the Golden Gate Bridge, Marion felt the strangeness of the gap between the legitimate and the illegitimate. Cars buzzed by her, station wagons with babies in car seats, Volkswagen bugs, teenagers' vans. Lovers hugged each other on the bridge walkway, bracing themselves against the wind. Tourists huddled at the lookout points. They were all—cars, vans, people—out in the open, free. She slowed down and tried to think through her discomfort. She thought of Jonathan. He didn't really matter to her. He hadn't mattered, she supposed, for years. He was husband to her wife, father, professional, jogger, man of action. She couldn't step back to put him into focus. She thought of Sarah. What did this afternoon have to do with her? She thought of Beth and of Ben and of all those people in her world who made tacit assumptions about her sexual fidelity. What concern of theirs were her deceptions? Why should she worry about them? Why did she envy those innocent lovers on the bridge?

As Marion took the Sausalito exit and wound down towards the bay, she realized what it was that she feared. It was the loss, the debris, the scatter of her once integrated life. It was the difference in her weeks and weekends, the Mary Ellis Moore gossip. Marion wanted to remain above the common censure. She wanted to be envied for the right reasons. If it were chic to have a lover, she wanted it suspected that she had one. But she didn't want to be ridiculous. And she feared that her alliance with José would be thought ridiculous. She must impress on him the need for discretion.

Marion had examined the map a dozen times and now drove up towards José's flat as if she had been there often. Up and around the hills she wove, feeling sick, hot, as little ready for passionate sex as she could imagine feeling. It was ten minutes to three. She had tried to be late but finally left in time to be early. She stopped the car and looked down at the bay. Sailboats cut back and forth at great speed. The wind was high and the water choppy. Jonathan loved to sail in these conditions. She hated it. In fact, although she'd never dared admit it, she preferred a cabin cruiser to a sailboat. She liked to lie back and imagine herself on the French Riviera, to have nothing to do with moving the boat from one part of the water to another. Sarah too was lukewarm about sailing and Jonathan allowed Sarah this. He never questioned the girl's likes and dislikes. To him they were authentic, sacrosanct. Marion, however, was expected to excel at all things, even sport. It suddenly struck Marion as strange that he felt so little threatened by her, that, unlike other husbands she'd heard of, he encouraged her to compete with him. He encouraged her, and yet, despite her abilities, something always seemed to come along, something of her own doing in fact, to reduce her triumph in his eyes and to take her out of the race. It was strange.

A car honked behind her. The street was narrow and the driver wanted to pass. Marion lurched forward and around the corner, looking at the house numbers as she went. She saw 523 and stopped. Again the car honked, and she moved on and around another corner to park up against the hill. She felt the grass and bushes of the hill scratch and grind against the side of the car as she backed into the space. Leaving the engine running, she jumped out to inspect. There were waves of tiny seismographic scratches across the two side doors, hardly noticeable, but definitely there. Marion's lip quivered. She felt like a child at school as she ran her hands lightly over the scratches, wishing them away. She leaned up against the hill and held her thumbs hard against her temple veins. Her head was throbbing. She could feel the tension tightening through her neck and shoulders. It was 3:04. She had managed to be late, after all. She walked around the car, switched it off, and then went back along the road, sick at heart, to number 523.

At the gatepost to the main house, Marion saw a piece of wood tacked to the mailbox. It said, "J. López " and had an arrow pointing to the stairs around the garage. She looked at the house and wondered whether anyone behind the sheer drapery was looking back at her. She wondered whether she looked as absurd to them as she felt herself. She had chosen her clothes with care, a jeans skirt and sandals, a tight blouse, a scarf at the neck, sunglasses. But she felt all wrong. And her stomach turned and turned. All the warmth and color seemed to have drained from her face. Her hands were chilled and even her teeth chattered. As she climbed down the steep stairs with the wind blowing sharply through her clothing, Marion wished with all her heart that she had the courage to flee. But she climbed down right to the bottom and knocked lightly on the door.

There was no movement on the other side of the door. For a few seconds she was wild with joy. Perhaps it was the wrong day, the wrong place. Perhaps he had forgotten. But she knocked again, louder, and this time she heard footsteps inside. The door opened and José stood there smiling, putting out a hand to help her over the threshold. Marion laid her hand on his and stepped into the room.

"José, this is beautiful," she said, standing in the middle of the room and looking around, carried out of herself by the loveliness of the place.

The apartment was one large, irregular room which seemed hung in air, suspended above the eucalyptus trees which grew down the hill between the houses. Far below, the bay spread out its waters like some great mist, fingering into coves and inlets between the juts of land. From here the sailboats seemed smaller, frail birds skimming the tops of the white caps. Marion saw the wind coursing around the building and through the trees. She heard the branches whine and sigh, scraping against the outside of the glass walls. A few kites bobbed above the marina. People moved in clumps along the sidewalk far below. It was like watching the snow on Broadway, standing in a slip, warm behind the double glass of the apartment. Suddenly Marion felt safe here. She had shed her terror at the door like a winter coat for spring. Somehow, in this room, with José and the Mozart string quartets playing softly out from somewhere, Marion felt at home.

"It really is beautiful," she said again, smiling.

"Thank you. Thank you for coming. You are very brave."

Marion accepted the glass of wine he handed her and sank down onto one of his numerous Oriental pillows. Navies and ambers, brick and burnt sienna blended into a soft-sculptured collage turned gouache by the bleaching of the sun. The only solid wall in the room, the back wall up against the hill and windowless, was covered floor to ceiling with books. In front of the bookshelves stood an ebony grand piano draped in an embroidered and tasseled black silk shawl. José saw Marion looking.

"That was my grandmother's shawl. See, here." He whisked it off the piano and laid it over her lap. Marion ran her fingers through the tassels and felt the soft stuff of the silk against her skin.

"It is beautiful, beautiful. This whole place . . . How lucky you are, José."

"Lucky? That's funny. You were telling me that first time on the grass how lucky you were, how powerful."

He smiled and sat down opposite her, watching her as she sipped her wine. She laid the shawl out beside her, turning away from him to admire and stroke it.

"I've been feeling less lucky lately," she said. "I don't know why. Perhaps one becomes more vulnerable with age."

"I don't think so. If we face it, age can be almost reassuring. Do you think Sarah feels less vulnerable than you do?"

Marion stiffened. Sarah didn't belong in here with them. She belonged outside, down at the water's edge, flying kites, shuffling along with the people. She looked at him.

"Why did you mention Sarah?"

"Because she exists. She is your daughter, my student. She is the reason I met you. We cannot turn away from that reality."

"No." Marion stared down into her empty wineglass. José stretched over to fill it. Then he lay back, conducting the music with his right hand.

"My father played this so often. He is a violinist," she said.

"I know."

"Oh."

"Sarah told me about both your parents, Berlin, the Philharmonic."

"How strange. She never mentions any of that at home. She shows no interest at all."

"She is very proud of her grandparents. She loves them both in a very wonderful way."

Marion saw Sarah now, sitting after rehearsal in the music room, standing with José on the steps, lauding her grandparents in her soft, halting voice. How dare she? thought Marion. How dare she exclude me?

"What are you thinking there so quietly?" asked José.

"Oh, nothing."

"That is not true. Your voice is tight, and I can see your stiff body."

Marion had never had anyone pay such attention to her voice and body before. In the Anglo-Saxon world, silence was a social shield which commanded respect. But José ignored the rule, if he ever knew it.

"Tell me," he asked again, sitting up cross-legged. "*Qué piensas?*"

"Oh, I don't know. I was just thinking about Sarah."

"I know. What were you thinking?"

"Why?"

"I'm interested in what you feel and think. I'm interested in you."

"I was irritated with her for idealizing my parents."

"But why? Tell me." José drew closer, staring.

"I don't know. She irritates me sometimes. My parents—my father, is the real thing. A fine musician. She has no business modeling herself on him."

"But she said nothing of modeling herself. She has ambition. That is good."

"Ambition, yes. But what about talent?" asked Marion, her color rising.

"She has talent," said José.

"Not enough though. Not enough to be what she wants to be."

"So what? Let her try. Are you jealous?"

"Don't be ridiculous," Marion shouted. The wine was churning in her empty stomach. She felt ill.

"Then what bothers you? What?"

"Oh, God!" said Marion, sinking her head into her hands. "What is it? Maybe it's that she lays claim to them and not to me. I don't know."

"I see. I see," José said. He laid his wineglass on a low table and placed Marion's next to it. Then he stretched out on his stomach at Marion's feet and began carefully to unbuckle her sandals.

Marion lay back in a swoon of confusion. Conflicting and inappropriate images flew through her head as José massaged and stroked her feet. She thought of Jonathan standing at the toilet, the scratches on her car, the hair growing on her toes. She felt José's tongue between her toes like a slug, prodding, sliding up and down. My God, she thought, how can he do that? She imagined the taste and the smell of her toes and she wished that she'd drunk more wine, that the room were darker. She couldn't see him, but she heard him moving on the rug, easing up towards her calves and knees.

Marion lay there listening to the quartet and to the scratching of the trees at the windows. She wished they could have gone on talking. He had taken off her skirt now, and underpants. He was unbuttoning her blouse. She felt like a patient on the gynecologist's table, like a sea beast washed up on the rocks for all the world to see. She tried to move around so that she could offer some reciprocation, even a token, but he gently held her where she was, intent upon raising her to a higher pitch. Marion tried to imagine herself again in the ocean, anywhere but here. His tongue was prodding lightly here, there, sliding, sinking, sucking. He was an artist. But she remained where she was, lucid, unmoved, punished.

She moved her hips slightly, moaned a little, a pretense she hadn't made since college. She wondered whether he knew, whether he could see through her performance as he saw through her conversation. But he was panting now, taking off his clothes, battening down his own eagerness in his desire to increase hers. Marion peeped at him as he wriggled out of his jeans and saw him there, uncircumcised, beautiful, against the light and shadow of the trees. But she remained herself still, Marion, lying there in a strange apartment, wondering how much time had passed since she had arrived.

José reached out and slid a cushion under her hips. "Beautiful, beautiful," he murmured, looking down on her. "You are beautiful."

His face was florid now, his eyes and hair wild. He parted Marion's legs again and entered her gently, staring into her face for her response. Marion closed her eyes and bit her lower lip, tossing her head to left and right in an imitation of the few pornographic movies she had seen. José's thrusting became more urgent. He moved her hips this way, that way, with his hands. His facility was extraordinary. Marion thought of Jonathan's bulk, his lethargy in bed. They had perfected their lovemaking to the lowest common denominator of effort and energy. Marion lay under José now, wondering whether she was addicted to the use of Jonathan in the dark as a prop of fantasy. She panicked now at her own inability to respond to the stuff and substance of her fantasy, to this Adonis devoting himself to her pleasure.

José crouched between her thighs, his heels together, his knees apart, his body upright above her. He drew her feet up over each of his shoulders and thrust rapidly, pumping in and out. He bared his teeth in a demonic grin and grunted with each thrust. Marion had never felt such a sensation, such a strange plumbing of her body. Closing her eyes, she willed herself to release. Then she looked up and saw José there crouching above her like some Aztec god waiting for the sacrificial beast to give up life, and she knew she would have to carry her charade through to the end. She moaned and gasped and then looked at him again.

"Have you? Have you?" he asked urgently.

"Yes," she answered.

And then he gave a final thrust, letting out a wild shriek as he sunk to her chest and bit her earlobe. He lay there for a second and then rolled onto his side, taking her with him, staying inside her. He looked more beautiful now than she had ever seen him. She felt like cradling him in her arms, covering him with kisses. She wished she had something to give him, some special gift, some jewel. Suddenly she was ready for him to make love to her, she was minutes from a complete release. But she knew, with a sharp spasm of sorrow, that it was over, that she was bound by her own fiction.

"You are a wonderful lover," she said, stroking his hair. She wanted to cry.

He smiled and leaned over to kiss her. "And you," he said.

"Who taught you?" she asked.

"Aha!" he shouted, and then laughed. Marion had embarrassed him. How odd, she thought, looking at him again. He talks of passion and fire, but he's embarrassed by his own technique. She felt quite powerful.

"I must go."

"Please don't," he asked. "Please stay with me, like this, a little longer."

"Will you play something for me?" she asked.

"Of course, madame. What do you wish to hear?"

"The 'Italian Concerto.'"

"No. Too loud."

"Ummm. Chopin's Prelude—F# major." She sang the first few measures.

"I love that one. Do you too? But, you know, they are solemn and sad, those preludes."

"I feel solemn." She smiled. "Please play it."

José opened a closet and took out a red silk robe for Marion. Then he took out a terry one and put it on. He rummaged around in the bookshelf and came out with the preludes. "Look here. Do you know what George Sand said of them? She said that 'shades of dead monks seem to rise and pass before the hearer in solemn and gloomy funereal pomp.' We said *solemn*. See? We were right."

Marion followed him to the piano and sat on the floor with her back against the bookshelves. He opened the piano and the music stand, laid out the music, and sat for a moment with his lovely hands spread on his thighs while he stared at the keys. Then he began to play. Marion sat up, shaken out of her tranquillity by his playing. It was wonderful. He was wonderful. She watched his hands. His technique was sure, his touch delicate. The music and the sight of him playing it made her throat tighten. She saw the room and the trees and the fading light through clouds of her own tears. They streamed down her cheeks. She could barely breathe for fear of disturbing him. He finished and then turned around to face her.

"Why are you crying?" he asked, pulling her up to him. She laid her head on his shoulder and wept into his neck.

"Please, please," she heard him say. "Are you happy or sad?"

"It is the music," she said, "and you. It's all so lovely."

He hugged her, kissing her hair, her neck, slipping his hands under the silk of his own robe on her. She stood back and smiled. Then she took her clothes into the bathroom to change. As she washed and brushed she heard him at the piano again, playing the "Three-part Inventions." Marion looked at her swollen face in the fluorescent mirror, the smudged eyes and reddened mouth. She put on her sunglasses and grimaced as she stepped back into the room, digging into her bag for her car keys.

"Stay there," she said. "Stay where you are. I want to leave while you're playing."

"But—"

"We'll talk tomorrow."

She walked over to him and kissed the top of his head. He leaned his head back between her breasts with his face up to hers to be kissed again. She kissed him upside down on his soft lips, feeling again the untimely desire to have him inside her, to be released by his touch, to start again. But he looked at her with the soft satisfaction and indulgence of a spent lover. His satisfaction was for them both as he smiled at her. He didn't doubt her and she felt like a cheat, herself the loser, alone in her sense of loss. Marion slipped out of the apartment as he played on. She braced herself against the wind and against the roaring of the traffic from the thruway. She started her car and wove down through the hills to the bay and out along the water to the thruway.

As she recrossed the bridge, she saw the ocean, the bay, the city, and she felt a stranger, an alien, a woman apart from herself. Marion switched on the radio and heard of an earthquake south of Los Angeles, a small one. She saw the bridge and all its cars plummeting down into the water below. She saw the buildings of the city buckle and crash, the hills heave and pulse in one mighty death throe. And then she saw the dust and the ashes settle and only herself left to wander on the beach.

4

The sun had almost set by the time Marion drove into the garage. Winter was not far off, bringing darkness and rain. She sat for a moment in the car wrestling with her reluctance to reenter her own home. She was weary and longed for a hot bath and a bed to herself. Sarah and Jonathan had had dinner already, she knew. She told them this morning she had a late meeting in Palo Alto, not an unusual event. As she walked up the stairs she heard the TV blaring and Sarah repeating and repeating two measures. Marion looked in on Jonathan sprawled before the flickering TV and then tried to leave before he saw her. She knew she was about to cry and that only sleep would cure her suffocating depression. But Jonathan had seen her and waved out from the couch.

"Hey, come here!"

"No, no. I can't stand that thing." She gestured towards the TV.

"Five more minutes of play," he said, never taking his eyes off the set. "Go see your daughter and then come back."

"No, thank you. I'm going to bed. I feel as if I'm getting the flu." Marion could barely speak the sentence. She had to struggle to keep her voice from flying out and up into hysterical weeping. She couldn't remember ever having felt this way. Not since childhood anyway, and then she had had her future to hope for, unknown things to comfort her. She climbed up to the bedroom willing herself not to think, not to start formulating solutions.

When Marion woke from a fitful sleep at 5 A.M. she knew she was ill. He head was on fire and her nightgown and pillow were soaked and chilled. She got out of bed and stumbled into the bathroom for the thermometer. Her fever was 102 degrees, her body sagged and creaked. Every joint, every hair follicle suffered and she felt dizzy and nauseous. She changed her nightgown and wrapped herself in a robe and waited for Jonathan to wake so that she could change the bed. But he slept on interminably, sprawling over onto her half of the bed now that the barrier of her body was gone. Marion got up, eased herself out of the room and went downstairs for a cup of tea.

The sun flushed the kitchen through with early light. Even in her fever, Marion enjoyed being there alone to see it. She laid her head down on the table and stared at her mug of tea, watching the steam rise out of it and dissolve in the chilly kitchen air. It hurt to move her eyes, so she closed them and held the image of the mug, the steam, the kitchen beyond, until it dissolved with the next wave of pain that washed over her body. She concentrated all her energy on not allowing herself to think beyond the mug of tea, and then just the tea, and then the steam alone. She was good at this trick. She had done it as a child and now she could recall the skill whenever she pleased, like riding a bicycle or twirling a hula hoop.

As Marion opened her eyes and watched the steam rise and dissolve outwards, she saw it curve suddenly towards the kitchen door. She felt a rush and a shuffling behind her, a presence, someone needing an explanation. Jonathan must have realized she'd left and come down to find her. Marion braced herself. He hated her to be ill. He seemed to take it as an affront, an indulgence on her part. And yet he was the hypochondriac in the family and she was seldom ill, never complaining without cause. His attitude didn't make sense, but she had no power to analyze it right now.

Slowly she pushed herself up from the table and turned her body around to face the door. She blinked. Sarah stood in the doorway like a doe transfixed by light. She stared at Marion and Marion was speechless in return.

"Mother?"

"Sarah! What have you done?"

Sarah stood motionless. Even her hands remained still at her sides. She had flushed purple now and bent her head to look out of the window, away from Marion. Her head was covered in small pink plastic rollers, rolled with neat precision, each one held in place by two shining chrome pincurl clips. Her face was almost covered with thick white cream, her abundant eyebrows plucked to thin jerky lines. She looked, in her fluffy robe and large sheep-skin slippers, like the "before" picture in some transforming process. Marion was too sick and too astonished to do more than stare.

"I didn't know you were here," Sarah said quietly, still looking away out the window.

"I'm ill. I came down for some tea."

"Oh."

"Sarah . . ."

"I cut my hair. I mean a friend did. She came over yesterday after school, and we bought these"—she patted a flat hand to her head—"on the way."

"A friend?"

"Marlene."

"Marlene?"

"The new girl. From Chicago. She's the percussionist. You saw her at the picnic."

"The eyebrows too? And the cream?"

Sarah thrust her hands into the pockets of her robe and turned to leave.

"Come and have some tea, Sarah," Marion said with so little energy that Sarah turned and shuffled over to the table. "Please make it yourself, and make me some more. I feel awful."

"What's wrong?" Sarah sounded as if she were responding to a nagging child.

"Flu. Why are you up at this hour?"

"I couldn't sleep—with these things in my hair."

"Can't you use the dryer? Why do you have to sleep in curlers? It's ridiculous."

Sarah didn't answer.

"Why?" persisted Marion.

"Marlene does. She said it stays in longer."

Marion let her head sink back onto the table. She felt nauseous again, and wildly irritated, as if her body would explode, burst its skin and splatter across the kitchen. Her fresh nightgown was soaked. Her hair stuck in strands to her head. Sarah moved slowly back and forth across the kitchen like Marion's mother, the rows and rows of pink plastic cylinders moving back and forth with her.

"How long have you been friends with this Marlene?"

"Not long. Actually, only since last Saturday. She only came this year, I told you."

"I hope she knows how to cut hair. Why didn't you tell me you were going to cut it? I would have taken you to Derrick."

"Her mother is a hairdresser."

"Oh." Marion lifted her eyes slightly from the table. Sarah kept her large back defiantly between them while she stood sipping her tea and staring out the window. Marion reached for her tea but gave up and let her arm hang loose at her side.

"What does her father do?" she mumbled.

"She hasn't got one."

"Her mother's a widow?"

"How should I know?" Sarah turned round to face Marion. She had face cream smeared over the teacup and on her hands, and she wiped it off on her robe.

"Oh, Sarah, use a paper towel. You didn't sleep in the cream did you?"

"Of course not. It's a masque, anyway."

"How can she afford Mary Ellis?"

"Who? Marlene? I don't know. I didn't ask. I wasn't interested anyway, and it's not the sort of thing . . . They have scholarships you know."

"Is she smart?"

"Not very. But that's not everything."

"I'd like to meet her." Marion stood up slowly, and Sarah stood back, watching her in her pain, staring at her patiently like a beast at its wounded quarry. Suddenly Marion staggered forward and grabbed the table, knocking over her teacup. It splashed her and dripped onto the floor.

"Oh, God!" Clutching her head, she flopped down onto the chair.

"I have to go get dressed," said Sarah. She stepped over the puddle on the floor and headed towards the door.

Marion felt the room tilt and sway. Her stomach and lungs seemed to swim from her head to her feet and settle nowhere. She swung around as Sarah passed her and grabbed her robe, almost pulling it off the girl as she did so. Sarah stopped and tried to turn, but Marion moved her grip to her waist, turning the girl like an unwilling mule back towards the kitchen. She felt her fingers sink through the soft robe into the flesh of Sarah's thick waist as if she were biting into her own anesthetized cheek. She knew there was pain, but she felt nothing.

"You!" Marion hissed. "You will go nowhere. You will get a sponge and a towel and clean that table and floor. And then—when you're done—you'll rinse out that sponge and that towel and put them back where you found them. Just who do you think you are?" Marion's voice dried up in her aching throat and she sank onto the floor, releasing the girl with a shove. Sarah staggered forward, wrapping her hands round her waist, hanging her head to stifle her sobs.

"I hate you!" she whispered. "I hate you! I hate you! I hate you!"

"And I don't give shit!" said Marion, trying to get up. She hung onto the chair and then the table and pulled until she stood to face Sarah. "That's your loss," she said. "It's a loss for us both. But to walk out, to leave me in my illness—no, my girl. Not while you live in this house."

"Then I'll leave. "I'd *love* to leave!"

"And become a hairdresser? A street musician? You'd better face facts, Princess Sarah, and then decide."

"What's going on here?" said Jonathan in the doorway. "Why are you two down here? Hey, did you see the new hairstyle?"

"No, I didn't. All I see is pink plastic. I have the flu, a fever of 102, and I'm going back to bed."

"Really? Oh, hell, not again."

"I haven't been sick all year."

"Are you sure you've got the flu?"

Marion shuffled past him and climbed the stairs. She heard Jonathan comforting Sarah. She knew it was he who would clean the table and the floor and then leave the dirty sponge and towel to lie in the sink. She heard Sarah's voice in a litany of complaint as she closed the bedroom door. Marion lay down on the unmade bed and closed her eyes. Early cars were starting up outside. She wondered where they went at six-thirty in the morning. Jonathan would come back up at any minute to dress and she'd have to put up with his whining on Sarah's behalf. She'd have to ask him to help her with the bed. The linen smelled of him, not of her anyway. By Thursday it was always rank, quite revolting. Maybe Carmelita would come today instead of tomorrow.

Marion reached for the phone and called Ben to tell him she was ill. Then she called Carmelita. Manuel answered and Marion's heart leapt into her throat. It was José's voice, his cadence, with a thicker, a richer accent. Carmelita had left already. Marion would have to manage alone.

Marion sat on the edge of the bed looking around her at the tangle of linen and yesterday's clothes. She decided that she hated this room. She hated sharing it with Jonathan. She hated the chaos of it, the discord between his side and hers. Even the pictures on the walls, even the color of the paint, the books, were alien to her. Her energies had been poured into the downstairs rooms, especially her study with its leather and wood and books. Their bedroom caught the residue. An Exercycle stood in the corner draped with a jogging suit and a sailing shoe drying out on each handle. How-to paperbacks lay around the carpet on Jonathan's side. Nothing matched, nothing blended.

Marion quickly unplugged the phone and took it with her to

the guest room. She closed the door, closed the drapes, and rolled back the bedspread. Then she slipped between the clean sheets and turned on the bedside light, looking around her at the pristine decor. She felt like a virgin here, a visitor in the house of a maiden aunt. The bed was narrow and tightly made. It smelled like the linen in her mother's cedar chest, woody and airless. She had forgotten the luxury of such solitude and wished only to have her mother there as once she had been in New York, nurse, caretaker. Marion dreamed herself back into adolescent illnesses, adolescent carelessness. But there was another note in her dreaming, some discord, that hammered just beneath her consciousness. Spoiling the clarity of the fantasy. Marion closed her eyes and tracked it down through the beating of her heart to José. José. Where did he belong in her world? How could he be there with Gertrude carrying trays and Jonathan on the Exercycle? What would he have thought of her savaging her own child in the kitchen this morning?

Marion stiffened. Jonathan and Sarah were coming upstairs. She heard Sarah close her door and start dressing on the other side of the wall. And she knew that within minutes Jonathan would come looking for her. She switched off the lamp, positioned herself as if asleep, and waited. Quite soon she heard the door open quietly, saw the light from the hall through her closed lids.

"Mother?"

Marion turned quickly and sat up. Sarah stood in front of the light like a specter transformed. Her hair framed the roundness of her face in a mass of glossy brown curls. They seemed to lengthen her neck, shrink the plumpness from her flushed cheeks by drawing the eye away from her face and into their infinite softness. Sarah held herself high, thrusting out her breasts and dropping her shoulders. She stood there, dressed for school, like a bride standing between ripeness and ravishment.

"Mother," she said softly, "I'm sorry."

"Oh, Sarah! Oh, darling, how lovely you look!" Marion's voice faded as the tears flooded her vision. She wept openly, gasping loudly for breath, and as she did so she felt Sarah's soft head on her shoulder, her long arms hugging Marion like a small child.

"Don't cry, Mother."

"I'm sorry. I'm sorry I grabbed you in the kitchen. Did I hurt you? I'm so sorry."

"It's OK, Mother. I'm sorry too. Lie down. Go to sleep. I'll see you when I get home."

"Don't go. Stay a while," Marion pleaded. She laid her hot, wet head back on the pillow and wiped her hand across her forehead.

But Sarah stood up and backed towards the door. She stood there staring, clasping her hands behind her like a child on stage.

"I'm being selfish. I know you have to practice."

"Yes."

"Tell Daddy, please, that I'm going to sleep. Tell him—"

"Don't worry, Mother, we'll manage without you."

"You look lovely, lovely. And I'm glad you have a friend."

"Thank you. Can I go now?"

"Of course."

The door closed. Sarah clattered down the stairs. In the dark as she lay there wrung through with fever and sweat, Marion tried again to see the steam alone, even the tea, the mug, to hear nothing at all. But she vibrated all at once with the tangle of her life, her lover, her husband, and her child. They played a ghastly symphony in her head to which there was no meaning, no rhythm, and Marion was ambushed on the podium with an amplifier in each ear and the baton in her hand.

Marion woke with bells pulsing through her head. The room was as hot and close as a tomb. Zigzags of weak winter sun slipped between the drapes and lit the wall beside her. She watched the stillness, the dark and the light around her, and then remembered where she was and heard the phone. She reached over to it, clearing the thickness from her throat. But it stopped suddenly, leaving only the pain of its coarse bell dying in her head. She lay back, awake, and switched on the lamp. It was eleven-thirty. Suddenly she wanted him there, her lover, kneeling anxiously beside the bed, stifling his misery at her fatal cough. She would run her fingers through his hair and comfort him. He would watch her while she slept. Even in her illness Marion blushed. She thought again of Sarah's blossoming. I have no right, at thirty-six, she thought, to play Camille, or the ingenue to his seducer. I am, in fact, more the seducer than the seduced. And she saw José again at the picnic, the sunlight on his hair, looking down on her with his sweet smile.

Marion lay stiffly in bed staring up at the ceiling. She wished that she could turn back and live again through her twenties. Her achievements seemed cheap now, leveled out, impotent in the face of middle age and death. She felt her youth, a youthfulness younger even than Sarah's, trapped airless within her aging body, refusing to die gracefully with the rest of her. It wouldn't allow her to settle back, like Beth, into accepting inevitabilities.

Marion sat up slowly. She shuffled to the bathroom for codeine or anything she could find to deaden the pain. While she was there the phone rang again. She dropped the cup into the sink and ran through her bedroom to the guest room.

"Hello?"

"Marion?"

"Yes."

"It's Ben."

"Oh."

Marion sat down heavily on the bed while her heart still danced and fluttered in her neck.

"How are you? What've you got?"

"Got? Oh, just a lousy dose of flu. I feel rotten."

"You sound awful. Can I do anything?"

"What?"

"Marion, are you really OK? You sound a little weird."

"Really, Ben! *Weird!* Only teenagers say *weird.*"

"Sorry."

"Ben, can I call you back? I was sort of asleep."

"Sorry again."

"Did you phone a little while back?"

"No. I thought you'd be sleeping."

"I was."
"I'll call again later."
"Thanks."
"Bye."
Marion dropped the receiver back into its cradle and sat for a moment staring at it. Then she went back to the bathroom and swallowed a codeine tablet. It was noon. She looked out of the bathroom window and saw the sky darkening. There were even some thunder clouds in the distance.

Marion stared at herself in the mirror and thought of José, of Ben, the power of the one, the impotence of the other. It's arbitrary, she thought, Why shouldn't it be Ben? He has the same gross attributes, the same apparatus. He too loves me. The deception is the same, the act is still adultery. But Ben is unthinkable. It would be an act of charity, eyes closed, head averted. José is more than a lover, more than an escape really. He is another life, a different set of rules.

She went down to the kitchen, wondering how she would kill the time between now and his next phone call. The house was silent, and the street. Everyone except her was healthy and vigorous and away from home. As the codeine began to work, Marion relaxed and went through to the living room to lie on the couch. Before she sat down she opened the record cabinet and sorted through her records to Chopin. She found a recording of de Larrocha playing the preludes and put it on the stereo. Then she lay back on the couch and closed her eyes to carry her back to yesterday and José's apartment in the air.

But she was carried beyond that, back to New York and to her room, to the lovely phrases from her father's violin, tea in winter, her mother's perfume, the loneliness of her own adolescent fears and dissatisfactions.

Somehow, Marion had always blended success and happiness into one solution. She had come to suppose they were inseparable. Anyway, her successes had seemed so full once, so potent. Like analgesics they had charmed away her misgivings; when one wore off, another came along dancing to a different tune.

But Marion now began to recognize in herself a subterranean legacy of uncontested, unexamined choices. They were leeching out, through careful layers of complacency, demanding recognition and more. She shivered and drew the afghan up over her shoulders. It had begun to rain.

The music stopped and the pickup arm scratched rhythmically over the same two grooves at the center of the record. Rain washed over all the windows. Wind and rain tossed shrubs and hedges up against the walls of the house.

Marion sat up and looked around her at the coordinated colors and designs of her living room. Her house seemed so formal compared with José's. It seemed adult, old, unloved. She wanted to throw out all the wood and brass and fill the room with cushions and furs. She wanted a fire in the never-used fireplace. She wanted to do it all now, yesterday in fact, to call in the Salvation Army and have it all gone by dinnertime. She couldn't imagine how all these things had ever given her satisfaction. There was no one thing she loved in her house, no thread which wound them all together into home for her. Marion shuffled towards the stereo to change the record. It was one o'clock. The storm outside had darkened the sky so that it felt like six. Gray light filtered weakly into the unlit room. She looked up as she walked back to the couch past the front porch window and she held her breath in horror.

A face was pressed against the glass, its white nose squashed like a snail, its black eyes staring wide into the room. Two pink hands spread out like spiders on either side. The porch was dark. Marion stood motionless, searching her memory for a weapon nearby. Then it knocked on the glass. It smiled. It stood back.

"José!"

Marion stepped away from the window and towards the front door where she stood for a moment unable to move. She heard the storm outside and then José's gentle tap on the doorknocker.

"Hey, let me in!"

She turned the lock and opened the door. José stood looking at her for a moment. Then he threw his arms around her and kissed her neck. He stepped back and held her face in his wet hands.

"Why are you sick? How can you be sick?"

Marion shivered. "You ask the most wonderfully ridiculous questions."

"No, I mean, *sick*—after yesterday."

"I know what you mean."

He touched her forehead with his cold hand, then her neck. "Go to bed. You should be in bed."

"I was."

"Where were you when I phoned?"

"Asleep. I was dreaming of bells. And then you hung up."

"How did you know it was me?"

"I guessed."

"No. You knew."

"OK. I knew."

"Come," he said, taking her hand. "Show me where your bedroom is and I will sit with you."

Marion looked back as he led her upstairs. Things had gone mad. Anyone could have seen him coming in. Mrs. Delancey could see them now if she looked out of her kitchen window. Marion couldn't seem to focus her mind on the enormity of this situation. It seemed natural for him to be leading her upstairs in her own home, up to her own guest room. He stopped on the landing and looked around.

"Which way?"

"There," she said.

He walked into the guest room and switched on the light. "Pretty."

"No, it isn't. It's boring."

"Go to bed and stop arguing." He smiled down at her as she sat uneasily on the bed and drew the covers over her.

"Now I will make you something. Tea and brandy?"

"José, anyone could come in. What would I say?"

"Say a friend has come for tea and brandy."

"Oh, for God's sake."

"Don't worry," he said, walking out of the room. "I'll take care of everything. I have come to bring music to my sick love. Where's the brandy?"

"Dining-room cabinet, lower left. And—" Marion lay back and gave up. It was too wonderful to resist. She couldn't think of consequences when she hadn't even figured out the causes. She heard the tinkling of china, the kettle whistling, and José's lovely tenor voice flying up and down with the Chopin. His presence somehow made her feel even more a stranger in this house. It was as if they were guests in a hotel, for the weekend, with no chance of interruption.

He appeared in the doorway silently, like a cat, and startled her. "Here is my medicine for you. Sit up."

He had found Sarah's old ceramic mugs somewhere. She clasped one in both hands and breathed in the lovely perfume of the brandy and tea. José smiled and sipped his noisily.

"Drink!"

She drank the tea and felt it warm her neck and chest as it slipped down into her stomach. The brandy twinged and tingled at her knees and elbows. She began to sweat.

"Good," said José. "You will sweat out the fever."

"That's a myth."

"If you know so much, cure yourself," he said, smiling.

"Oh, José," she said, lying back with her hands behind her head. "*You* are a cure. You're like sun in the storm." Then she raised herself on one elbow to look at him. "How did you know I was ill?"

"Well, first I phoned the clinic before school this morning and the secretary told me. And then I saw Sarah and asked her."

"*You asked her?*"

"Calm down and drink."

Marion obediently sipped and then looked up at him again for an answer.

He sat on the other bed, spilling tea on the bedspread as he bounced down. Marion tried to care about the tea stains but couldn't. She only thought of Sarah and the touch of her soft curls this morning.

"I told her I had to speak to you about my shoulder. She said you were very ill, home, with the flu, that I could call you here. So I tried, but you were asleep. So here I am to cure and be cured." He smiled.

"Did she seem suspicious?"

"About what?"

"About us."

José stopped smiling and came to sit on Marion's bed. He took her cup and put it down on the bedside table. Then he put his hands on her shoulders. "I think that I have much to teach you. You are so confident on the outside, so proud. But inside you are a rabbit, running this way, that way, frightened you will be eaten by the fox. What fox? You must stop this or it will destroy you—and us."

"That's all very well for you to say. You have nothing to lose."

"I don't measure out profit and loss." He looked away, round the room, taking in every object. Marion reached out and touched the sinews of his neck. She remembered his distorted face, his sleek brown body above hers, and she shivered.

"Are you still cold?"

"No."

"You shivered."

"It was you, not the cold, that made me shiver."

"*That* is power." He kissed her lightly on her wet forehead.

"So," said Marion, "you are not averse to power?"

"Not human power, the power of feelings. I do not understand your kind of power, your control."

"I don't know whether I understand it any more either." She looked at him, trying to break out of her false sense of security. She reminded herself a half a dozen times of where they were, who could call or come by. But she couldn't make herself believe in the danger. She kept returning to his smile, his soft hands.

José cocked his head on one side and went to the door.

"What's that scratching?"

"What?" Marion sat up. "Is someone there? Oh, Lord, José, what will we do?"

He held an arm back towards her to keep her quiet. "No, not someone. A radio, or record player, or something."

"Oh! I left a record on. Downstairs, in the closet in the living room."

José bounded off and she heard clicks and snaps. She heard him putting the record away and putting on another. Then she heard the harpsichord, the "Italian Concerto," and he was back upstairs, sitting next to her.

"Your stereo doesn't deserve that treatment," he said. "The needle's shot."

"Oh, what a relief. I thought it was Sarah or someone."

"Here," he said, reaching into a pocket for a small packet, "here's a string for Sarah. She needed it for tomorrow. That's why I came by." He winked and sat back against the wall, arching his knees over her legs. He closed his eyes to listen. Marion closed hers too. The music reached them in waves from downstairs. It filled the room and then emptied it again with the ebb and flow of the pattern of each movement. They were silent.

The phone rang and Marion made a convulsive grab for it. José looked at her with curiosity, moving his ear near to the phone to hear.

"Marion?"

"Yes."

"It's Ben, again."

"Oh, hello, Ben-again."

He laughed loudly. "Things are slow, believe it or not. I thought I'd pop by to see you after work. OK?"

"Oh, Ben, I feel so lousy. You're sweet, but I wouldn't be very good company."

"I'm not coming for company. I'm coming to see you. You sounded real weird this morning."

"*Real weird!*"

"Sorry! I'll be there at about four."

"OK. OK. See you then."

Marion put down the phone and looked up into José's face with a smile.

"Who was that?" he demanded. His face was dark and closed, his mouth a stiff line.

Marion arched an eyebrow, an old trick. "That was Ben, the other clinic doctor. He's coming to visit—like you."

"He loves you. I could tell."

"Don't be absurd."

"You allow him here while you are alone and sick?" He raised his voice in menace.

Marion scanned his face for a trace of humor. There was none. "Are you joking?"

"Joking? You are alone and sick and you allow that man who loves you to visit you—in a nightgown."

Marion bit her cheek hard to prevent herself from laughing. "He doesn't wear nightgowns. And who said he loves me? Are you crazy?"

"I heard. I heard his voice. Who is he? Why do you let him come here?"

"José, José, this is lunacy. Don't you see? *You* are here. *You* are the danger, not he. He's nothing but an old friend."

José turned away. "It's not right." He shrank down into his shoulders.

Marion reached out to touch him but he shuffled her off.

"José?"

"I'm thinking."

"OK." She lay back looking at him, suppressing her desire to laugh off his anger. Clearly his response was something beyond her control. She felt like an anthropologist in the field watching the strange behavior of a dangerous tribal chief. Finally, he stood up and faced her formally.

"I must leave now."

"José, please!"

"I hope you feel better. Don't forget to give Sarah the string I brought."

Marion now turned away from him to face the wall. She pretended to be hurt.

"Good-bye," he said. She didn't reply. She heard him walk

heavily down the stairs and take the record off. Then he went out, slamming the door behind him and leaving her in a wake of shock waves. She lay there, motionless, staring at the patterns on the wallpaper. This was beyond her comprehension—this moving so readily from adoration to adolescent jealousy. It made no sense. All she knew was that she didn't want to lose him, that she would sacrifice anything now, anything she could think of, to keep him loving her.

The doorbell rang. Marion jumped and looked at her watch. An hour had passed in five minutes. She threw on a robe and went downstairs to open the door.

Ben stood outside, wet from the rain but spruce and neat, holding two dozen red roses. She smiled bleakly and held the door open for him. As she closed the door, she looked out into the dark afternoon sky. An old black Pontiac was parked opposite with a man at the wheel. It was José. He stared at her for about five seconds through the open window of the car, the rain running off his face. Then he turned on the ignition and roared off down the street, leaving her to face Ben and find a vase for his flowers.

5

Friday was the second time since she had been nine or ten that Sarah had invited a friend home voluntarily—last week, and now again this week. She seemed to have arranged for the visits to coincide with times when Marion would be away.

But Marion had decided to come home early. She had been back at the clinic all week but was pallid and enervated, without any interest in her patients or their complaints. They didn't seem worth the effort to cure. Nothing seemed worth the effort. She had been over last Thursday's events hundreds of times, every phrase, every turn of feeling. Nothing that had happened seemed to account for José's behavior and now his silence. She had heard nothing from him or about him from Sarah. Sarah, in fact, seemed more secretive than ever, and happier, lighthearted even. Marion considered it a perverse response to her own gloom. Her depression seemed to cheer the girl up.

Marion sat in her coat at the kitchen table drinking coffee and staring at the phone. She'd been staring at it for a week now, reaching for it, even dialing a few digits and then hanging up. What was there to gain? Even if she saw him again, what did he promise for her life but more distraction and anxiety? It seemed to her now that she had been almost happy before the picnic, that she could be happy, or at least satisfied, again. There was no logic to this liaison. It didn't fit. It was untidy. Nothing led on from it. It started nowhere and promised to end in chaos. So why was she so miserable and without hope? Why did she want nothing more than to see him again, to spend an afternoon in his apartment?

The front door opened and Marion heard Sarah and her friend laughing in a forced, hyperfeminine cadenza. They spilled into the hall, giggling, dropping their books and coats on the hall table.

"Your place is *so* neat!"

"You think so? I hate it, with all its color coordinations," Sarah shrilled.

Marion turned her head to hear more accurately. Her stomach churned acid in anticipation.

"Mother's into tone and class. She calls them *standards*." Laughter. "Dad doesn't seem to mind, though. You'd like him."

"Where's your mom?"

"Playing doctor."

"What do you mean? Isn't she a doctor?" The girls were approaching the kitchen.

"Oh yeah. But she only works half-days. Except Fridays. She's a doctor, but she really gets off on shopping and having lunch with her—"

Marion stood up to greet them with a firmly held smile. "Would you girls like some hot chocolate? It's so grim outside." She opened the refrigerator for the milk, biting down to stop the tears from filling her eyes. The girls stood silently where they were. She could feel them breathing behind her, exchanging glances, stifling comment.

Marion poured the milk into a pan and spooned in the chocolate, trying to hum something to herself. But no tune came. Her voice droned off-key like Jonathan's, without rhythm or melody. She pretended to forget the measurements and reread the instructions aloud. Still, no word came from the girls. Finally she stirred the mixture and turned to face them. Sarah stared solidly at some point beyond her shoes.

"I thought you would be at the clinic today," she said.

"Evidently. No, I was still feeling hungover from my flu, so I came home. Sarah," said Marion, demanding eye contact. "You haven't introduced me to your friend yet."

"Oh, uh . . ."

The girl stepped forward boldly. "I'm Marlene," she said in a singsong. Marion reached out and grasped the girl's flabby palm. Marlene stared curiously at her, fortified by her own potent teenage sexuality into a slow appraisal of Marion's person. Marion felt the girl's eyes on her face, her neck, her carefully chic clinic outfit and wanted to defend her pallor, her careful makeup, her Gucci shoes. She wanted to shout at this impertinent nothing, this gaping neophyte, that she had won the right to her home, her clothes, her career, her choices, the right to work as she pleased and to return home early if she needed to. She wanted to challenge her to return at the age of thirty-six. She wanted to see the blossom blown and withered, to see the bold light dimmed.

"Mother?" Sarah stepped in front of Marlene. Marion looked up into her daughter's face, questioning. "Um, Marlene is the percussionist. Remember, I told you?"

"Oh, yes," said Marion returning to the chocolate on the stove. "And you're quite a hairdresser from what I see."

Marlene snickered in satisfaction.

"Who taught you?" Marion asked.

"My mom."

"She's a professional?"

"Yeah. I mean, she's a hair stylist at Magnin's. Been doing it since she was my age."

"My goodness, you must give me her name."

"Who cuts your hair?"

"Derrick. At Universe."

"Oh."

"Heard of him?"

"Yeah. Mom has. She says he stinks."

Sarah whooped and snorted into her palms. As Marion turned with the hot chocolate she saw her nudging Marlene. Both girls stiffened into expressions of false seriousness.

"Well," said Marion, setting the mugs down with purpose, "I

shall have to try your mother and see how she measures up." She took her mug and walked quickly out of the kitchen and upstairs.

As Marion sat on her bed, holding the mug between her knees, she heard the girls come up, talking in low voices. They went into Sarah's room and closed the door firmly. She heard their muffled voices, their laughing, and she felt like the cripple in the playground. She drank her chocolate and drew her coat around her. The afternoon was already sinking into dusk and the bedroom was chilly. Jonathan objected to the use of heat during the day, not so much because of the cost, but because he had adopted a moral stance on the energy crisis and on soft American habits. He had been demanding honey and fertile eggs lately and Marion couldn't even find it funny.

The talk from Sarah's room became low and urgent. Marion stood up silently and crept across the hall. Slowly she turned the handle of the guest room and slipped into its dark interior, closing the door behind her. She rested her head close to the wall, cupping her hand around her ear.

"Who?"

"Dunno."

"—his jeans!"

"Tight!"

Laughter, giggles. Drawers and closets opened and closed.

"Let's put on a record."

"Stereo's downstairs."

"What've you got?"

"Nothing really. Only classical."

"Oh, yuck!"

A forced laugh from Sarah. "I like it. Sort of."

"It's OK. But I'm not in the mood. I feel like dancing. I'll go with you to Tower after rehearsal Saturday. Will your mom let you buy some records?"

"Oh, yeah. But I'll have to get out of sailing."

"Sailing?"

"Yeah. We have a boat."

"Can I go sometime?"

"Oh, sure. It's not that much fun though. Cold. You get seasick?"

"I've never been."

"I'll ask my mom."

"Let's go downstairs. Haven't you got any rock or disco?"

"'Saturday Night Fever,' that's all."

"That'll do."

"It's my mom's, if you can believe it."

The door opened and Marion heard them clopping downstairs in their Mary Ellis oxfords. She heard the familiar beat, the tunes. She heard Sarah and Marlene thumping on the living room rug. Her forehead was wet against the wall. Her mouth tasted of chocolate and vomit.

When Marion had come home with the record several years ago, Sarah had sniffed and made a great show of closing doors and stuffing her ears with cotton, especially when she tried to practice. But Marion had listened to the record again and again until she knew every note, every word. She had swung her body to the music, a natural dancer, flinging her arms up and out as she'd seen in the movie and on TV. Her head swayed against the beat, her feet flew back and around in timeless, passionate rhythms. The music and the dancing shifted her into her own realm of possession, she and the music, she and the rhythms of her own body.

Quietly, Marion opened the guest room door and stepped out in the hall. She walked across to her room, stopped in the doorway, and then turned abruptly and went downstairs. At the foot of the stairs she sat and watched.

"Well, you can tell by the way . . ." sang out the stereo. Marlene struggled to help Sarah swing forward in time to the music.

"Here," she said, "kick this leg out. Look, watch me." She flung herself gracefully into the beat, stylizing her movements, pursing her lips. Marion shrank back before she turned to come back. "Now you try."

Sarah jerked herself forward like a robot, holding her neck and head stiff and serious. When she lifted each leg, she held the foot vertically, a storm trooper in training. Marlene collapsed onto the couch.

"No, no, no. Relax! Just swing your body. You need something to relax you. Got any sherry?"

"What?"

"Sherry. Alcohol."

"No. Well, yes, of course, my parents do. But—"

"Oh, yeah, your mom's upstairs. Oh well. Look. Watch me again." She went back to the stereo and moved the needle to the beginning of the song.

"Well, you can tell . . ."

Marlene threw off her shoes and flew into a round of twirls and dips. She thrust out her pelvis, flung back her head, and stalked across the room. She had a perfect figure, from what Marion could see, under the midi and navy stockings; a small waist, plump, firm breasts. Her skin was dark-olive, her face peppered with the bumps and red scars of teenage acne. But her large black eyes and sensuous mouth, her thick black hair cut beautifully around her face, compensated for the imperfect skin. She was sexy in a cheap way that Marion imagined would give her currency among boys her own age. She seemed to dare to give vent to her own sexuality without regard for its potency. Marion watched in fascination.

"Now, you," said Marlene, falling back onto the couch. Sarah, blushing and perspiring with the effort, executed a hopeless parody of Marlene's routine. She kept her arms stiffly bent, as if she carried a shopping bag on each, shooting out her fingers with the beat of the music.

"Well, anyway," said Marlene, "it's hard."

"I'm hopeless, I know it," said Sarah, sitting stiffly on the chair opposite.

"No, you're just uptight. I told you before. You have to relax."

"I know. But it's hard."

"What shall we do now."

"I have to practice."

"OK. I'll go."

"No, I'll ask my mom if you can stay for dinner. Can you? I'll only practice for an hour."

"Um, no, thanks. I think I'll go on home. Ask her about the sailing though."

"My mom? Sure. Next Saturday?"

"Yeah."

"And tomorrow we'll go to Tower."

"Oh, yeah. OK." Marlene had put her shoes back on and was doing her hair in the reflection of the window.

"You're so lucky to have your hair," said Sarah, trying on the singsong voice in vogue among teenagers.

"It drives me *crazy*!" said Marlene, shaking out her hair and lifting her chin in approval.

"Well, you're lucky you don't have mine."

"I think yours is just gorgeous since I cut it."

"Really?"

"Yeah. Listen, I've got to go. See you tomorrow."

Marion strolled down into the hall and smiled. "What've you girls been doing?"

"Oh, just messing around," said Sarah, shepherding Marlene out of the house, shielding her from Marion with her large body.

"Bye! Thanks!" shouted Marlene.

"Bye," said Sarah. She closed the door quickly.

Marion stood back and watched Sarah avoid her eyes. The girl went into the living room and took the record off the stereo and then tried to circumambulate Marion to reach the breakfast room.

"Tell me about Marlene," said Marion.

"There's nothing to tell."

"Well, for one thing, she's the first friend you've brought home in years. There must be something special about her."

"I like her."

"I know that. What is it about her that you like?"

"Oh, Mom, please. I just like her, that's all. I need to practice."

"All right, my dear, go ahead."

"Oh, do you mind if I don't go sailing tomorrow?"

"No, of course not. But why?"

"I have things to do."

"*Things?*"

"A project."

Marion cocked her head. "For what subject?"

"Music."
"I see. Well, fine. You do what suits you."
"Thanks."
Marion sat down heavily on the couch and stared out at the dying light. The phone rang. She heard Sarah answer and mumble in her soft, low voice, reverentially. "Tuesday . . . Thursday . . . three o'clock, then. That's fine. Thank you."
She got up and walked to the kitchen as Sarah put the phone down.
"Who was that?"
"Mr. López."
Marion took a quick breath. "What?"
"He canceled the rehearsal tomorrow."
"Why?"
"Dunno."
"Will it be another time?"
"Tuesday and Thursday after school."
Marion switched on the lights in the kitchen and the hall. "Did he call you from school?"
"How should I know?" Sarah vanished into the breakfast room and Marion heard her unsnapping the cello case, tuning, screwing and adjusting the strings. She stood there for a moment in the fluorescent light of the kitchen and then ran out and upstairs two at a time. She dialed quickly.
"José?"
"Yes."
"It's Marion."
There was a long draw on a cigarette, smoke exhaled under control, a final sniff.
"Why haven't you phoned me, José?"
"I don't know."
"You do know."
"Well, you know why."
"Because of Ben coming over?"
"Not just that."
"What then?"

“I had to think.”

“About?” Hope surged up and around Marion’s neck, head, ears, hope combined with a sour note of bathos, the stupidity of this all, the inappropriateness of her week of suffering, the muffled suspicion that there was more to her dejection than José’s withdrawal.

“Marion, there is something special about you for me—”

“And you for me.”

“There’s something—something strong and weak about you that I love. And then, when that other doctor phoned, I realized that he is part of your world, your class, your interests. He is safe. Even if he didn’t love you—as he does, don’t deny it—he is more *appropriate* for you, as you would say, for an affair even, than I am. I am another world. For you I am a dangerous toy. I think that for you that is my appeal.”

“Why did you cancel rehearsal tomorrow?”

“Do you not have anything to say to answer me?”

“I do. I do. But I have to see you to tell you that you are no toy to me. You are the best thing that has ever happened to me. Can I see you tomorrow?”

“I will be home all day. Come as soon as you can.”

“I’ll be with you before I wake up.”

They both hung on for a few seconds and then hung up without saying good-bye.

Sarah’s cello strained through scale after scale, muffled by closed doors and carpeting. The sun had set, leaving only its red afterglow over the horizon. Friday evenings used to be genial, the night before two days of restaurants, sailing, friends, the opera, the symphony, Sarah a silent presence. But tonight and Fridays to come promised to be unbearable. Marion felt snared by her own predictability. She thought of the women featured in the “New Scene” section of the paper, women who demanded and took weekends for themselves, months off, not commune types, not the hot-tub set, but women who saw their lives eddying in the safety of the shallows and decided on a periodic plunge. Some had husbands who spoke up under their photos. They talked of threat, trust, reciprocal respect. Did she want that with Jonathan? Marion sank her head between her knees until her face flushed hot. Then she sat up, dizzy from the plunge. No, she didn't. She wanted to be twenty-five and childless or, failing that, thirty-six and free. She wanted a gregarious, extroverted daughter and six lovers. She wanted Jonathan to melt away without litigation. She wanted him eliminated without fault of her own.

"How far along are you?"

"I'm not absolutely sure. Five or six weeks, I guess. Not more than seven."

Gertrude wiped her hands again on her large-flowered apron and sat down at the kitchen table. Marion sat down too, trying to catch her mother's eye, seeking out the warm gleam, the special loving glance. But Gertrude seemed not to notice her. She was calculating, muttering in German, producing a solution.

"Tomorrow," she said at last, looking up at Marion as if she, Marion, were a distant cousin asking a great favor. "I'll phone Steinberg and fix it for this week. He'll have to do it this week. You will just have to take a day or two off from classes. But," she sighed, slapping her flat hands on her thighs, "it can't be helped. Now, let's have some tea."

Gertrude stood up and filled the kettle, humming her favorite theme, the "Ode to Joy."

"Fix what, Mother?"

Gertrude turned, kettle in hand, to stare at her daughter.

"What are you asking?" she whispered.

"Fix what for me with Dr. Steinberg, Mother?"

Gertrude walked over to the table and set the kettle down between them. Marion could hear the water slapping up against its sides, like the turbulence in her own stomach.

"What are you asking me, Marion?"

Marion looked down at the table and traced the familiar grooves and ridges in the wood with her fingernail.

"I won't have an abortion," she mumbled.

"What? What is this?"

"I won't have an abortion."

"Marion, do you know what you are saying? Don't say it! An abortion is nothing. Nothing! And think. Think what is the alternative. Adoption? An illegitimate child! Think of the child!"

"Jonathan wants us to get married." Marion stared down at her finger as it moved back and forth in the same groove. She could hear Gertrude drawing in breath, holding it, letting it out again in small puffs.

"Do not have this child, Marion. Finish your studies. Wait until you find a man who is right for you, worthy of you. Not this one. Believe me. You are young and what you do, you think you can undo like that!" She snapped her fingers. "But marriage, children, medical school, *all* together—you are not ready. You do not understand what you would have to give up."

"I would go on with medical school. I'd never give it up."

Gertrude smiled, a thin unhappy smile. "Not just school," she said. "Not just school."

Marion wiped the thin film of sweat from her forehead with the back of her hand. She felt Gertrude's anxiety like a stranglehold around her neck, a grip from which she couldn't struggle free without agreeing to get rid of the child she carried. Yesterday, she would have agreed with Gertrude. Yesterday, an abortion had seemed right, logical, sensible. But now she felt equally sure that what Jonathan offered would be better for her. He had conjured up a life for her in which she would have everything, and on her terms. Why wait? he asked. And she asked herself the same question. Why? He loved the idea of the child. And he seemed to value her career more even than his own. Pregnancy was nothing, he said, nothing for *her*, Marion Klauber, anyway. She could have it all. Everything was easy for her. Why shouldn't this be easy too? She would get her childbearing over and have her thirties to herself. Marion had looked at him as he knelt next to the bed, stroking her wet sticky hair away from her forehead, and had felt a sudden surge of delight at the neatness of his solution. Perhaps this pregnancy was providential. Jonathan would be a different sort of husband from the one she had supposed she would one day have, but he was also different from any man or boy she had known before. She was comfortable with him; she was herself as she liked herself best. And with him, she saw now, she could continue to be herself, the self she chose to be, without being subjected to the critical insights of a more substantial, a less frivolous husband. The whole issue was being overplayed by Gertrude.

"How old were you when you were married, Mother?"

"Twenty-eight."

"That must have been old, then."

Gertrude smiled. She knew she had lost, and she tried to hide the quiver in her lip by stretching her mouth into a smile. "Do you love this man, Marion?"

"Yes." Marion folded her arms and stared at Gertrude. "Well...yes. And he adores me."

"Things change."

"You mean he'll change?"

"It could be."

"Mother, this is not the end of the world. You think I'm perfect, a great beauty, a genius. I'm not. I know what I am. Sooner or later I'd get married, and you'd have the same response."

"Perhaps. Perhaps not."

"What are you worried about?"

Gertrude cast her eyes around and around Marion's face, like a lover taking a last look before the flight is called.

"I'm worried, Marion, my darling, that in your innocence and your lust for always something new, the gambles you take—I am worried that sometime, a long way off maybe, five years, ten years, you will look back and regret. And there are only a few things in our day-to-day lives more terrible than that."

They were married on the hottest October day ever recorded in New York. Marion stifled in her long white dress. Her head seemed light, giddy, and she had to sit down more than once so that she wouldn't fall. Everyone knew, of course. The haste of the wedding, the innuendos of Jonathan's mother, all added to the general conclusion that Marion had landed her catch with ease.

Marion herself was unaccustomed to this subtle dislike and exclusion. She had always counted on her charm and intelligence to win over people she wished to impress. But with these women she had no power. They seemed to misunderstand her deliberately. At least four of them had assumed she was a nurse and didn't seem to hear her when she corrected them.

She looked across the room at Beth, the only guest whom *she* had invited. Beth had the demeanor and dedication of a nun. She was burdened, it seemed to Marion, by common sense. But there she was, burdened and free, while Marion, the one most likely to succeed, was now strapped down, by her own extravagance and would have to be more than a magician to set herself free again. Marion looked around her at her own wedding, and a chill settled over her heart.

The phone rang and Marion picked it up slowly, without a word.

"Hello? Sweetie? You there?"

"Yes."

"Listen, I have an emergency C-section and a bleeding partial. No way I'll be home before ten or eleven. Did we have anything on?"

"Only a movie with Beth and Alex."

"Beth's staying to help me. Why not go with Alex? That'll keep you both out of mischief."

"Mischief!"

"Well, go. Enjoy yourself. You've been run down lately."

"I've had the flu."

"Yeah. Well, I must go. Kiss Sarah for me. See you later."

"Oh, Jon, about sailing tomorrow. Um—Sarah's got some project going with a friend and I've got things to catch up on. Do you mind?"

"No, that's OK. I'll ask Beth if she and Alex want to go."

"Fine idea."

"Must run."

"Bye."

"Bye."

Marion held onto the receiver in its cradle. José might be home tonight. But that would leave tomorrow like a black hole. No, she would sit through a movie with Alex and a box of chocolates, keeping José for tomorrow, like an undershirt against the cold, to warm her cadences, her smiles in response, to convince Alex that her temper and outlook had improved in the two weeks since they'd last seen each other. She picked up the receiver and dialed quickly.

"Alex?"

"Yup. How're you?"

"Fine. Jonathan just phoned—"

"I know, Beth phoned me."

"Want to see a movie tonight?"

"Did Jonathan suggest that too?"

"Yeah."

"Well, do you want to?"

"Yeah. There's that old Lina Wertmuller at the Surf—*Swept Away*," she said. "I've seen it, but I wouldn't mind seeing it again, and it's the only thing worth seeing."

"I don't think I've seen it."

"You'd remember if you had."

"OK. Let's go. What time?"

"Well, the movie's at eight and I'd like a bite first, wouldn't you?"

"How about if I pick you up in ten minutes?"

"Fine."

Marion pulled on a pair of jeans and a sweater. She hastily put on some make-up and ran downstairs. Sarah was still laboring over the Bach.

"Sarah?"

"Mmm."

"Daddy and Beth are caught up at the hospital, and I'm going to a movie with Alex. Want to come?"

"No, thanks."

"Well, there's lots of food in the refrigerator. Some lasagne, soup—"

"Don't worry. I'll fix something."

"Are you happy to stay home tonight?"

"Happy?"

"In a manner of speaking, of course. God forbid you should be happy."

"Can I ask Marlene to spend the night?"

Marion paused. She looked at the girl's closed face, her legs spread around the cello in hopeless vulnerability. She saw the quick flash of anxiety in her eyes.

"Why not?" Marion said.

"OK."

Marion stepped backwards out of the room, mumbling something about checking supplies. She walked through to the dining room where the alcohol was kept. The door to the cupboard had no key. There was no where she could move the vast quantities of alcohol that were stored there now anyway. Quickly she walked through to the kitchen and printed a message on the scratch pad: TEENAGERS DO NOT DRINK ALCOHOL IN THIS HOUSE. She tore off two pieces of Scotch tape, walked back into the dining room, stuck the notice onto a bottle of Johnny Walker and a bottle of Campari and closed the cupboard door. The doorbell rang and she heard Alex trying the handle. Quickly she flung on her parka and opened the door.

"Bye, Sarah!"

"Bye!"

Alex stood in the hall in his corduroy-and-leather jacket, smiling, the counselor in repose.

"Does she want to come along?"

"No, I asked her."

"Will it make a difference if I ask her?"

Marion cocked her head and smiled. She ushered him out and closed the door behind them. "Alex, you're a darling, but not even you can compete with what she's got lined up for tonight."

"What's that?"

"The newest addition to Mary Ellis—a sexpot from Chicago whose mother is a hairdresser."

"Snob."

"I know. But you should see her. And you should see Sarah transformed in her presence. I can't imagine what's happening to her."

"She's growing up."

Marion slumped down into her parka. Marlene made her uncomfortable. She didn't want her in the house. She felt invaded, imposed upon, unnaturally vigilant, unsafe. They drove to the movie in silence. Several times Alex glanced over at her, questioning, but Marion smiled back and continued to worry. Something about Sarah and this new girl, something discordant about their liaison, made her wary.

The movie was diminished the second time she saw it. But Alex was pulled into it, straining in his seat for every inch of screen. He wanted to discuss it afterwards over coffee; he wanted her opinion, the feminine, the feminist perspective. Marion was too bored to give him what he asked. She couldn't find opinions on master-slave sexuality that had any fire in them. She was flying from Marlene to José—from tonight to tomorrow—and her distraction finally convinced Alex to take her home.

"I must take Bethy to see that," he said, seeing her through the door with a smile. "I think she'll find it provocative."

"Thanks, Alex, dear. I'm anxious to check on the girls. Want some coffee?"

"Thanks, no. But look, relax. You'll give yourself an ulcer."

"Good-bye. Thanks. See you soon!"

Marion closed the door and went straight to the liquor cabinet. The note was still there. She peeled it off and went upstairs to Sarah's room. The door squeaked slightly as she opened it, and Sarah sat up.

"Sarah?"

"Hi, Mother."

"Is Marlene here?"

"No, she couldn't come. Daddy phoned to say he'd be back around midnight."

"OK. Thanks, darling. Good night." She brushed Sarah's forehead with a kiss.

"Night, Mother."

Marion closed the door and went to her own room. She sat down, reached for the phone, and dialed José's number.

"Yes?" He had been asleep.

"José, I called to say . . . to say good night. I wish I were with you."

"*Dios mío!* And so do I. Can you come now?"

"No, but I'll be there tomorrow."

"Early?"

"Early."

6

Saturday mornings had always made Marion feel lucky. For other women, a Saturday was just a Saturday, more of Monday to Friday, more people to account to, to listen for. But by Saturday Marion had done a week's work. She had written her term paper, passed her exams, and she could play house in good conscience. Jonathan and Sarah seemed to play along. Jonathan would creep out of bed early, killing his alarm before it buzzed, off to the hospital for his rounds. And Sarah would wait for her to come down before starting her practicing. She'd even smile as Marion appeared at the kitchen door, with a hint of patronage, benignly, like Jonathan smiled, just a little too quick to relax back into full-lipped nonchalance.

But this Saturday, as Marion watched the clock move through to the hour of six when Jonathan would wake, she felt manipulated, the object of a tacit conspiracy to make her and women like her feel lucky. After all, what did she really have to show on this middle-class balance sheet of hers for her weekly sense of well-being? Nothing she did or had seemed to hold in itself a spark of real satisfaction. It was rather, she thought, that she used her assets as twigs and branches from which to weave her elevated web. She would peer down at the others scuttling around below and feel lucky—lucky and safe. She, Marion Roth, had found a safe way of growing old. But now there was a snapping of dead wood and she wondered where to catch on, which way to fall and how.

Jonathan's alarm buzzed out and Marion leapt over him to kill it. He stirred and clutched towards her, deep in sleep.

"It's six," she said. "What time did you come in last night?"

Jonathan turned away and drew the pillow around his ears. It was still dark, but Marion could see by the light of their two clocks the tortuous trail of his clothes from the door to his side of the bed. White coat, shoes, slacks, shirt and tie, lay mangled and lifeless on the carpet. She curled back on her right side, watching the second hand sweep around the minutes, waiting for Jonathan to wake and leave. Someone tried to start a cold Volkswagen outside, over and over, until it was flooded.

Jonathan stirred and then jumped up. "Christ! Six-thirty! Why didn't you wake me?"

"I tried to—"

"He was hopping one leg into his pants, slapping out last night's wrinkles, grabbing at his tie. "I've arranged to meet Alex and Beth at nine at the marina. No chance that you can come?"

"No, sorry. What's the weather like anyway?"

Jonathan stalked across the room and parted the curtains.

"Shitty. Looks like rain, but the forecast last night said clear."

"Well, good luck." Marion tried not to sound impatient. "Take warm clothes."

"Mmm." Jonathan was cleaning his teeth and came out with the brush in his mouth, spraying toothpaste as he talked. "How was the movie?"

"OK. Fine. Alex was a bore. How was the C-section?"

He stopped and looked at her quizzically. She looked at the clock, wondering how long it would take him to leave, pondering the cliché of time's relativity, the endlessness of the last half hour.

"Why do you ask?" He was shouting through from the bathroom.

"Polite conversation," she shouted back. "Quid pro quo."

Again he came through, wiping his face on her towel, looking at her, wide awake.

"Why, why, why can't you use your own towel?" Marion sighed and rolled away from him.

Jonathan didn't move. "Listen, what's gotten into you lately? Or should I ask who?"

"If that's a joke, it's in very poor taste, especially at this hour."

"Well, I don't know. You've been bitchy, uncooperative, not giving a damn about anyone except—"

"I've been ill."

"Yeah, yeah, yeah, I know. But not that ill. Ill in the head maybe. Permanently premenstrual maybe. Even Alex commented that you've been uptight."

"Oh Alex!"

"A psychiatrist!"

"So? So? A friend, not a psychiatrist, to me."

"Well, anyway, I'm warning you to shape up."

"Warning? Warning!" Marion sat up and stared at him, feeling as she did the pull of gravity on her cheeks, on the soft flesh under her eyes, on her breasts, her thighs, feeling her age, her openness to pain, the viciousness of the life they shared.

Jonathan threw the towel into the bathroom, put on his jacket and walked out into the hall, leaving the door open behind him. Marion leapt up and slammed it closed, standing alone on her side for a moment, listening as he clattered down to the garage and drove away.

She hated him. And yet, quite unreasonably she knew, she could not bear him to hate her back, to call her on her state of mind. His unquestioning readiness to accept the surfaces of things had always provided her with a measure of privacy, a measure of freedom. And she seemed to count on his being that way. When he gave vent, as now, to his own unexamined anger and resentment, she could not but feel the lash of it across her heart, the snap of another support that left a limb, or a lung, limp and flapping in the hostile air.

His resentment wasn't new. It was as old as the birth of Sarah, she supposed. It was just that she'd forgotten, over the past ten years or more, the bully inside her worshiper, and her own flash of teeth in response, like a vixen caught fast in a trap. She had seen him watch her as she stuffed chocolate into her mouth while the baby nursed. She marked his distaste, his disappointment, at the sight of his goddess, like fine porcelain, breaking out into a craze of flaws and fractures. She knew then that her new helplessness, her dependency on him made him want to crush her, to stamp her out like an ant or a slug.

Marion walked through to the bathroom and ran herself a hot bath. The sun was rising through the stipple of the bathroom window, setting the tile, the towels, and everything in the room on fire. She eased herself by inches into the water, the sweat beading up on her lip and forehead. And she lay there staring as her body lost its own solidity and her blood matched the heat of the water surrounding it. She heard a scratching at the door.

"Yes?"

"Mother, it's me. Are you awake?"

"Sort of."

"I'd like to practice now, before I go out."

"Oh, sure, go ahead."

"Thanks."

"Oh, Sarah—"

"Yes."

"Come in."

The door pushed open about twelve inches with Sarah on the other side.

"Come in, come in, for heaven's sake."

Sarah came into the small bathroom. She stood still, looking at the floor. Her head was once more bound in pink plastic; cream covered her cheeks.

"Have you phoned Grandpa and Grandma yet?"

"No."

"Well, phone today."

"I will."

"And Grandpa will wonder about the Bach."

"I'll do it this week."

"Make sure you do. He loves those tapes you know."

Sarah shuffled, waiting to be dismissed.

"Sarah?"

"Mmm."

"Would you do me a favor and scrub my back?"

"What?"

"Scrub my back. Really hard. Here's the cloth."

Sarah stood motionless. Even her hands remained still at her sides.

". . . Unless of course, you'd rather not—"

One had plunged into the pocket of her robe and then pulled out again quickly, like a rodent fleeing from the wrong hole. She stepped over to the sink and picked up the soap, slipping it from one hand to the other.

"Mother, do you mind, I'd rather not?" she asked softly.

"Well, of course not, of course not." Marion splashed her feet and sank her head into the water, reaching for the shampoo.

"Would you pass me the shampoo, darling?"

"It's in front of you, in the corner on the right."

Marion grasped the bottle and squeezed the shampoo out onto her head, then she massaged it into her hair. She repeated silently again and again to herself like some mantra of painful flagellation, "She cannot bear to touch me. She cannot bear to touch me." Her hair felt coarse and stuck in the slits of a few fingernails. She tore through it, finding strands of it woven amongst her fingers as she reached for the towel to dry her eyes. Sarah had gone, escaped while Marion's eyes were closed, closing the door silently behind her. She had fled in the face of an intimacy beyond her own desire, beyond what flesh would tolerate.

Marion touched her thigh with her fingertips. She stroked the instep of her foot, wrinkled and swollen as it was with water. They seemed to belong to someone else, and yet she felt her flesh as her own, hers, and yet not hers, something there to be touched, to be kept alive. How could she bear to be shunned by her child, the only person as close to her in blood as her own mother? How could she stand by? How could she bear the strangeness of it?

And then she remembered. She felt again those years of competence and control, wheeling Sarah into the elevator and down to Gertrude's apartment, down through floors and floors, handing her over without a last touch, without a moment's remorse. And Sarah's face when Gertrude opened the door, her arms open, straining at the leases that tied her into the stroller. Marion felt a fool to hope for more now, an abject fool. She had freed herself without a thought; so sure, so sure was she of her own good fortune.

And then Marion wept in pity for Sarah and for herself. Tears splashed down her cheeks and onto her chest as she gasped for breath, hanging her head and then tossing it back to stare through veils of misery at the ceiling. And Marion knew in her loneliness that it was not her luck that had changed or her life or her people, but her own vision that had cleared. She looked in on her world and she saw the bits and pieces that passed for success. And she felt like a beggar, nothing in her hand, who would be grateful beyond reason for the willing touch of her own child.

The sun now glowed well above the horizon and had turned the bedroom from scarlet to gold. Fresh light fell over yesterday's books and clothes and unmade bed. Between six and seven Jonathan's rain clouds had dissolved, casting the whole day into a new mold. Children began to come out onto the street to celebrate the beginning of another weekend. Marion strained above their shrieks and shouts to hear the cello below, but no sounds came from her own house. No hammer pounding nails into the back fence. No kitchen clanging. There was not even the smell of bacon and coffee. The Roths were different, and their differences removed them from the normal expectations of middle-class weekends. The oddness of their hours, their child, their priorities, had singled them out on the block for a special reserve. No one assumed that Marion would or could help out with a few eggs or a can of tomato paste. No husband could rely on Jonathan to have that special tool which, in most neighborhoods, was owned by each for all by tacit agreement in the spirit of teamliness and the American dream.

Marion stood nude at the door of her closet and stared in at the skirts and blouses, the boxes of shoes, the evening wear in dry cleaning plastic, and she knew she didn't want to go through the charade of clothing herself for José again. Somehow the deprivation, the anticipation, the snatches of time on the phone precluded which blouse to choose, which bra, which earrings were easiest to remove in a hurry. She wished she could fly off as she was, clean, shaved, and plucked, ready for deliverance. And yet it was this ritual of approach and unveiling that had kept her in misery and anticipation, which had led her along relentlessly like a cow to the slaughter.

There was another scratching at the bedroom door. Marion turned and stepped out of the closet to hear.

"Mother?"

"Yes, Sarah."

"Can I come in?"

"Just a minute." Marion grabbed her robe and plunged her arms into it, tying the sash roughly around her waist. "Come in."

"I can't. Can you open the door?"

Marion ran to the door and opened it. Sarah stood on the other side holding a tray which was propped over one raised knee. She hopped slightly as she tried to keep her balance and coffee slopped from the little coffeepot onto the tray cloth.

"Sarah! How very lovely!"

"Where shall I put it down?"

"Oh, oh, here, next to the bed. What have you made?"

"Oh, just grapefruit and a muffin and coffee. Nothing much. Don't fuss."

Sarah hovered over the tray, shaking out her hands as she always did after hours of practicing. She had removed the cream and the curlers and her hair bounced around her head like a small child's—soft, inviting the adult hand to sink in and caress the head underneath. She seemed golden in the golden light. All her surfaces looked soft to the touch, young and resilient. She was even beginning to look a little thinner, or maybe it was the angle and the light. Things always seemed a little distorted in the morning.

"What time are you going out?" Sarah asked.

"As soon as I'm dressed. And you?"

"After I've practiced."

Sarah stared at the coffeepot as Marion poured the tepid liquid into her cup.

"Sorry, it's probably cold by now."

"No, it's fine. I don't like hot coffee." Marion spread marmalade over her muffin and then began on the grapefruit. "What a treat this is. Have you had breakfast?"

"I had something."

"What?"

"Grapefruit."

"Is that all?"

"I'm not hungry."

"I've always said that if we all ate only when we were hungry, we'd be much healthier for it."

"I know."

"Marion munched on the chewy muffin and poured out the last of the coffee. Her stomach rose in revolt, but she drank it down in one gulp and sat the cup back on its saucer as she looked up at Sarah. The girl hadn't moved since she had set the tray down. She seemed to want something for which she dared not ask or to say something in a language unknown to her. Marion stood up and walked back towards the closet.

"Thank you again, darling. I have to get dressed. I'm late. Don't worry about the tray. I'll take it down when I go."

"No. I'll take it. I'm going down now."

Sarah took the tray and left, hooking the door almost closed behind her with her foot. Marion quickly slipped into some old jeans and a cashmere sweater. Her hair had dried into wayward wings and wisps, but she ignored it and rummaged through her drawer for rouge and eyeliner. Her face in the mirror stared back at her in wild defiance. Dress me if you dare, it said. Soften, blend, tint. Her eyes blazed out, small and mean; her nose seemed swollen, her teeth yellow. New lines ran across her forehead from one eyebrow to the other and her skin itself seemed coarse with the scales of sun and age.

She set down the pot of rouge and closed the drawer. The phone rang and she got up to answer it, but by the time she picked it up, Sarah already had it. Marion hung on, listening.

"Hello."

"Sarah?"

"Mr. López."

"Yes. No rehearsal today. Did you remember, I hope?"

"Of course, Mr. López."

Silence.

"Uh—is there anything—?"

"Yes—my shoulder. Sarah, is your mother at the clinic?"

"No. She's upstairs. Should I call her?"

"Yes, please."

Marion heard Sarah put the phone on the kitchen table, heard her run upstairs two at a time, and stop outside her door.

"Mother! Mr. López, on the phone for you." Sarah was out of breath. She pushed open the door slightly and saw Marion at the bedside holding the receiver at her side.

"I have it, thank you, Sarah . . . Hello?"

"You were on the line!"

"Yes."

"Why aren't you here?"

"I can't . . . Wait, the phone is off—uh." Marion heard Sarah plod downstairs. She heard the click of the receiver replaced on its cradle. "Are you crazy?"

"No. Impatient."

"I'm coming now. For God's sake—"

"Hurry up!" He rang off and Marion shouted above the dial tone. "Aspirins. There really is nothing more I can do for you, I'm afraid. Just rest it. No, don't play the piano. Fine. Come and see me if it still bothers you next week. Yes. Good-bye."

Marion replaced the receiver and sat down heavily on the bed. She heard Sarah's muffled scratching at the door.

"Mother?"

"Yes."

"Can I come in?"

"Of course, for God's sake."

"Is he OK?"

"You mean Mr. López"

"Yes."

"He's fine. He has bursitis or something related, and he's a bit of a hypochondriac."

Sarah stared at Marion. She seemed again to be muffled, muted by her own tight corks and seals. "I think—I think—"

"What do you think?"

"I think that he's—not a hypochondriac."

Marion looked up at Sarah. "Well, maybe not. I'm not used to these sensitive types."

"No, I guess you're not."

"Well . . ." Marion stood up. "I'm late. I'll see you later." She took her sunglasses out of her purse and put them up on her head.

"You're going out like that?" Sarah mumbled.

"What do you mean?"

"Oh, nothing."

"No, what?"

"Your hair—it's sort of messy."

"I know, but I have no time to fix it. I must rush. Bye, darling. Enjoy your morning with Marlene."

Sarah nodded. She tried to walk out behind Marion, but they both met at the doorway and Marion stepped forward to go through first. Sarah was stepping back though at an angle to move out of the way and they crashed together, hips and breasts, arms flailing. Marion's glasses fell to the floor and Sarah, in her confusion, crunched them under a slipper.

"Oh, hell! My glasses!"

"I'm sorry," Sarah said, dropping to her knees on top of the broken frames. "I'm sorry, Mother. I didn't mean—"

Marion felt her blood rise and fall. She knelt to face Sarah and groped under Sarah's knees for the pieces of plastic.

"I'll get another pair, Mother. OK?"

Marion looked up into Sarah's face and shook her head.

"But I'd like to!"

"Another time," Marion said. Don't worry."

They both stood up and threw the pieces into the wastebasket. Sarah left quickly, heading back to the breakfast room, without a word. Marion took her keys and ran down to the garage. It was eight o'clock and the children on the street had gone in for breakfast.

Marion blinked into the sun as the garage door rolled up. The street seemed lit for a symphony. Sarah's cello began overhead. Quickly Marion climbed into the car, turned the key, and then roared out in the new morning, bound for Sausalito.

After the wedding, Marion and Jonathan had taken an apartment in her parents' building, ten floors up. Marion had decided to ignore her pregnancy until the academic year was up. She hid her nausea, cross that she should have to succumb to such a cliché. And then she insisted on bike-riding, sailing, dancing, even walking twenty blocks through the wind to school. When old ladies asked her what she wanted the baby to be, and smiled, and put their thin, freckled hands on her stomach, she was surprised, and slightly repelled. It was as if anticipation of the baby was supposed to be the mainstay of her success and happiness. Anyone, any fool, she told herself, could get pregnant. It was absurd. Pregnancy seemed to turn a woman's most intimate hopes and fears, and, more than that, her body itself, into public property. As the pregnancy progressed, Marion became even more determined to hold herself aloof from the statement of her own shape.

But there was something in the fact of her pregnancy, the misshapenness, the softening and plumping of her proud body, that changed things with Jonathan. Perhaps it was his unmasked scrutiny of other women, unpregnant women, that made her work at pleasing him, made her suddenly fearful of losing him, of losing his worship of her.

And with Gertrude, there was a new restraint. Marion had felt, since that first argument about the abortion, a retreat by Gertrude, a sort of discretion, she supposed. Even Jonathan seemed to pick it up. He responded to Gertrude's formality with gushes of patronizing friendliness, the sort of indulgence, Marion had noticed, that he reserved for women. And then Marion, seeing the superior set of Gertrude's jaw in response, the cock of her head, the cold measure of her eye—Marion herself would feel her blood rising against him and then subsiding into a confusion of impulses and aversions.

A few days after Marion's finals, Gertrude arrived at her door, wearing her downtown hat and handbag.

"Come," she said. "Get dressed. We are going shopping."

"What for?"

"Baby things."

"Oh." Marion stretched and laughed. "Gertrude Helga Klauber, grandmother-to-be, we've got weeks."

"Three weeks, not a diaper, not a sheet, nothing."

"Do I have to come?"

"Marion! Get dressed."

"OK. OK."

On the bus, Gertrude looked at Marion closely. "Marion, who will care for the child when school starts again next year, and all the years to come?"

"I'd thought of Winnie. I spoke to her, in fact. She's prepared to give up her other days. I'll pay her the equivalent of course. On Friday's she can just take the baby down to your place—if that's OK with you."

"No."

"What do you mean no?"

"No. No, no, no!"

"Winnie has raised nine children, Mother."

"They raised themselves. She cleaned other people's houses." Gertrude stared out of the bus window at the steamy grayness of summer in New York. "Marion, will you let me care for the child?"

Marion heaved herself around to stare at Gertrude. "You! Don't be crazy, Mother! What about your own life?"

"What life? What life? A few patients, your father's lunch, and dinner. What life?"

Marion felt the child turn in her stomach. Something about

Gertrude these days, an edge, a dull flash, chilled her own sense of well-being, made her fearful of nothing.

Until recently Marion had disregarded her mother's profession, the odd women who slipped in and out of her apartment in the mornings. That Gertrude was a psychoanalyst had always seemed like some foreign fiction. It didn't fit the elderly woman who, as far as Marion was concerned, had devoted her mind and energies to her daughter's well-being.

But suddenly now, for the first time, she saw her mother as a woman apart. Suddenly, all those certificates on the wall in strange languages, those familiar well-worn bookspines neatly ordered and out of reach on the shelves—suddenly, her mother's past and all its faded promise leapt into vision and, without knowing why, Marion felt herself culpable.

"Mother," she asked. "Why did you give it all up for a cottage-industry practice?"

Gertrude looked at her and smiled. "Before you were born," she said, "I never considered giving up. My work was as important to me as anything else in my life."

The bus lurched and strained. People got on. People got off. Marion felt sick. She felt the blood rushing to her ears and cheeks. Suddenly she didn't want to hear what her mother was about to say. She knew it already. It was as if Gertrude had told her the same tale all her life, weaving and embellishing to make Marion herself the heroine, the princess, the prince charming, the savior and the salvation all in one. She didn't want to hear. She felt like Rapunzel, locked in the tower, scanning the forest wildly for a way out.

"Then you were born, my Marion. A blessing." She sighed, looked into her lap. "I outgrew my ambition. I didn't want you to grow up a stranger."

Marion heaved herself up and rang the bell. "I'll never give up like you did," she said coldly. "Come, let's go."

Gertrude stood behind her, waiting for the bus to stop. She touched Marion's shoulder lightly, as if she were a stranger with something to say. "You won't have to, Marion," she whispered over her shoulder. "You have something I never had."

“What?” Marion asked, twisting around.

“You have me.”

The bus stopped and they both climbed down into the hot street. Gertrude clasped a hand around Marion’s arm. “Marion, my Marion, let me do this. Let me take the child. It’s what I want with all my heart.”

José stood up to kiss Marion when she stepped out of her car. He had been sunning himself against the mailbox post, watching her carefully as she edged her car along the side of the hill. There were, perhaps, people who would know her here or who would at least have the curiosity to wonder who she was, but she felt, in the grip of José’s strong arms, in the cloud of his foreign and unmasked masculine smell, none of her old concern. She was here, by some miracle, with a strange man in a strange place without even the customary masks and veils of female presentation, and she was yet herself, Marion Roth, choosing to be loved if she wished.

They linked hands and walked down the stairs, José first, to the apartment. The door was open and the morning sun filled the room. There were a few books opened on the floor, and the smell of fresh coffee beans and the strong coffee brew itself perfuming the air. He left the door open and went through to his kitchen while Marion sank down onto a cushion, folding her hands behind her head in wonder. There wasn’t anything in this room that seemed subject to the routines and functions of daily life. There wasn’t even a regular table or, it seemed, a bed. She wondered where he slept and ate, where he would mark papers or write a letter. She felt happy here, in the strangest way, unpushed by anything but her desire to examine her own happiness and to wonder at its context. It was not so much the place itself as the mood of the place that affected her—a mood of opulence without self-consciousness, of culture without pretense. Books, fabrics, all the surfaces and smells seemed to belong together, to be bound organically into one nest, a nest in which she found herself more naturally accommodated than in any of those she’d been born to or had made for herself. Perhaps, she thought, I don’t have the talent to make a place for myself—or even a life for myself—that fits. I can't make that leap from object to illusion. I have made a business in my life of literal translation. There's been a logic to all my choices, an insane logic, that has directed me away from myself, so far away, in fact, that it has left me without the courage to return. She looked up as José came in with a tray of coffee. Ah, she wondered, the courage for what?

"Coffee and sweet rolls for you—Mexican style," he said, closing the door as he passed it.

Marion sat up and reached for a mug. The coffee was hot and sweet, almost like Turkish coffee. The rolls looked soft and moist and smelled freshly baked. She ate one quickly and reached for another without his offering it.

"They are quite delicious. Everything is, you included."

"Thank you," he said, smiling.

"Aren't you having one?"

"No, I had three while I was waiting for you to arrive."

"Oh."

"What happened at home this morning?"

"What do you mean?"

"I mean what bad thing?"

"How do you know?"

"I know. Tell me."

"Tell me how you know first."

"Tell me what first?"

And so Marion told him about Jonathan and Sarah, the bath, the breakfast, the sunglasses, and he listened, giving her his whole body in attention, not bothering to murmur in comment until she had finished. He now lay back and stretched out his legs. He sighed and then reached over with one foot to touch hers.

"I knew," he said, "because your hair is not styled. You are wearing no makeup. You are eating without hunger. I think your heart was not with me this morning. It was with your daughter."

"José, what can I do?"

"Wait. Let her come to you. Let her be herself. You think it is because you are the strong professional woman, full of drive and ambition. But it is she who is ambitious. She is driven. It is your other strength, your real strength, that burns her when she comes too close."

"What strength is that, for God's sake?"

He smiled and leaned towards her until she could smell him over the sweetness of the coffee. "It is you," he said, baring his teeth in a tight smile. "You, you, you."

Marion felt the familiar tug of desire in her womb, a flash, quicker than light, from her pelvis to his. This, she thought quickly, is what men feel, how they feel when they want a woman. No analysis, no mood tricks. It bypasses the cranium. And then she refused to think further, she blotted out everything but the unquestionable promise of his smile when he leaned towards her and began to slip off her jeans.

This time Marion was there and back so silently that he never even knew. And then she rushed him through the preliminaries, as if in desire, because in fact she wanted him properly, inside her, for the pleasure of it and for the pleasure of knowing she had nothing to strain towards, no goal, no triumph to achieve. She could watch him building up, withholding, releasing, and she could feel his pleasure because she still felt her own. She could lie back with him and love him really, holding in no secrets or regrets.

"What are you thinking?" he asked.

"That I love you very much."

José leaned over and kissed her ear, her neck. He propped himself up on one elbow and looked down on her, posed like Clark Gable or Marcello Mastroiani, so beautiful she had to move her head to see him at another angle.

"I have not dared to hope for this all this past week," he said. "I have tried to tell myself to give up the thought of you, but I cannot. You are like a drug to me. It even made me sick."

Marion smiled. "You made me sick."

"I know."

"Why? Why were you such a madman over Ben of all people?"

"You know why," he said, rolling back, his hands behind his head. "I felt as if I didn't belong in your life, as if he belonged, fitted you more naturally."

"Oh, Lord! Nothing could be more wrong. He's tight, uptight. And boring."

"But an old friend?" José smiled.

Marion sat up and looked at him. If she had to slaughter Ben for him, she would. She knew just then she'd do anything to have José with her, to have him here for her like this, to make him feel as safe with her as she felt with him.

"An uptight, boring friend," she said, smiling back. "There are friends and friends."

The wind blew around the house and Marion heard the trees again, whining against the wood, squeaking and banging without rhythm, providing a counterpoint to the regular thumping of her own heart.

"I wish I could stay here with you till Monday."

José sat up. "Can you? Could you?"

Marion shook her head.

"Find a way!"

"I can't."

"So it must always be like this? A few hours around sex?"

Marion was startled. Sex was the unspoken core, the nexus between them, and yet she had divined that he didn't want to name it. He preferred, as most women did, to fur out the edges into the general romance of the affair. "Is that how you see it?" she asked.

"That's how it is."

"I suppose—"

"Mariana! Mariana!" He sat up and grasped her hands. "Can we go away together—a week, a few weeks? Can we?" He was looking at her, willing her to assent.

Marion sat up too. She had thought of this, but only in fantasy, never as a possibility. "Where to?" she asked.

"Does it matter? Anywhere! But, better, somewhere beautiful—a beach, a mountain."

She stared at him. The thought of moving their time together to another place, the thought of stretching it over days and nights, now filled all the categories and corners of the neatly ordered mind that she kept for her other world, testing and probing for a place to rest. She smiled suddenly and looked up at him.

"José, there's a meeting in February, a family practice meeting that I'd actually thought I might go to. In Puerto Vallarta. But I'd sort of dismissed it because it's during ski vacation."

José jumped up and leapt over the cushions, pouncing down next to her on the other side. "*Mía Madre!* For a smart woman you are sometimes dumb! *I* will be on vacation then. Easy, easy, easy! Will you do it? Will you?"

Marion's heart began to gallop. It did seem easy. It seemed possible. Images flashed through her head, hotels, breakfasts, one room or two, colleagues, passports, Jonathan, Sarah. Would they want to go along? How would she fly? With him? Alone? And Ben. He'd probably be going and she'd have to stay at the clinic. Oh, no, he was going to his wife's family. They had hired someone to cover for him at the clinic.

"I'll try," she said. "I'll look into it."

"Not try, DO! Which hotel is it?"

"I don't know. I'll look it up."

"I know Vallarta. I can fix everything."

"Oh, José, wouldn't it be wonderful?"

José looked at her and then held her hand at arm's length. His face was on fire, flashing out life and energy in his complete devotion to her, to the idea of a week with her. "It would be more than wonderful," he said. "I promise you. I promise you that."

On her way home, Marion drove out to the Mission and found a Mexican bakery she had passed years ago. She had been looking for a *piñata* for one of Sarah's birthdays and remembered clearly the smell that had come through the door, the shelves and shelves of oversized cookies and cakes which she had seen when she looked through the window. She hadn't gone in then because of the flies and because of the slovenly woman behind the counter. She had hovered outside like a tourist and then moved on, unwilling to take risks.

But now she walked in and pointed to the shelf with José's sweet rolls. "Six," she said, and held up six fingers.

The woman smiled toothlessly and put six on a tray and then

into a bag. As soon as Marion was in the car, she opened the bag and sniffed deeply. She felt as if she were already with him in his alien place, without speech or sight or desire of her own except through his interpretation. She felt like a swimmer in warm waters, buoyed up and floating without effort, counting on the gentle tide to send her back to shore. And she wanted this. She wanted to give up the control of her life to him, even for a week. She wanted to open herself to risks and dangers for the sake of her own waning youth. She wanted to know for sure whether she had any right to be at odds with what the world saw as her own good fortune.

7

Sarah had been dieting for weeks and even though Marion disapproved of the radical self-denial, she was pleased. She was pleased that Sarah's attention was directed outward, that the girl seemed so suddenly concerned with her appearance. But, like everything else that Sarah did, this diet was being carried to extremes. After each meal, even if she ate only a salad or a few steamed green beans, she would excuse herself and run upstairs to the bathroom scale. She had managed to lose a remarkable amount, though and Marion noticed quite soon that her breasts were smaller, that her face, and particularly her cheeks and chin, seemed thinner, more adult looking. Marion had offered several times to take her shopping for some new clothes, but Sarah had refused. She seemed to be waiting to reach some goal, as yet beyond her, before she rewarded herself with clothes. And Marion thought she saw an element of satisfaction in the way Sarah pinned in the waists of her skirts to make them fit, or moved over the buttons on her blouses. Sarah seemed to like shrinking within her old mold, liked to be reminded of what she once had been.

Marion noticed Sarah's new obsession, she acknowledged it, but she gave it only moments of her time. For the most part she was molding her days and weeks around her meetings with José. They met regularly now, in Sausalito, mostly at his apartment, but they had also become bolder. They began to meet for a drink first at the No Name Bar. They walked along the water, side by side. They stopped to chat with friends of his, a writer, a few artists he knew, a street musician. Marion would stand back as he smiled and shook their hands with both of his and she would nod when he pulled her in and responded to their unasked question with, "Bill, this is Mariana, my friend." Marion tried not to speak. She wanted to be considered foreign, without any familiar mode of reference. She wanted most of all not to spoil these times with worries about disclosure. And so she smiled and listened and felt part of his world, lost to the cares of her own wold, so transported in fact that, like Alice, she needed the right ritual to bring her back to her other self.

The return journey from his place to hers served as Marion's ritual. As she recrossed the bridge to go home, with the sun on her right firing up the hills of the city, as she approached the tollbooth and slowed down in the traffic, she would sit back to enjoy a new pleasure, one that she recognized as such only after she had been making the crossing for over a week. It was a slow rush of hope that had the power to carry her out and up, above the water and the hills on either side. It suspended her high above herself, lighter than her most unformulated wishes. It was like the ritual uncorking of champagne, the first glass of wine felt behind the knees. It gave her a sense of power like none she'd had before. It had no reference, no object, only the promise of things to come, the feeling that she could choose, that she could change. She felt free. And this freedom carried her almost to her garage door where it set her down gently, ready to face herself again.

Things had seemed to slip into place for Marion, to change gear so smoothly that she felt blessed by providence, sanctioned in her deceit. Beth, for instance, had sounded almost grateful when Marion canceled their first few lunch dates, and after that, neither of them had assumed that the other could find the time during the week. They restricted their meetings to the weekends when they could be together, coupled, with Jonathan and Alex.

And Marion had arranged the trip to Puerto Vallarta without

difficulty. It had been so easy, in fact, that it lent her boldness for her meetings with José. Jonathan seemed to welcome having Sarah to himself. He even promised to take time off to be with her during the week that Marion was away.

"I thought you might like to come with me," Marion said when she was quite sure he wouldn't go.

"Naa! Much rather go to St. Thomas for the big meeting next September. You can sail there and at least you don't have to put up with those Mexicans and their God awful food."

"Oh."

"Disappointed?"

"No, no. I'll be at the meetings all day anyway."

"I figured you would. And anyway," he said, putting his arm around her with brotherly concern, "I think you need to spend some time on your own, away from here. I mean I told you you've been—uh—distracted lately. And we both need time to think."

"About what?"

"About us, about where we're going and how we're getting there."

"What do you mean *going* and *getting there*?"

"I don't know."

"Well, if you don't, how—"

Jonathan had moved away and was sitting down carefully, a hand on each knee, looking up at Marion. He gave her a look that seemed hopeless, appealing for her help. He had none of his usual optimism, his childish reliance on action to eliminate doubt. Marion sat down too.

"We have everything," he said. "We have careers, enough money, a lovely kid, a house, a boat, best city in the whole God damn world, and what have we got?"

Marion stared back at him, dumb.

"I mean, I always thought," he went on, "that I had it made. Great job, bright sexy wife, none of the usual hassles. I mean, look at someone like Ben, married to that lightweight. I imagine myself sometimes married to a lightweight like that and I'm grateful."

"Thanks."
"No, really. I'm being serious."
"I didn't think you were joking, I'm afraid."
"Well just hold off till I'm through, OK?"
Marion bit down, crossed her arms, and sat back, waiting.
"What I'm saying is that something has happened. I don't feel so damned grateful any more and I don't know why."
"Perhaps you haven't got as much to feel grateful for as you thought you did? Perhaps you're waking up? And anyway, grateful—who to? Why *grateful* for God's sake?"
"'Cause I felt grateful."
"OK, what's changed?"
"We've changed. *You've* changed."
"Aha!"
"You have. You're so damned irritated with everything—Sarah, me. I mean you've always had a chip on your shoulder, but it's never been this heavy."
"I've—"
"No, let me finish. Might I say you *were* irritated? Lately you don't seem to give a shit about anything. I mean you sail around like Lady Muck on Toast as if you're in another world and we're beneath your notice. Admit it."
Marion looked at her sandals and said nothing. Her eyes were filling with tears. They seemed, these days, to betray her even before she could find the reason. Perhaps it was the conjunction of her mornings and evenings, the exclusion of her afternoons, the slipping away of life as she had known it, before she was quite ready to let it go. She looked at Jonathan as he sat there, hurt, puzzled, wanting her assurances, and she smiled as if at a child who had discovered gratuitous evil, undeserved punishment.
"There you are crying and smiling. I dunno. You've gone nuts. I've gone nuts too, I suppose." He fell forward onto his knees, grasping Marion around the waist, burying his head in her lap. He was inviting her to run her fingers through his hair, maybe even to take him to bed, but she was paralyzed. As his head turned in her lap, she looked at his hair and she couldn't touch it. It stuck

together in thin clumps, too long, too thin to leave unwashed, as it was, and salted through with dandruff and loose scalp. Marion grasped the polished arms of the chair she sat on. She could feel in her fingertips José's thick, healthy black hair, the luxuriance of his smooth firm flesh, and she wondered whether, finally, it takes one man to drive another out. Jonathan had become repulsive to her. She could not have him touch her and had for weeks been finding ways to warn him that sex was unwelcome. After a while he seemed not to need the warnings. They hadn't made love since her first visit to José. But this gesture now, this culmination, she knew to be an invitation to begin again.

"Jon. Jonathan! Please sit up."

Jonathan unwound himself and sprang back into his chair. His face was flushed, as if he'd just made love. His hair stuck out like pampas grass. Marion looked away.

"Jon, I don't know what it is that's changed. I don't know exactly. But I do suspect that it's not as recent as you imagine. We've been coasting along for years, feeling so damned fortunate—grateful, if you like—that we haven't stopped to look at what we're so grateful for. I look around me and I see different sorts of people who affect the way I think about my life. There are the ones who have always sent me into deep gloom—the Junior Leaguers, the housewives on this street. There's no point in going over them. Then there are the ones like us—Beth, others, the doctors and the lawyers—who seem to do the same things and want the same things. But there's a third group that I never noticed before. It's hard to describe really, but I have the craziest feeling that they've been laughing up their sleeves at our smugness all along."

"Who? Who are they?"

"I don't know. Yes, you can shrug and wave your arms, but there are people out there who read and know things and feel things we never even imagined. There are people for whom other people, experiences, music, fresh things are more important than . . . what we have. I suppose I mean that they take risks. They avoid the safe choices we've made."

"You're beginning to sound like a laid-back loony. What in

hell are you talking about, Marion? Safe choices! What safe choices?"

"Medicine, San Francisco, the clinic—every choice I've made has been safe. And boring. And I'm beginning to feel that my time's running out."

"Was I a safe choice too?"

"Yes! You were the safest of all. I fell into marrying you, into having Sarah, like some programmed automaton."

"You didn't fall into having a second child though, did you? You weren't so damned automatic then, were you?"

Marion stared at him and he sank his face into his hands, winding his fingers into his hair.

"Why do you bring that up again?" she asked. "I thought you'd accepted my position. I thought you'd agreed."

"I never agreed. You know that. I gave up, but I never agreed. Look at that kid of ours, just look at her. You're always saying she has no friends, that it's not normal . . ."

"So?"

"If we had another one, things might be more normal."

"*More* normal! I want things to be less normal."

Jonathan shook his head, shrugged. He seemed to be having a conversation with himself, talking himself into or out of something. Marion felt like the prisoner in the dock, watching while the jury deliberated.

Finally, Jonathan looked up at her and smiled without conviction. "You've won, you know. You always win. Nothing I want ever seems important enough."

"Oh, for God's sake, Jonathan, spare me the melodrama. Who's talking of winning and losing anyway? Are we at war?"

"I mean we'd never even have gotten married if you hadn't been pregnant," he went on, ignoring her question. "I have to remind myself of that every now and then when I try to remember how good things were. Even when you were so God damned moody and suspicious of me, at least you tried. You seemed to care. We were happy."

"Were we? *Were* we? I—" There was a rush and a scuffling

from the foot of the stairs. Marion jumped up and spun round just in time to see Sarah move away from the doorway. "Oh, Jon! Oh, my God! She's home! She was there listening!"

"So?"

"She *heard!* She heard us arguing. She heard about the pregnancy."

"She's got to grow up and face facts. Now's as good a time as any." He seemed cheered up.

Marion was running away, after Sarah, but she turned to face him, breathing quickly, dropping her voice to a whisper. "I want to say this to you now, while I feel it in its most distilled form: I hate you. I hate your obtuseness to everything important in this world. I hate your concern only for yourself, yourself in others, and in things that show. I hate the clichés that you live and feel and speak. I have not heard one fresh thought from you in fifteen years and I don't hold out much hope for the next fifty. I hate your snap solutions, your reliance on action, your respect for success. I hate the fact that you can't hold a tune, that you come to bed unwashed, that you have not a graceful bone or muscle in your body and don't even know it. But most of all I hate your viciousness masked in humor, your boomerang criticisms. And I want to tell you this: if that child heard what we said, as I'm sure she did, if she suffers, as I'm sure she will; it will be nothing compared with the realization that you and I hate each other and that neither of us, *neither* of us, has ever loved her more then we've loved ourselves." Marion swung out of the room to find Sarah.

"Speak for yourself!" he shouted after her. "I don't need you to speak for me. I'm quite capable—"

Marion heard the cello and saw Sarah's familiar shape through the curtains. She paused before she went in. It was odd. Things seemed so much the same—the cello, the voices of children, a lawnmower buzzing, and yet she felt like Anna Karenina sneaking into her own house past the servants and along the halls. Marion was forced to explain the inexplicable to a child to whom she felt she had no right, who probably wished to hear nothing at all, who probably wanted to be left alone to enjoy the shreds and snatches of her childish fantasies. She pushed open the door and stood in front of Sarah.

"Sarah—"

Sarah stopped playing, holding her bow in place. She looked up at Marion's face and then fixed her eyes on her belt.

"Sarah, I—"

"Mother, I don't want to know."

"But—"

"I heard. You know that. I guess I should've figured it all out before, but it never crossed my mind. Or about being an only child. I never thought about it. It just sort of seemed to fit in with everything else we did differently from everyone else. I just wish—I just wish—"

"What? What, Sarah?"

Sarah lifted her head to face Marion. Tears were spilling over the girl's cheeks, splashing onto the cello, but she stared through them as if she were caught out in the rain far from home and had forgotten her umbrella.

"Please, Mother—please believe me. I just wish you would leave me alone."

"Sarah clasped the cello in both hands and rested her cheek against it, sobbing openly, crying like a baby. Marion ran forward to hold her, stepped around the cello to enter the magic circle of her child's grief. But Sarah saw her coming, raiser her bow and slashed it upwards across Marion's cheek, laying open a two-inch ragged cut.

"Marion's hands flew up to her face, to the burning, bloody line under her right eye. She opened her hands and saw the blood on her palms and fingers and then closed them up again like dead spiders. Drops of blood ran down her cheek and onto her collar. Sarah stared at her mother as if entranced by her own violence. She watched the blood fall and followed the splotchy patterns on the fabric of Marion's blouse. The lawnmower buzzed on in the distance. Blue jays squawked noisily in the oak behind the house. The house itself creaked and sighed as it warmed in the midday sun.

"You could have cut my eye!" Marion whispered. "You could

have—" She lunged forward and grabbed Sarah by her sleeves, shook her, and thrust her back against the chair. "You goddamn bitch!" she shouted. "You could have blinded me!"

"Hey, what's going on in here? Sarah! Marion! Jesus! What's happened?"

Marion turned to face Jonathan, the blood now oozing over her cheek, but as she did, Sarah dropped her cello and ran into his arms, burying her head in his shoulder, sobbing, shaking, clasping him around the neck with both long arms. Marion watched them, listening to the resonating of the cello where it had fallen on the wooden floor. She noticed the pins in Sarah's skirt. She saw the dirt under Jonathan's nails as he patted Sarah's back, the familiar tilt of his head as he whispered in her ear. Marion stepped over the cello and around them both. She walked upstairs, washed her face, dabbed the wound with hydrogen peroxide, and combed her hair. Then she sat on the bed, looked up a number, and dialed.

"Betty? It's Marion. May I speak to Ben, please?" Marion waited. She coiled the cord around her little finger and then pulled it off again. She stared unthinking at the wall ahead of her. "Ben? It's me. Look, I'm sorry to bother you on a Sunday, but I have to talk to you urgently. Anywhere. I'll come to Marin if you like. OK. Then how about Moishe's. M-O-I-S-H-E-S. On Union Street, near that underground garage. Yes. Forty-five minutes, OK. Thanks. Thanks, Ben."

Marion stood up and went downstairs. She heard Jonathan and Sarah in the kitchen talking in low voices. She unhooked her parka, flattened herself against the wall, and slipped through the door down to the garage. It smelled like Sunday down there, dank, disused, the cars nose to tail like elephants in the circus. Marion opened the garage and jumped into her car, thanking god that it was last in, first out. She roared out into the sunshine and, as she turned, looked up. Sarah stood at the long front window of the living room, her hands locked into the fabric of her skirt, watching, too late, too slow to say what she had to say. Marion looked ahead of her down the street and changed gears. She rolled off away from the house and drove to Union Street to meet Ben.

The restaurant was crowded with Sunday people. Marion edged her way up to the hostess and put her name down for a table. She left a message for Ben and walked through to the bar. There were no chairs or even bar stools available, so she milled with the other standers, sipping a glass of white wine and avoiding eye contact. She noticed several people look at her cheek and then look away. She'd forgotten to change her blouse. Her parka needed cleaning and her jeans bagged and pulled in the wrong places. These people, by contrast, seemed groomed for a show. Marion stared at the women as they laughed and threw back their heads. It was a gesture picked up from the TV ads: the woman as wild horse inviting a male to mount and tame her into submission.

Men laughed too, young men with moustaches, but their laughing was more of a snicker, a hint at the sophistication they didn't possess. And over all, like an intoxicating cloud, hung the scent of their perfumes and lotions, women's and men's, the blending of each hope that something in the care, the expense, of this Sunday presentation would pay off with a mate.

Marion caught sight of herself in a mirror behind the bar, staring back out of the mass like a long stake driven deep into the ocean bed, the only thing fixed among the waves and ripples. And yet she felt invisible, sealed out, like a refugee whose country no longer exists and who is permanently displaced, with no village, no people, no language of her own. She surged forward through the crowds to the edge of the bar and gestured for another glass of wine. As she did, a hand touched her shoulder gently and she looked up into the mirror. Ben stood behind her, scrubbed and shining in a coat and tie.

"What happened?" he asked as he paid for her wine. Then he took her gently by the elbow and led her towards an empty bar table. "You look as if you've been in the wars."

Marion smiled. Sometimes his platitudes were a comfort. She felt with Ben as she imagined she would with a brother. He stared at her now, though, with more than brotherly concern. There was something like dread in his eyes, the look of a lover who is being told to go.

"Ben, I'm quitting," she said, swilling the wine in her glass and then staring boldly at him.

"Quitting what, Marion? Your marriage?"

"Maybe that too. I'm quitting medicine."

"Marion!"

"I know what you're going to say." She stretched her hand across the table and closed it over his wrist. She could feel her cheek smarting as her face reddened under his stare. "Ben, I'm no longer sure that it's the right thing for me. I have to look around at the alternatives."

Ben twisted his wrist out of her grasp and linked his fingers under his chin, resting his elbows on the table as she had so often seen him do when he talked to patients. He looked old, much older than she, fatherly, brotherly, she couldn't place it.

"Marion, how old are you? Thirty-four? Thirty-five?"

"Almost thirty-seven."

"OK. Thirty-six. Do you know what you're doing?"

"What?"

"You're regressing. No, don't withdraw. You listen to me now. You're behaving like an eighteen-year-old, like my Clifford—growing his hair and fingernails to see whether he can bear to look unlike me. You're unhappy, restless, dissatisfied, and you latch onto the easiest change to make, something that I wager holds the least responsibility for your present state of mind. What do you think you'll find? Happiness? Nirvana?"

Marion pressed her lips together and shook her head.

"Marion, you're a natural physician. In fact—as you know, you must know—you're wasted in that clinic. It's always been a mystery to me that you settled for that. You belong in academic medicine. Oh, I don't know . . ." Ben called the waiter for two more glasses of wine. "Why am I wasting my time telling you what you already know? Tell me what happened to your face and we'll take it from there."

Marion saw the waitress beckoning them out to the patio and she got up, steadied her wineglass, and followed the waitress towards the corner table hidden under a vast cascade of maidenhead fern. They each took a menu and then settled into hooded basket chairs.

"Blintzes, please," Marion said, handing the menu to the waitress.

"Is that all?" Ben was staring at the menu as if it were a rare book in a foreign language. "Isn't that a dessert?"

"No, not necessarily. I feel like blintzes. But their sandwiches are really good. Try the pastrami on rye."

"Sounds good to me," he said, snapping the menu closed. "One blintz and one pastrami on rye."

"Tell me, please," Ben said. And Marion settled back to tell him everything from the beginning, from Barnard and medical school, the wedding, Sarah, Gertrude, even José, and then the scene this morning. Her tale was orderly, neat and sequential, and he listened like one who had been deprived, never interrupting, hardly touching his sandwich. The waitress came and went, brought more wine, coffee, crackers. But they were sealed into the story, both of them, and Marion heard her own voice fashion it, saw herself revealed in the space that lay between them.

Ben stared at her in silence.

"That's all," she said. "That's it."

The coffee was cold, but Ben drank it as if it weren't, taking small sips, alternating it with his wine. His face was flushed with the wine and the sun.

"Do you mind if I loosen my tie?"

"Oh, for God's sake, Ben, of course not."

He thrust out his chin and tugged at the knot in a masculine gesture that had always appealed to Marion. She smiled. He smiled back.

"Where's he now?"

"Where's who?"

"This José guy."

The way he pronounced *José*, his use of *this* and *guy* worked instantly on Marion. She froze her smile and sat up. "He's at home, I suppose, playing sonatas."

"Oh."

"Why do you ask?"

"Well, I'm wondering whether he'll shoot us both in a fit of jealousy as we leave the restaurant."

Marion laughed at the incongruity of Ben in his loose tie eating pastrami and José in his Pontiac glaring through the rain. She laughed until tears rolled down her cheeks. People turned to look at her and smiled. Even Ben smiled, laughed, and sat back to look at her.

"What a woman you are. Lord, you have such a talent for complicating your life."

"I know. But really, Ben, what would you do?"

"What would I do? I'd kiss that jerk José good-bye for one thing. Excuse me—that's just the way I feel."

"And then?"

"And then I'd go to work on my marriage."

"What kind of 'work'?" Marion was still amused.

"Therapy. Family therapy. Does the Jewish church have an agency?"

"Who knows? The Jewish 'church,' as you call it, would be the last place I'd go."

"Well, whatever. I'd try to save my marriage and my job before chucking up both for some musician."

"It's not for him. It's for me."

"Garbage!"

"Oh, Ben, why are you so predictable?"

"Sorry."

"This is more than an affair. It's a revolution for me."

"I wish I could get hold of him and give him a piece of my mind."

"Ben! Stop being the super Scout and answer me. I want to quit."

"No!"

"Yes! The sooner the better."

"Look, Marion, listen to me. OK. OK. I'll make a deal. Let's consider this a sabbatical. Cut out the mornings, but come in on Fridays. I'll find someone for the other days. Take four days a week to examine your alternatives or whatever it is you're going to do. Take as long as you like, weeks, months, but keep your hand in. Don't give up entirely. You have to come in on Fridays."

"Why?"

"Because I count on you. And you have patients who count on you."

"I've always done that though, compromised, branched out and then turned back at the last minute. There are always people who count on me."

"For me, then, six months. How's that? Six months, one day a week. Isn't that branching out? Please. Please, Marion."

Marion looked down into her lap. She swallowed down the disappointment that rose in her throat, like a child who had counted on parental consent. Why couldn't she tell him no, Fridays were out? Why couldn't it be a clean break? Why couldn't she simply disappear, vanish? She didn't want to hang on. She wanted no guidance or therapy. She wanted to start the destruction somewhere and the clinic seemed the easiest place. She wanted the courage to turn her back on her own career and somehow she had counted on Ben to give it to her.

"Marion?"

Marion looked up at him. The waitress was wiping off the table impatiently.

"Bring us two more coffees, please," Ben asked and then stretched his hand across the table, palm upwards, to hold her hand. She laid her hand there and he closed his around it.

"Marion, I'm going to tell you something I thought I'd never say. But I'll say it now. I love you. I've loved you for ten years and, as far as I can see, I'll always love you. I'm not telling you this for any other reason than that I don't want to see you ruin your life for some nonsensical love affair, or romance with yourself, midlife crisis, or whatever it is. The fact is that you must know how I feel or you wouldn't have asked me here today. I think that, despite what you say, you counted on me to save you from yourself. And, to the best of my ability, I will do so."

"Ben—"

"You will take four days a week to do whatever you have to do, but the fifth you will give to me."

"Oh, Ben, you're so sweet. You're such a bear, such a sweet, sweet man!" Marion bent her head down to his hand and kissed it. "How can I refuse you?"

Ben took his hand away and folded his napkin neatly, corner to corner. Then he looked up at Marion.

"I hate being sweet and predictable, Marion. I hate speaking in clichés. But that is the way I am, I'm afraid. If I could choose, I'd be dark and mysterious and moody and know just when to be passionate and how to drive a woman like you wild. But I don't know how, and it's hopeless even thinking about it. I accept myself the way I am. I feel happier, safer, this way." He stood up and tightened his tie. Then he smiled. "I must run. I'll have to do some penance for missing Sunday at home on my free weekend."

Marion trotted behind him, out of the restaurant. They stood outside awkwardly, like teenagers after the matinee.

"See you Friday, then," he said. "My car's a few blocks away."

"I'll keep my old hours until we can find a replacement."

He touched her cheek lightly and then walked away down the street. She watched him until he turned a corner and vanished. It was four o'clock already and the air was chilling. Marion drove her car out of the garage and headed towards the bridge. She needed to see José and, even more than that, to be in the other world of his apartment, to have its smells and sounds and comfort within reach. She had never been there on a Sunday before. But today she was in special need and the risk seemed irrelevant.

8

Marion drove along the familiar route, stopping and starting, edging through the jam of tourist cars and Sunday drivers, unaware of the time and the place through which she drove. She was thinking of José's apartment and it was just a matter of crawling over the earth to bring her within touch. She could even hear him playing Mozart. She could see the angle of the sun through his window, could smell the sweet coffee brewing.

There was a parking place two blocks before José's and Marion took it. On Sundays everyone apparently stayed home in Sausalito, filling the parking spaces with their cars. She zipped up her parka and ran along the road to his house. As she approached she saw a group of blond teenage boys hovering over a motorcycle in the garage above José's apartment. She hesitated for a moment and one boy looked up. He was square headed, muscular, and Germanic in a way that had always repelled Marion. She found these bull-like, dull suburban boys unapproachable.

"Need help?"

"No, thanks. I'm just going down to Mr. López's."

"Uh—" He loped towards her, rubbing the grease from his hands onto his jeans. "Want me to tell him you're here?"

Marion stepped back, suddenly irritated. "No, thank you. I know my way down."

She walked quickly to the stairs and climbed down into the wind. She heard the boys raising their voices in a vulgar laugh above her and knew that she was the object of their humor. But she didn't care. All she wanted was to be inside José's apartment.

As she turned the corner down to his front door, she realized that it must be open. She heard the piano first and then, over it, a voice, a girl's voice or a woman's, arching and lilting through a Schubert song. She stopped three stairs from the bottom, barely breathing, sweltering in her parka despite the wind. They played and sang on interminably until the end of the song, including each chorus and repeat.

"Oh, José, let's do it again!"

"OK. Then some coffee."

"How lovely."

"Like you. Always!"

They laughed. Marion grabbed at the railing for support and slipped down one more stair. José began again, rolling through the first few measures, and then the girl sang with a voice like one of the kites along the shore, dipping and soaring but perfectly controlled. The song was magic and so beautiful that Marion almost forgot the singer. She crept across the step, close to the side of the house, and then down to the door. The piano was out of sight behind the open door, so she could look into the room—her room—undetected.

There were two plates on the carpet, two empty wineglasses, the piano shawl thrown over a cushion. Sunlight cut across the pillows just as she had known it. She stood there with the wind and her own blood setting her damaged cheek on fire. The song was almost over. Snatches of it were strangely familiar, like the evocative whiff of an old perfume long out of use. Quickly she stepped across the doorway and stood in the shadow on the other side to look in.

José sat on the piano bench in his silk robe, barefoot, like Bacchus, his hair flowing out, his head thrown back in sheer pleasure. But she, she was like no one Marion had ever seen. She stood in front of the piano looking out to the bay like some angel, some fairy incarnate. She was taller than Marion, but thin, honey-skinned, with a round perfect face, blue eyes, a rosebud mouth and apple cheeks. Her hair cascaded out and down around her shoulders in a profusion of untamed blond corkscrew curls. A long white woven muslin shift emphasized her body's curves and domes, and suggested the soft contours of her pubic hair. Marion guessed her to be no more than twenty-five or twenty-six, but she had no way of judging such beauty. The girl was perfect, so perfect, in fact, that Marion stepped out of the shadow to look at her more carefully.

They had finished the song and sat together on the piano stool. She leaned up against his shoulder and played with the tassel of his sash. Then she picked out a few phrases in treble.

"That's where I have the trouble. Why can't I get it right?" She looked up at him like a child.

"Because you have never learned to let it bubble out, like water. You rush in and grab at it, and it runs through your fingers. You've always been like that."

She sighed and drew up her knees, clasping them to her chest. José buried his face in a handful of her curls and she tilted her neck back to rest her head on his shoulder. Then she sat up again and shook out her hair. She rolled her head around and around three or four times, and then suddenly held it still and stared before her directly into Marion's gaze. Marion stood there blinking in the sunlight, like a member of the audience spotlighted and called up to go on stage. For a few seconds they stared at each other transfixed until the woman released her by turning away, and Marion fled.

She heard their voices raised in question to each other as she stumbled and ran up the stairs. Then José was behind her.

"Marion! Marion! Wait! I will explain! Everything!" He was toiling behind her in his robe, tripping, swearing in Spanish. "Marion! Stop! One minute!"

But she ran up blindly with the wind behind her. She stopped for a second at the top of the stairs and then ran across the garage ramp where the boys still tinkered with the motorcycle. They looked up for an instant as she ran past and then again when José followed. She heard a primitive roar and wail from them, a loud, forced, cruel chorus of teenage masculine laughter. Even in her frenzy she wondered whether they had witnessed such a scene before. She remembered the boy's awkward offer to warn José of her arrival and decided that they had. As she ran along the road with José shouting behind her she thought of her first day with him and his expertise, her conviction that she had then that he had had endless women. And she felt more than anything else a fool. In that first flush of pain and disappointment, it was a sense of her own stupidity and childishness that emptied her stomach and clamped a vise around her throat. It was the shame and regret of her own naïvete, the madness of her chasing after the fulfillment of her soul when the independence of her heart hung by such a frail thread.

Marion reached her car and fell against the hood. She had a searing pain in her hip and her ears ached from the coldness of the wind. José caught up with her within seconds and smothered her, covering her body with his.

"Go away," she gasped.

"No. Never."

Marion lay her damaged cheek on the hood of the car and stared back towards the road. She could see a few of the boys hanging around the curve in the road, watching them, laughing, and slapping their sides. José still lay above her, holding her still and resting his face on her parka.

"Marion, I want to explain—"

"Go to hell."

"Don't say that please."

"GO TO HELL!"

He stood back and grabbed her by the shoulders, turning her expertly without letting her go. They faced each other, his pelvis pinning hers against the car, his strong hands holding her arms on each side.

"She—"

"I don't want to hear." Marion turned her head away from him, away from the teenagers on the street.

"Dios mío. What happened to your face?"
"Nothing."
"What?"
"Sarah got me with her bow."
"When?"
"Oh, I don't know. This morning."
"Why?"
Marion said nothing. He stood before her with his robe parted down to his waist. His chest heaved. His hair blew in the wind, and his face was a vision of concern for her. Even now, with the full force of his deception still before her in every detail, she wanted to forgive him.
"You will tell me later," he said. "But first I want to explain about my wife."
"Your wife!"
"Well, my ex-wife."
Marion stared at him in awe. How was it possible that he made such an art out of life? She began to doubt her own perceptions.
"She's on tour and stopped with me for the weekend. She came last night. She comes, sometimes—twice a year. Marion"—he lifted her chin again towards him—"we have been good friends since the divorce. We are good friends now . . ."
"Evidently!"
He looked at her, narrowing his eyes, and released her from his grip. The muscles in his cheeks flexed rhythmically. Marion felt him withdraw under her sarcasm and she wanted him back, feeling in the wrong, apologetic. She wanted him back as supplicant, to cure the void in her heart.
"What do you want from me?" he asked. "Absolute fidelity? The kiss of death? The middle-class marriage?"
Marion thought of Ben with the roses, the black Pontiac in the rain, the softness in José's voice when he said to his wife 'always' and she tightened her own voice. "I want from you exactly what you want from me—no more."
"Ah!" he said and turned away to look out over the bay. His arms were crossed. "You have not earned that."

"*Earned?!*"

He turned back to face her. "You have not been true to yourself. You have run your life, given and withheld your love, according to programs. Things don't work that way. You have to be open to love and to life and to the hurt that they each bring before you can make exceptions."

"What exceptions? I don't know what you're talking about and neither do you." She started to search for her keys but he stopped her arm.

"I have a relationship with Marta, a long one. It's a friendship now that once was love. And there's still love, but calmer, without the possessiveness that haunts new love. That possessiveness is really insecurity."

Marion felt a surge of irritation flood upwards, exploding in her head. "My God! You have a damned nerve! I have never heard such self-serving drivel. First you blab on about middle-class fidelity. Then you make some unbelievable statement about earning the right to make love to more than one person. And then you, *you*, who behaved like a two-year-old about Ben—you have the nerve to pronounce on possessiveness!"

"Exactly! I am possessive with you because I am insecure. I feel that Ben is a threat. And I want you with me always. Marta has many men. I don't want her to be with me more than two weekends a year. I know how terrible it is to live with her. But we are friends, more than friends. Making love to her—"

"I don't want to hear about your lovemaking."

"No, of course not. Of course not. You too are possessive and insecure. I understand, and so I won't explain any more. In fact, I know she would like you. She wants to meet you. She said so. Will you meet her?"

Marion thought of the angel in the white gown, her skin, her mouth, her eyes. She shuddered. "No, it's out of the question. I'd scratch her eyes out."

José laughed. "That's honest. There, you see." He opened her blouse and kissed her on the neck. "We could give each other so much. We both have so much to learn."

Marion allowed him to caress her. She drew him close to her and laid her head on his shoulder. She could hear the teenagers cheering in the distance, whooping and laughing, but she could only wonder at her own idiocy. What he said made no sense to Marion Roth, M.D., the keeper of records. It sounded like special pleading at best, like the soft open-ended phrases of modern greetings cards. And yet, when she plumbed his meaning, when she glanced at her marriage, at Beth's, at Ben's, she saw no possibility for Schubert songs, for a friendship with love only twice a year. She saw no hope for a bond above the level of the practical division of labor, the middle-class marriage contract.

"José, I must go."

"No!"

"I must, and you have your Marta. But anyway, I'm dropping out of the clinic for a while, except for Fridays."

It was his turn now for surprise. He stared hard at her to see if she were joking. He could not yet judge the possibilities of humor in his adopted country.

"Are you joking?"

"No."

"What will you do?"

"Take up the piano again."

"Marion, you are joking."

"I'm not. I'm telling you, I'm going to take piano lessons."

"With who?"

"I don't know. Any suggestions?"

He was in her palm now, so easy to carry off with her in his fascination.

"Marion, why?"

She found her keys and opened the car door. "We'll talk about it another time. Look at the sunset."

"What about Vallarta?" He looked in through the window urgently.

"We'll still go. I'm still a doctor, you know."

"And I love you. Dr. Roth."

She smiled and started the car. Then she touched him lightly on his cheek and drove off down the road, past the group of boys, past the garage, down towards the bay and back across the bridge to face her husband and child.

When Marion turned into her garage she looked up and saw Sarah standing where she had left her, staring out of the living room window like a dismal sentinel. From the street the girl looked gaunt, almost wasted. Marion was shocked. She tried to count the weeks since this diet had begun. There could not have been more than three, four at the most. And yet Sarah had already lost her sheen of health. She looked old and haggard and worn down.

Marion stopped the car and ran upstairs. She wanted to preclude Sarah's apology by forgiving her in advance. She didn't want any more scenes of withdrawal or viciousness in the face of her physical overtures.

Sarah met Marion at the head of the stairs. Her face was gray and smeared across with dried tears. Her slacks hung precariously from her hips and bunched around her ankles. She picked fluff off her old brown sailing sweater.

"Hi, Sarah. Where's Daddy?"

"He went sailing with Beth and Alex. He asked me to go but I didn't want to."

"Well, let's have some hot chocolate or something. I'm dying." Marion stepped deftly around Sarah and walked into the kitchen. She heard Sarah plod in behind her. She could feel her standing waiting in the doorway.

"Mother."

"Mmm."

"How's your cheek?"

"Oh, much better." Marion turned to face Sarah. She stopped herself from reaching out to her, holding the kettle firmly between them.

"Want some?"

"No, thanks."

Marion set the kettle on the stove and turned up the flame. Then she sat at the table and beckoned Sarah to join her. They sat there facing one another, naked, silent.

"Sarah, we must talk."

"I'm sorry, Mother. I'm so sorry." She bit her lip.

"Not about this morning. That's over. I won't mention it again. I mean about your diet. You are looking ill."

Sarah shuffled around, turning just enough of her shoulder in Marion's direction to indicate how she felt about this intrusion.

"I realize that you are doing this in the interests of beauty and perhaps even health. And I don't quarrel with dieting as such. What worries me is the radicalism. I don't think I've actually seen you eat a morsel in days."

"I do eat."

"But not enough."

"I still need to lose lots more."

"Nonsense! To get too thin too quickly is dangerous." Marion got up to make the chocolate, but she turned suddenly and leaned across the table, smiling into Sarah's bloodshot eyes. "Sarah, is it that you're dieting *for* someone? Do you have a special boy you like?"

"Oh, Mother, how gross!" Sarah leapt up and stood behind her chair. "It's just like you to think that. Why can't we have a sensible conversation without you making insinuations about boys?"

"But, Sarah, to the best of my knowledge I have never asked you about boys before. I don't recall ever mentioning a boy."

"You think it then. You're always thinking it." Sarah looked desperate to leave, but she obviously wanted to stay. She hung onto the back of the chair and rocked it against the table.

"Sit down, for God's sake, and calm down." Marion was sure she was right and the conviction helped her to keep her own anger in check. "Your relationships with boys are your own business—"

"There *are* no boys!"

"OK. OK. What troubles me at the moment is our relationship, yours and mine."

"Are you and Daddy going to get a divorce?"

"Good Lord! Why do you ask that?"

"Because you seem to hate each other so much."

"What nonsense! I haven't thought about it, frankly. And anyway, you can't live with someone without hating them at least part of the time."

"Clichés! There's one for every topic under the sun. Why don't you ever tell me the truth?"

Marion looked up sharply. "Like about what?"

"Like, you and Daddy *do* hate each other. Like, you find me weird, and ugly, and disappointing. Like, you'd rather be anywhere than here now, his wife and my mother."

Marion looked into her daughter's face and fought down her desire to confess. She knew she could start with José and work backwards. She could explain her own confusion, her amorphous desires for herself, her fear of dying out quietly. But she saw there, in the girl's confusion, her own impotence with Gertrude, the impossibility of candor between mother and daughter. She understood the gap between what the girl knew and what she wished to hear. If she revealed herself to Sarah, if she laid her problems out on the table between them, how could the girl not rear back in panic when she saw herself so small in comparison with Marion's other concerns?

"Sarah, you are the most important person in my life."

"Lies! You are the most important person in your life."

"That is possible, for all of us. If it is myself first—*if*—then you are second."

"So?" Sarah's lower lip protruded like Jonathan's, like his mother's. It always had the effect, in all of them, of galvanizing Marion into irritation.

"OK," she said, slamming her fist down onto the table. "OK, my girl, tell me how you would like me to be!"

Sarah was toying with the sugar bowl, stirring, spilling, showering the sugar down into a heap from above. It spilled, flying across the table in a full circle. She blushed and dug the spoon back into the bowl.

"I'd like you to be a normal mother."

"Hooray! And what the *hell* does that mean?"

Sarah's eyes were full of tears again. But Marion's irritation had steeled her heart against sympathy. "Well?" she asked again.

"I don't know. It's just that I—I mean I wish—"

Marion softened despite her exasperation. "What do you wish, Sarah?"

"That you'd grow up! You're ridiculous! Everyone says so."

"Who's everyone?" Marion felt the sting of public chastisement and ridicule for her most private thoughts and hopes. She felt exposed, betrayed by this daughter who had the unfair advantage of choosing just the right weapon with which to wound her.

Sarah swung her head away to avoid Marion's eyes. She seemed unable to face the consequences of her own hostility. "Oh, Marlene, the girls at school."

"What girls?"

"Can't remember."

"You can. And will!"

Sarah faced Marion. "Mother I made that up. *I* find you ridiculous. Even if they did, they'd never say so. But I can see it in the way they look at you. And I wish—"

"I don't give a damn what you wish!"

"You *look* so ridiculous!" Sarah had raised her voice above the squeak that tears brought into it. "You should see yourself! Why can't you be more normal?" Sarah dropped her head onto her arms and wept. There was no other sound in the house but this foreign weeping, like the gasping and coughing of a tortured animal. Marion stared at her daughter's tossing head and suddenly felt nothing. She was detached, wondering whether to wash out her mug, what to make for dinner.

Sarah mumbled something into her arms.

"What?" Marion asked sharply.

"I said I'd like to go live with Grandma and Grandpa."

"Don't be ridiculous. They're far too old to take care of you." Marion got up and washed out her mug. She took some soup out of the freezer and then decided on a cheese souffle to go with it. She took out the eggs, the cheese, measured out the milk and butter. The orderliness of the activity absorbed her. While she stirred and measured, she considered Sarah's request as if it were an appeal for a bizarre dinner guest or a weekend in the mountains with people Marion didn't know. It seemed out of character. And yet Marion began to see, when she had absorbed its full impact, that it was not beyond reason. It was, in fact, understandable. Between Gertrude and Sarah there was nothing to hide. There was the sort of love, the sort of one-way focus that a child needed, that she herself had had as a child. And Sarah sensed this. She understood that for her own full blossoming she would either have to nudge herself into Marion's spotlight or retreat into the only situation she knew where she could stand in the full beam of parental adoration.

Marion carried the bowl of eggs and milk to the table and stood opposite Sarah, whisking furiously. Sarah had stopped crying and looked up at Marion like a child without the words to ask for the help she needed.

"I don't ever want to get married."

Marion put the bowl down. "Well, you're certainly full of surprises today. Isn't it a bit soon—"

"No, it's not. I have reasons. It's disgusting."

"What? Marriage or sex?"

Sarah turned away in silence. She was sniffling now and shuddering after her long cry.

"I used to be worried at your age that I'd never find anyone to marry me."

Sarah looked up quickly.

"I used to feel so different," Marion went on, whisking. "I thought no one would want me."

"Well, they did, didn't they?"

"Yes. Sooner than I'd thought."

They were silent. Too much had happened to allow such a topic to do more than rise and fall quickly. The sun had almost set and the kitchen was cold and dark. Marion went out to switch on the lights and the heat.

"Daddy's awfully late."

Sarah didn't reply.

"Why don't you go and have a bath? It'll make you feel better."

"I feel fine. And I like showers," said Sarah, getting up to leave.

Marion heard her climb the stairs and run a bath. She stopped to listen. Jonathan was opening the garage. The children were off the street. Everything seemed usual. Sunday night, public television, family night. Marion poured the mixture she held into the souffle dish and put the dish into the oven. She suddenly felt tired, overcome by fatigue after her day and in the face of a night of explanations. She would happily have put off any discussions of the clinic until tomorrow. But that was impossible. She would have to tell, and the sooner the better. Suddenly, with all the force of a childish fantasy, Marion wished that she could turn away from her own irritations, leave this house and this child and these slow changes, and flash into another life like the phoenix, using the ashes of the old to feed the new flames.

At first Marion had put it down to love. She reached this conclusion deductively, really, as she had never experienced anything like it before. It started soon after their wedding. She found herself hurrying back from school, rushing through the supermarket, and then paging through Julia Child to find a recipe to fit the ingredients she had for dinner. With any spare time she arranged flowers on the table or polished the brass knobs and latches or oiled the furniture. And she took care with herself, washing her hair every day, putting on makeup, perfume, earrings.

Then she would watch for him. She waited at the window, looking down at the sidewalk opposite, scanning the block for his car. Once she had seen him stop on the corner to talk to a woman he seemed to know. They had stood together for ten minutes or so, laughing, slapping each other's shoulders, and then finally waving and drifting apart in the crowds. Marion waited.

"Hi, there! I'm home. Marion? What are you doing there? Why are you staring out of the window in the dark?"

"Who was that woman?"

"What woman?"

"The one you were laughing with across the road."

"Oh, not again! For God's sake!"

Marion heaved herself up to face him, but he snatched up the morning paper and dashed for the bathroom. "Nancy!" he shouted over his shoulder. "She's an X-ray tech. Nice kid. We should have her over."

The door slammed and clicked and Marion walked through to the living room. She closed the drapes and set the table. She felt herself in the firm grip of a disease, subject daily to its unpredictable fevers and chills. It could bring her down—her, Marion Klauber—in the face of Nancy or Bonnie or Sue, take away her power in the marriage, remove her from her own control and cast her into the dark realm of female despair.

"Do you like the chicken?"

"Chicken? I thought it was veal." He poked around the scallops of chicken left on his plate. "It's OK. Fine. But I'm getting a bit tired of chicken."

"I'll get some steak tomorrow. Would you like steak? Or lamb?"

Jonathan glanced at the TV. He liked to keep the game on during dinner with the sound off. "Ever thought of taking cooking classes?"

"I don't think I have the time."

"Well, in the summer then. After the baby's born. You'll have time on your hands."

Jonathan came in soaked and smelling of salt and sweat, and he busied himself immediately unzipping and pulling off his gear.

"How was it?" Marion asked.

"Superb! Super duper!"

She grimaced. Jonathan had a penchant for British public-school expressions, which he had picked up from the movies. "Didn't you go with Beth and Alex?"

He was rummaging in a bag, fishing out dirty clothes, throwing them down the garage stairs onto the pile of laundry at the bottom. "What?"

"Did Beth and Alex go with you?"

"Only Beth. Alex had a paper to write."

"I don't know why they don't buy a sailboat. Beth's become a fanatic."

Jonathan looked up at her. "They don't need one. They have ours."

"You're right. Why duplicate that sort of asset?" Marion stirred the soup and then set the table. "I haven't had lunch with Beth for weeks. I must phone her tomorrow."

"Don't know if she'll have time. You know she's coming in full-time now?"

"No! Really?" Marion sat down. "She said she'd never do that. I wonder why she didn't tell me? I thought she wanted balance, time for Alex and Alfred and so forth."

"Well, she wants to be a successful professional, and as I see it there's only one way and that's to take the work seriously. And anyway," he said, looking up, "her patient load has just about quadrupled. She's a wow with this new breed of women. She doesn't laugh when they want to inspect their own crevices."

Marion slumped down. She felt an old pang, the familiar stab of envy when she was confronted with Beth's textbook successes, her just rewards. It was the narrowness of Beth's demands that paid off, the proximity, the tangibility of her goals. She had always seemed so happy to settle for less, to confront her abilities four-square, and to make the most of them. Marion felt like a butterfly beside her. She felt dissolute, extravagant, trivial.

"You're lucky," Beth had said, over and over, from the beginning, without malice, without envy.

"Lucky?" They were in the cafeteria, their second year together in medical school.

"To have a mother like yours, and a husband like Jonathan."

Marion said nothing.

"He's unusual, Marion. He seems to want more for you than even you want for yourself."

"But, you know, sometimes I get the feeling there's no room for failure."

"Who's failing? You're both carrying it off. It couldn't be better, Marion. Marion! You still have your silver spoon!"

Marion smiled and shrugged. Beth always reassured her. She

had only to look at the grayness of Beth's life and beyond her at everyone around to feel fortunate again, more than competent to cope, hopeful, even euphoric about the future.

"How bizarre our lives have been, Beth's and mine," Marion said, looking up at Jonathan with a smile.

"Why do you say that?" His own triumph was very sweet.

"Because today I decided to give up the clinic and take piano lessons."

"You what—"

"Ben persuaded me to continue with my Fridays. But Monday to Thursday, I'm out."

It was Jonathan now who slumped down at the table and stared at her. "Why?"

"I'm taking an open-minded sabbatical."

"But *why?*"

"To find out more about what I am and what I want."

"Find out—Marion! I need a drink!" He walked through to the dining room and poured himself a double scotch. Then he came back for ice and stood in front of her.

"Piano?"

"Yes."

"Four days a week?"

"Yes." She began to flush under his glare.

"What about money?"

"I have six weeks of vacation and half-time for three months after that. I'm entitled to that."

"Half half-time, you mean!"

"We have enough, more than enough, Jon."

Jonathan shook his head and went for some club soda. She followed him.

"Jon! There's another reason. I didn't mention it. The most important as a matter of fact."

"What?"

"Sarah." Marion spit out the lie like purulence from a festering wound.

"Sarah?"

She bit her cheek until she could taste blood. "I feel she needs me. And that I can help her by taking a more active role in her life and interests."

Jonathan stared at her with his head tilted forward pugnaciously. He was playing the role, she knew, giving the drama time, keeping her waiting for his blessing. She stood there staring back without a word. He repeated her words as if to himself and then stopped at last, lifted his head, and gave her a pontifical smile.

"Now that's different," he said, pulling out one of the dining room chairs and sitting down. "That's a sacrifice. That's not to be sniffed at."

Marion looked away, sick, but he would not let her go. He pulled out a chair and gestured her to sit down.

"Does she know?"

"No."

"Well, I think we should tell her together, don't you? I think she should understand what you're giving up and how much she means to you." He smiled. "Why didn't you tell me that first? You're a funny woman, you know." He looked over towards the door as Sarah came in, and he stood up before her with all the dignity of the winning team coach.

"Marion," he said, "there's just a chance you're on the right track at last."

9

Sumiko had suggested the conservatory to Marion, and Marion liked the idea. It was orderly, it was a place to go to, like the clinic, but better. She would go every morning at ten, after an hour of practicing, and have a two-hour lesson with a break in the middle. Then, on the days she did not meet José, she would go home to practice again before Sarah returned. Her hours were, in fact, more rigid now than they had been at the clinic. But she didn't care. She threw herself into her new regimen with so much vigor that even Babs, her teacher, suggested she relax a little.

It was late November when Marion decided to change her life. The sun was weaker and the rain beginning. But to Marion, this year, it was like springtime in New York. She noticed the trees still green, the flowers and shrubs with early winter blooms. And she felt light-headed, light-hearted, her old response to spring. As she drove along the hills and down towards the conservatory, looking out over the undulating rows and rows of pastel houses at the sun on the sea, she felt a redoubling of the hope which her visits to José had inspired. Anything seemed possible now. Everything.

She and José began to play the piano together. José brought out some simple duets, a Clementi, a Von Weber, and they sat side by side at the piano, with José coaching softly, nodding the beat, hushing and then singing for the piano and the forte. At first Marion was embarrassed and played too loudly and too fast. But he understood this and tricked her into relaxing, showing her how to play each phrase and having her copy his playing. He never flattered her. If anything, he was ruthless. And she felt safer this way, never expecting undue praise or getting it. They were happy, bound together into the music they made, like two worshipers communing with their god, side by side at the ruins of an ancient temple.

"And to think that I could be taking a pulse," she said, laughing.

"And to think that I could be making a speech."

"A speech?"

"Or a bribe. Or a threat. All my family are politicians. Only I am the failure."

"I love failures like you," Marion said, laughing and kissing his ear. "I'm also a failure, you know, as failures go. I was Miss Promising Career. And look at me now, happy and unpromising. I haven't even had the guts yet to tell my parents."

"Wouldn't they approve of the piano though?"

"No, it could never be a career for me. And it's dangerous. I'm playing, amusing myself, you see, making choices I have no right to make, and that does no one any good except me."

"It does me good."

"But you don't exist for them—and even if you did, you wouldn't count."

"Thanks," he said, standing up and walking off to the kitchen. She heard him crashing around with the kettle, clicking his tongue. Marion followed him in there and stood in the doorway.

"José! Don't start again, please. I'm telling you the truth. Don't you want to know what really is?"

He ignored her, stirring, sipping, adding sugar to the coffee. "I am nothing I suppose," he said finally to the wall.

"You are everything," she answered softly and went through to the main room to sit down. She looked out over the bay, so bright now that the reflection of the light hurt her eyes. Then she lay back to think about José and what she had just said. She cleaned her head and then peopled it carefully with the main sets and characters of her life. She staged them all before her and then eliminated them one by one—her mother and father, Jonathan, and Sarah, Beth, and Alex, then the house, the clinic, the car, the boat. Could she settle for José, this room, and her music to fill the space they left behind? She opened her eyes and looked around her. She turned to watch José bring in the coffee, his jaw set into a sullen resistance. And she knew that she had not told him the truth, that he could never be enough, however much she tried to shrink the space around him. She sat up, strangely happy, reaching out to him with a smile, loving him more than ever, taking away the tray and pulling him over with such fierce passion that he forgot his sulking and made love to her in just the way she wanted him to.

It was Thursday, the last day she could count on seeing him before Monday. The sun had begun to set and they both turned away from it, moving the cushions so that they looked back into the crimson room. José lit a cigarette and Marion kissed him softly on his chest as he blew the smoke up to the ceiling. She could hear the familiar cues of his heart, his lungs, his stomach. Every muscle and mole was now intimate to her, the strange assortment of toes, the patterns of his hair. She knew his body by sight, by touch, by smell. And she was always watching for more of him, learning to anticipate his behavior.

"Will you pick up Sarah from rehearsal Saturday?" he asked.

"Yes. But I'll have everyone with me." Marion had learned not to mention Jonathan by name, or Alex or Beth for that matter. They were all going sailing again after morning rounds.

"I hope it rains."

"So do I."

They smiled. Marion pulled on her jeans and breathed in to zip them up.

José covered himself with an afghan and watched her, his hands linked behind his head. She had long ago unmasked his quaint modesty about his body, his need to drape a towel or a shawl around his waist when he walked around the apartment, and his slight shock at her abandoned prancing without clothes. It was a paradox in each of them, this inversion of physical modesty and sexual exhibitionism, but he would not discuss it. He did not have the Anglo-Saxon ability to abstract sex and passion into dinner conversation.

"You know," he said, watching her dress, "Sarah looks sick."

Marion stopped struggling with the snap at her waist and came over to sit down. "How, sick? How do you mean?"

"Pale, thin. You know, sick! How much weight has she lost?"

"I don't know. She won't say. She simply won't discuss it. I thought that if I ignored her condition, she would stop. But it's gotten worse, hasn't it? I mean, over the past month?"

"I think so."

"José, what can I do with that girl? She won't even see a doctor, not even—"

He looked sharply at Marion and then looked away.

"—she won't even go to Beth for a chat. She nearly bit my head off when I suggested it."

José narrowed his eyes at her and then smiled. "I love you."

But Marion was too uneasy to respond to his magnanimity. He had brought Sarah into their afternoon and Marion could not dismiss her again. She could not even resent the intrusion in the face of Sarah's obstinate embrace of ill health.

"Has she dieted?" he asked.

"Dieted? Starved is more like it."

"Well, make her eat. Tell her it's unhealthy to be so thin. You're the doctor."

He got up and pulled on his briefs and then his robe. He seemed suddenly bored with the subject, anxious to have her gone now that Sarah had replaced him in her concern. He busied himself with piles of music, turning his back on her, ignoring the tears which had filled her eyes.

"José—"

"Why are you crying?"

"I don't know."

"Because of Sarah?"

"Partly."

"What else then?"

"It's just that—just that whenever I turn my back on things, when I am just happy, something like this comes along to drag me back." She blew her nose loudly.

José stopped his rummaging and turned towards her, still distant, still aware that her tears were not for him. "It is your problem and Sarah's. Only you can solve it."

"Why are you so callous?"

"So what?" His body was thrust forward in challenge.

"So uncaring? Why have you cut yourself off from me since you mentioned Sarah? You are the one who always told me she was part of us and that I couldn't ignore it."

"I care. I care! But what can I do? I am not the doctor or the parent."

"That's obvious, but—" Marion looked at him and stopped. She didn't want him retreating from her just when she was facing her own isolation. She needed to have him interposed between her and the edge of the precipice on which she was standing.

"But, what?"

"Nothing."

"Tell me!"

"Nothing, nothing. You are right. It is my problem to solve. It has no bearing on us."

She put on her parka and felt for her keys in the pocket. José bounded over to her and swept her to the floor, kissing her everywhere, sending her keys flying.

"I love you! I love you! *Estoy encantado contigo!*"

Marion closed her eyes and waited for him to release her. She had no way of swinging so radically with him from low to high and was only beginning to understand the relatively simple mechanism that triggered these swings.

"I must go," she said. But he wouldn't release her. He snuffled in her neck, murmuring in Spanish. He pleaded with her for a few more minutes.

"Is she practicing well?" he asked, still holding her hands in his.

"Practicing? What do you mean?"

"Is Sarah practicing as before?"

Marion thought and then looked up at him. "No. As a matter of fact, she's been less hysterical about it lately. Isn't that funny?"

"Funny? No. She's goofing off in the orchestra. I had to bawl her out yesterday for the first time ever."

His words hit Marion like falling bricks. She felt the violence of them, the inappropriateness of American slang in his speech. She recoiled from his slurred cowboy pronunciation and heard her own voice rising in Sarah's defense. "You chastised her in front of everyone?"

"Yes."

"That's cruel. Why did you do it?"

"She was playing badly and giggling with her friend when I showed her how to play the first few phrases of the second movement."

"Marlene?"

"Yes."

"I dislike that girl."

"Of course. She's cheap and lower-class."

"José!"

"Is it not true?"

Marion looked away. "I don't approve of their friendship."

"Because she's cheap and lower-class!"

"Perhaps."

"So, what will you do about it?" José sat back, challenging her, playing with her in her discomfort.

"I'll do something. I'm not sure what as yet. First I have to deal with this dieting, then find out what's up with the cello. I wonder whether Sumiko has noticed anything."

"She phoned me last week to ask about Sarah."

"José, why didn't you tell me?"

"Because she asked me not to."

"She asked *you* not to tell *me*?"

"Well, she said she didn't want to mention it to you because of your piano. She thinks you took up piano to please Sarah." He began to suck her knuckles, looking up into her face.

Marion withdrew her hand and crossed her arms, as if she were questioning a patient. "Let me understand you. Are you saying that Sumiko didn't want me to know because she thought I might be disappointed for myself or angry with Sarah?"

"I think she meant disappointed. But she wasn't all that worried. She was just hoping Sarah would settle down and you'd be playing duets with her in her June recital."

"Duets!"

"Well, that's logical, isn't it? Look," José said, "it's not that serious. She's just growing up. They all go a bit crazy at this age. Even Sumiko said so. Maybe she likes a boy."

"I thought of that already. She nearly went crazy when I mentioned it."

"Then she has got one. That proves it."

Marion thought it through. "I suppose it's possible. But who? Where would she meet boys?"

"That Marlene seems to have a few. They hang around after school for her. Maybe she passed one on to Sarah."

"Oh, José! What kind of boys would Marlene know? What did they look like?"

José sat up soberly and faced Marion as if she were a student out of line. "Marion, don't ask me to spy on your daughter. It's *inappropriate* as you would say and it is not right. If she has a boyfriend, you must find out who. I cannot give you advice."

He stared at her and then stood up. He began puffing up the cushions, folding up the afghan. She knew he wanted her to go, but she sat there staring at him as he progressed through the room. Finally, he turned to her with his hands on his hips, his biceps flexing.

"OK. I'll do it, even though I think it's wrong."

"Do what?"

"I'll speak to her. I'll find out what's bugging her."

Again, Marion recoiled from his words. It was all wrong, this plotting and maneuvering around Sarah's aberrations. It was too vague and imprecise for there to be any hope of success and she could only feel exasperated when faced with her own impotence to make order out of this confusion. "On second thought," she said, "I'd rather you said nothing."

José shrugged. "Up to you."

Marion kissed him lightly and left. As she drove home she was oppressed by the flatness that had descended on them with Sarah's intrusion. There was something about the girl that deadened her, that dulled her radiance and made her hopes seem ridiculous. She edged towards the tollbooth trying to swallow down the lump in her throat. And when she did she was left with a residue of anger at Sarah that churned her stomach into acid. She drove into the garage behind Jonathan, attempting to turn her anger once more into indifference or, failing that, to confine it to Sarah's absurd dieting. But the sight of Jonathan walking toward her in his trendy office-hour clothes and sporty good cheer, his indifference to the subtleties of mood, his naïve assurance that the world would fit his expectations and that if it didn't it could be made to, these all combined to make Marion explode.

"Have you taken a look at your daughter lately?" she asked, standing across the stairs up to the house.

"What the hell's up now?"

"She's sick."

"Sick? What is it?" He tried to step around Marion, but she blocked the stairs.

"She's in some crisis, Jon. She must have lost at least thirty pounds."

"Nah! Come on!"

"*Look* at her! She's skin and bones."

"I've looked. She looks fine to me. Now let me go. I need a drink. And I want to run before I get ready to go out."

Marion walked upstairs with Jonathan behind her. At the top of the stairs she spun around to face him again. "Please Jon, please notice what's going on. Do you know that she's letting her cello slide? Sumiko—"

"Come on, come on, let's go in. Leave her to me."

Marion walked across the hall and up to the bedroom, waiting for Jonathan. She heard him greet Sarah in the kitchen. They were chatting and laughing over the noise of the rock station on the radio. Marion sat down on the bed and tried to control her breathing. She knew that her anger only served to make him deaf to her concerns, and she needed him now to share her burden. She got up and stood at the top of the stairs. They were still down there, but in the dining room. Jonathan was pouring a drink. She heard Sarah rocking the chair against the table in time to the music from the kitchen. It was unusual to hear rock music in the house at this hour—practicing and homework time—but Marion liked it. It seemed to bring life into the house, to make theirs like other people's kitchens and dining rooms.

"Jonathan!" she shouted down into the cavity. "Jonathan!"

"Yeah?"

"Come up here, please!"

"Yes, ma'am!"

She heard them laugh and knew he had saluted the ceiling in mock seriousness. Marion spun around and went back to the bedroom. She sat at her dressing table, and looked in the mirror, and then saw Jonathan in the doorway, cradling his drink in his hands.

"What's up?"

"I'm worried about Sarah."

"I know, you said so. She's too thin or something, and she's goofing off at the cello."

Marion jumped up. "Close the door."

"Yes, ma'am!"

"Oh, for God's sake, stop that adolescent nonsense. One adolescent is quite enough in this family."

"To which one do you refer?" Jonathan winked at her. "You've been a little adolescent yourself lately, you know. But I know"—he held up his hand and closed his eyes—"we're gathered together to discuss Sarah. Shoot!"

"She maintains there's nothing wrong with her."

"Well, she's right. She's lost some weight. Probably got some guy in the wings, lucky fellow." Jonathan was changing into his running clothes. She knew she had to hurry.

"Well, I think that if she doesn't look better in a few weeks, we should take her in for tests."

"Tests!" Jonathan stopped pulling on a sneaker. "What are you talking about?"

"I want her checked out by Ben, a complete physical. If nothing turns up, I'm going to have Alex suggest a therapist. She could be anorexic."

"For God's sake, Marion," said Jonathan, raising his voice, blasting her with his own irritation. "There's absolutely nothing wrong with that girl. When she's heavy you're disgusted; when she diets, you're worried. She's obsessed with the cello and then she's goofing off. You're never satisfied."

"No! Because she's swung from a relatively safe extreme to a relatively dangerous one. And I wish you wouldn't use *goofing off*! I can't stand that phrase!"

"You want a fight, don't you really? You don't want to discuss Sarah, you want to attack me!" He slipped on his headband and stopped at the door. "I've had about as much as I intend to take of your damned gratuitous aggression. Leave me alone! Leave us both alone! Sarah and I manage perfectly until you start interfering. Just shut up! Try for once to control yourself. *Goofing off!*" he mumbled, loping down the stairs. "Jesus Christ!"

Marion stood at the door stopping the insults that filled her head. It was hopeless. There seemed to be a momentum to this degeneration of her family that defied control. She felt propelled into conflict at home as forcefully as she was filled with optimism when she turned her back on her family. And she lived between the two extremes in growing despair of any resolution.

Marion ran herself a bubble bath and slipped into it. They were going to the theater with Beth and Alex and then to dinner afterwards. She wondered how she would stand the predictability of it, the drive downtown, their questions about the conservatory, the piano, their innocence, their sweetness, the parking, the running through the wind and then the choosing of a place to go afterwards. She could even hear Alex wanting something light, Beth being easy, Jonathan sniffing the wine and making mild objections. And they would discuss the play, each of them dragging phrases out of yesterday's review.

"What a bore," she said aloud. "What a fucking bore."

But, in the car, after they dropped Sarah off to mind Alfred and Beth and Alex had climbed in, Beth leaned over Marion's shoulder from the back seat and said softly, "I was shocked to see Sarah. How much more has she lost since last I saw her?"

"Ask Jonathan," Marion tossed back. "He's the expert on anorexics. They don't exist you see."

Marion missed the glance between Beth and Jonathan, but she heard the silence.

"Marion's uptight," Jonathan said. "That kid's no more anorexic than I am."

Marion stared out into the night, fixing her eyes on empty sidewalks and Victorian houses as they flashed past.

"Has she been inducing vomiting?" Alex asked.

No one answered. Jonathan shot a look at Marion, but she stared ahead.

"I don't know," he said, "not that we know of anyway." He accelerated through a yellow light. "But what's all this about anorexia and vomiting? The kid's a normal adolescent girl trying to be gorgeous for the boys. She's got a new friend. She listens to rock music now. She's growing up, for Christ's sake. I vote we leave her be."

They parked the car and ran up to the theater. But when they went in, they found that Marion had bought tickets for the following Thursday, and that this night was sold out. No one blamed her. They huddled in the doorway for a few minutes and giggled like children. Then they walked over to André's for a good French meal and excellent wine.

It was ten o'clock when they drove up to Beth's house.

"Come in for a brandy," Beth asked. "Please. It's early."

"I'd love to," Marion said. "We'd love to, wouldn't we, Jon?" Jonathan reached over to give her a conciliatory squeeze. The wine and food had softened them both back into their old good-humored ease. Marion had entertained them all during dinner with a caricature description of the conservatory faculty and students. She laughed at herself and they all laughed with her. But even as she had them there laughing, taking their cues from her, she had felt the burden of her responsibility for the tone of these evenings they spent together. When she talked, they found things to talk about. If she was silent, the evening fluttered and fell.

They climbed out of the car and up to the front steps. It was a crisp night with the moon and stars lighting up a dark sky and promising clear weather for tomorrow.

"Oh, isn't it lovely!" Marion said, tilting her face up to the sky. "I've never seen it so clear." She turned and walked away from the house, crunching the gravel of the driveway under her feet. She had forgotten the others already. She was learning to catch moments like this and to hold onto them, to open herself, as José could, to the swells and rushes of the spirit. Marion looked up at the sky stretched over her and she felt blessed, rewarded, even in the chaos that surrounded her. She felt she really did have the chance to start again.

She hadn't really heard their voices until they ran up behind her.

"Marion! Marion! Come inside!"

It was Alex, running towards her and then back across the driveway, looking over his shoulder like a retriever to make sure that she was following. Beth had already reached the doorway with Jonathan behind her and they both turned to stare blankly out into the dark night in Marion's direction.

"What's up?" Marion asked, smiling at their concern. "I was only out there looking at the—"

She stopped dead in the front hall. Before she even saw Sarah sprawled across the living room carpet, she smelled the vomit. It sickened her instantly, like the fear that rose in her throat. She ran across to Sarah and knelt beside her. Part of her skirt brushed through the vomit on the floor as she arched over Sarah, bending her ear to the girl's mouth, taking her pulse.

"Thank God! She's alive!"

"She's alive, all right," Jonathan said with a hint of amusement. "She's dead drunk."

Marion looked up quickly. They stood in the doorway like a

trio of mimes on a street corner, each staring at her, waiting for her to set the proper attitude. She sat back on her haunches and looked around. The room was in disarray. Cushions had been flung all over the floor and some of Beth's evening dresses and a few scarves were draped carelessly over the couch. There was an empty bottle of gin and two glasses on the coffee table. A record turned endlessly on the stereo with the needle running in jarring rhythm over the paper in the middle.

"Where's Alfred?" Marion asked.

"Asleep," Beth said.

"Who else was here?"

They looked around.

"Someone else?" Alex asked.

"Two glasses," Marion mumbled. She stood up and walked past them to the kitchen. When she returned with a bucket and sponge, she found Sarah propped up against Jonathan, gasping something into his ear, drooling down her blouse and onto the floor.

"She's asking for Marla," he said. "Who's Marla?"

"Marlene. It's her friend from school," Marion said. "It must've been her. Get her outside, please."

Jonathan and Alex hoisted Sarah up and dragged her out into the cold air. Beth brought a sponge and knelt beside Marion, dabbing at her Persian rug.

"Why do you think she did it?" Beth asked timidly. "She must be going through some real crisis. Do you think she's so very unhappy?"

Marion sat back on the rug and smiled without amusement. "Bethy, I want to tell you something. You are a saint—"

"No! I'm not, Marion. Don't, please!"

Marion ignored her friend's strange vehemence and went on. "If it were your daughter who carried on a debauch when she was sitting for my retarded child, I would not bother to find out the reason why. I would press her face into the vomit she spewed onto my beautiful rug, and then I would drag her out into the cold air to wait for the police."

"You would not!"

"I would indeed. And what is more I would despise you for raising such a child. I would advise you to seek therapy. I would—" Marion sunk her head onto her chest and began to weep. Her whole body shook with the violence of her thwarted satisfactions. She shook off Beth's arm, turned away from her comforting phrases.

Jonathan peered around the front door. "You girls cleaned up the mess?"

"Yes," said Beth, gesticulating with her sponge.

Marion felt them discussing her in looks and glances. She heard Jonathan come over to her and felt his hands on her shoulders.

"Come. Sarah's in the car. Let's get her home to bed."

Marion stood up and looked down at Beth as she sat there on her soiled rug smiling up at Marion, wiping her sleeve across her forehead.

"Go on," Beth said. "It's all wiped up. It'll be dry by tomorrow. Please don't bother yourself about this nonsense. And get a good night's sleep. We all have to work tomorrow."

Jonathan led Marion to the car. He opened the door and handed her in. Then he walked round to his side and looked back towards the house.

"See you in the morning," he called out softly.

"For sure," said Beth.

10

It was strange for Marion to be walking through the front door of the clinic shepherding Sarah, to feel herself more parent than doctor. It was Monday and she had taken Sarah out of school for this appointment. She had canceled her own lesson too. But in the flurry of arrangements and phone calls, she had not stopped to consider how she would feel stopping at the front desk to announce herself. On Fridays now, she always affected her old efficient style, as if nothing had changed, as if the secretaries and nurses were not gossiping about her from Monday to Thursday and as soon as she turned her back.

"Good morning, Dr. Roth."

"Good morning, Nancy. I've brought Sarah in to see Dr. McCarthy."

"I know. Hello, Sarah! Long time no see!"

"Oh, hi, Nancy!" she said without a smile, twisting her arm out of Marion's grasp. She backed away from them and went to the waiting room where she stood in front of the magazine rack staring at the assortment of outdated glossies and children's books.

Marion reached for the appointment book and glanced without seeing through the list for the day. She was groping for time. She couldn't sit in the waiting room with the crowd, many of whom had been her patients. And she knew her office was occupied by her replacement in the clinic, a pert southerner, fresh out of his residency in New Orleans and recruited without difficulty to fill the void left by her absence. She pushed the book away and looked up. Nancy was waiting.

"Dr. Roth, I'm afraid your office—"

"Yes, I know. I have a few things to do. Do you know how far behind he is?"

"Well, it's ten-twenty now, and Sarah's appointment's for ten-thirty. Let me see . . . he should be on time. He usually is."

"Would you give him a message?"

"Sure."

"Tell him I'll be back at about eleven-thirty—twelve. Perhaps I can see him then."

"I'll tell him for sure."

Marion walked out into the daylight, got into her car, and drove along California and up to Sacramento Street. She strolled for a few blocks down one side of the street and up the other, past four or five boutiques, stopping and looking in through the windows. And then she chose one quickly and pressed the door buzzer to be admitted.

At first, in the dim light, the place seemed deserted, but after a while she noticed a silent young woman sitting on a step, leaning back and smiling up at her. The woman was dressed in layers of bright purple and green silk and had stretched her long, stockinged legs in front of her across the step. Marion noticed her nails, her dark rouge, the careful accents of jewelry, and wondered, as she stood before her in her own straight office clothing, how long it must take to dress for such a job each day.

"Can I help you?" the woman drawled, in a voice just above a whisper.

"I hope so," said Marion brusquely. She was excited at the prospect of what she was about to do, and excitement always gave her an efficient presentation.

"I'm going away, to Mexico, and I want a new wardrobe. In fact, I want a new wardrobe period."

The young woman peeled herself away from the wall and stood

up, smiling, never taking her eyes off Marion's face, far too practiced in her craft to allow her survey of Marion's shoes, skirt, and old Coach bag to be noticed.

"Well," she said. "We have just received our first spring shipment and there's some *super* stuff in it. What are you, an eight?"

"A ten."

"Why don't you just take your time and look through here and here," she said, sweeping her arm across racks of clothes. "Pick out what you like and we'll take it from there. I'll see if there's anything in the new stuff that you might like. What sort of things do you want? Day? Evening?"

"I don't know." Marion looked around at the profusion of colors and fabrics. "I suppose I need beach clothes and things for the evening. Something sophisticated, but not too wild."

"I'll see what we've got." The woman vanished behind a curtain.

Marion was left alone amongst the clothes. Some soft Brazilian music piped in above the silence of the store. Quickly she put down her bag and took off her jacket, and then began riffling through the racks, starting with the evening wear, taking out anything that looked hopeful or so unimaginable on the hanger that it had to be tried on to be judged. When she had scanned the entire selection, she carried the batch of clothes through to the dressing room and took off her skirt and blouse. She stood in the center of the cubicle viewing herself from every angle in the mirrors. Her body looked sallow and lumpy. Her underwear didn't match, and her stockings had a run. She turned and turned, looking over her shoulder, standing on her toes. Nothing helped. Marion took off her bra and climbed into the first dress, a black chiffon, one-shoulder extravagance which emphasized the droop of her breasts. She was taking it off in despair when the saleswoman reappeared, hung up the clothes she had brought out from the back, and then returned with a selection of scarves and earrings, blouses, belts, bras and hair combs. Like magic, everything that Marion had tried on now was tucked up, tied back, embellished, shown to its best advantage. The woman seemed to know better than she did how she looked best. She had even removed a few of the dresses before Marion could try them on, and substituted others in colors Marion had never thought of for herself before.

As Marion worked her way through the pile of clothes, she found herself transformed in French underwear, evening sandals with ankle straps, and a one-piece bathing suit that had her staring at her own image in disbelief. She was enchanted. She set aside more and more clothes to try on again, then tried them on the second time, even though she knew she would take them all.

The saleswoman carried out her purchases in relays and wrapped them at the front counter while Marion tried and retried the clothes, then finally began to put her own clothes back on. Suddenly, Marion stopped as she was zipping up her skirt and, wrapping the changing room curtain around herself, leaned out into the showroom.

"I think I'll wear that red dress—the bouclé. It doesn't need a thing done to it, not even the hem, and I just feel like a change."

"Great idea! Will you wear the brown sandals and bag with it?"

"Why not? Can you bring them up?"

"Sure thing."

Marion stepped out of her tweed skirt and folded it neatly. Then she took the dress from the woman and put it on. It was lovely, fitting, sophisticated, with padded shoulders, long sleeves, and a profusion of French tucks down the front. She buckled the belt and eased into the snakeskin sandals. She swapped her shoulder bag for the small snakeskin envelope and then looked at herself in the mirror, turning to catch every angle.

"May I make a suggestion?" the saleswoman asked.

"Of course."

"Some eye makeup. You've got lovely eyes. They need some emphasis."

"Oh. I haven't got any with me."

"We carry a whole range . . . Want to have a look?"

Marion followed the girl to the front, holding onto the wall for balance on her way down the stairs. She chose some mascara, eyeliner, shadow, rouge, and a dark scarlet lipstick to match the dress. And then she allowed the girl to help her apply it. Her eyes flashed and glistened under the thick black lashes. Her face seemed thinner, more sophisticated, the face of a diplomat's wife, a French film star. One side of her hair was swept back in a comb. The other fell casually over her forehead as if it had been styled that way.

The saleswoman gathered up Marion's old suit, shoes, and bag and packed them neatly into a shopping bag, while Marion glanced at the three-page sales slip she had been given. She wasn't really interested in the money. Nothing seemed to her, as she stood there, looking at the neat lists—items purchased, the tallies, subtotals, tax—less relevant than money. She wondered vaguely, while she pulled out her American Express card why she had ever taken any account of it at all, why she had let Jonathan concern her about security and retirement and stocks and bonds. How absurd, she thought, as she signed her name to an amount exceeding the total that she had paid for clothes over the past five years, how ludicrous to care. It's just money, she thought. It's earned. It's spent. It's nothing.

The boxes were all neatly stacked and tied, and Marion stood waiting while the saleswoman phoned to check her credit. She peered through the glass of the display cabinet that served as a counter at an array of bangles, earrings, and sunglasses.

"May I look at those?" she whispered, gesticulating towards a pair of white-rimmed sunglasses. The woman hooked the phone onto her shoulder and smiled, reaching into the cabinet for the glasses. Marion tried them on and nodded.

"A gift!" the woman said, smiling.

Marion smiled back. "Thanks."

She looked at herself again, this time through a brownish haze, and she was delighted. She loved everything about this place. The saleswoman hung up, wrote something on the slip, and handed Marion her copy.

"You look stunning!"

Marion scooped up the first few boxes and took them out to the car. Then she returned for the rest. As she was buzzed back into the store she saw that another woman stood at the counter chatting to the saleswoman. They both turned as she came in.

"Marion Roth?"

"Hello, Dede."

"Marion! Heavens! I didn't recognize you at first. You look *neat*!"

"Thank you, Dede."

"Wow! I haven't seen you since the *picnic*, but I've been *hearing* about you!" Her voice chirped up and down, emphasizing the appropriate words like the singsong of a bad actress. "Is it true you've given up medicine?"

"Well, not quite. I go in on Fridays."

"And you've taken up the *piano*! What—"

"Yes, I love it."

"*Well, it obviously* suits you!"

Marion smiled.

"How does Sarah like the change?"

"Frankly, I haven't asked her."

"I saw her downtown the other day. She's looking *great*!"

"Dede, I'd love to chat, but I must run. I have an appointment at eleven-forty-five." Marion grabbed the remaining boxes and turned to leave.

"Boy, you look like you've been shopping for *Christmas*!" Dede called out after her. "Did Susie here sell you the store?"

"No! I bought it!"

Marion heard the door snap closed on its spring behind her. She struggled up to her car, opened the door, and threw the boxes into the back seat. She turned the key and backed out of her space quickly; then she did a U-turn in the middle of the street and drove straight back to the clinic.

Ben was in the front office when Marion came in. He looked up quickly as she opened the door and then stood up straight, holding onto the counter.

"Marion!"

Nancy looked up from her desk and the secretary popped her head through the hatch from the office.

"Dr. Roth!" they both chorused.

Marion smiled and walked up to Ben. "Sorry I've taken so long. Where's Sarah?"

"She just left. Went back to school, I think."

"Do you have a minute, Ben?"

"Yes—uh—let's—well, how about lunch? Have you eaten? James is taking over for me this afternoon. Are you free?"

"Certainly."

Marion was enjoying the chaos she had caused. She smiled at the office staff and glanced into the waiting room. "I just need to use your phone a minute, Ben," she said, walking back to his office and closing his door behind her. She sat down behind his desk and crossed her legs, smiling. She felt like a second wife, a mistress, an exotic scandal in the drab routine of the office day. But more than this, she was on stage for herself, enjoying each turn, each effect that she produced, herself the author, the actress, and the audience.

Marion folded Ben's blotting paper over the mouthpiece of the phone and dialed Mary Ellis. She asked for José in a loud Brooklyn accent and then doodled hearts on Ben's calendar as she waited.

"Hello?"

"José," she said, removing the blotting paper. "It's me."

"M—Oh. How are you?" he purred.

"Listen, I can't make it this afternoon."

"But—"

"It's about Sarah." She dropped her voice to a whisper. "I can't talk now. See you tomorrow."

"*Why?*"

"Can't talk! I love you." She gently replaced the receiver and then blotted her face with the blotting paper and went out to find Ben. He was waiting for her at the front desk.

"Ready?" she asked.

"Yes. Just let me change my coat." He went into his office and emerged in his Brooks Brothers blazer. "Let's go."

They walked out to Ben's Mercedes and he handed her in. He backed out of the parking lot and drove down California Street in silence. Marion looked over at him as he drove, but he ignored her and stared ahead. She leaned over and snapped on the radio. It was tuned to KABL. Easy listening for commuters. Marion twirled the buttons and found the jazz station.

"Is that OK?"

"Fine, fine."

"Ben?"

"Mmm?"

"Where're we going?"

He shot a side glance at her. "I booked a table at the St. Francis."

"Why?"

He drove silently.

"Well, anyway, that's lovely." She sat back. Everything seemed lovely at this moment, even Ben. He was being mysterious. And Sarah had receded into an excuse—the ostensible reason for the lunch.

Ben parked under Union Square and they walked over to the St. Francis. When they had been seated at a table, he called over the waiter.

"Two martinis up."

"Ben! Martinis! I don't drink martinis!"

"Well, there's always a first time."

"Oh, Ben."

He gave her a pale smile and sat back to look at her. This was his world, the world of mixed drinks and crab cocktails, and it was she now who was looking for cues.

"What happened?"

"What do you mean?"

"I mean all this—" He gestured with his hand at her hair and dress.

"Oh, I went shopping. I decided to change my image—branch out!"

"Well, you've certainly done that. And in more ways than one."

"Don't you like it?" Marion leaned back in her chair, smiling at him.

"You know I do. You look gorgeous." He toasted Marion with his martini and then drank half of it in one gulp. "Now, let's talk about Sarah and get that over with."

Marion put down her glass and sat forward.

"Marion, I checked her out thoroughly. We took urine and blood, of course, but apart from a possible mild anemia, I don't think there's a thing wrong with her."

"Well, thank God for that."

"Physically, that is."

"What do you mean?"

"I think she's showing signs of real anxiety. Oh, she didn't say anything, of course. She's too clever for that, and she knows she can't talk to me, but I have the feeling there's a pathology behind this unhappiness of hers. And the drinking episode the other night—she wouldn't talk about it. She told me it was just a mistake, something stupid. She wouldn't even tell me about the other girl."

"What do you suggest I do?"

"Ask Alex to refer her to someone; if she's willing to go, that is. I just know I'm not the one to handle this. Marion, it could be a real problem."

"*I* know that, but it's Jonathan who keeps insisting that her behavior is 'within normal limits of adolescent experimentation.' I mean, Ben, can you beat that? He refuses, absolutely refuses, to confront the problem."

"I'm afraid, my beauty—"

He stopped. Marion had reached over, suddenly, in the middle of this sentence, and grasped his left hand. She twisted his wedding band on his finger, turned his hand over and traced its lines with her forefinger. Coming from Jonathan the same words would have irritated her; from José she would have taken them as her due. But from Ben they came like roses from a pauper, dearly bought and offered with gentle devotion.

"Are you hungry?" he asked softly.

"Not one bit."

"Then let's go now."

"Where?"

"Wait here. I'll be back."

Ben pushed back his chair, walked over to the waiter, and gestured towards the table. Marion saw him take out his wallet and hand over a bill, waving off the change as he left the restaurant. After a few minutes the waiter came over to her with another martini and took away her empty glass. Marion smiled. Ben wanted her drunk, but she was drunk already. She had been drunk all day, all week, all month, and for months on end. She sipped at the cold bitter liquid and felt its added effect immediately. As she looked out through the double glass of the window at the city below—blue and gray and black—she felt her old power return, but with an added expanse. Nothing now, nothing except Sarah, seemed beyond reach. She felt she could stretch out and seize whatever she chose, whenever she wished.

"Shall we?" Ben stood behind her and touched the back of her head. She turned quickly, her cheeks and ears flushed from the alcohol.

He took her elbow and steered her quickly between the tables and out to the elevator. They waited in silence and then stepped in together. He pressed a button and held open the door for her when they reached the tenth floor. She waited for him to lead the way and waited again while he took the key from his pocket to check the room number. They walked along the corridor together, watching the numbers pass until Ben stopped and opened a door.

Marion walked in and stood at the window, staring out over Union Square, as Ben locked and bolted the door. Her knees were weak from the martinis and lack of food, but she was calm and quite casual in her anticipation of the next few hours. It was as if they had been doing this for years, old hands, good friends. There was none of the frenzy that she felt with José, no racing heart, no need to fill the silence with reassurances.

Marion turned to face Ben as he walked over to her at the window.

She smiled up at him in a haze of benign affection. He bent his head and kissed her on the mouth, so gently that she drew her arms around his neck and pulled him closer. She felt his hands reaching for her zipper, felt her dress open. She lowered her arms to let it slip from her shoulders onto the carpet around her feet.

"Oh, Marion! God!"

Ben stood back and looked at her. She smiled, a queen, a star, and turned to catch her image in the mirror opposite the bed. She did look wonderful in her new bra and panties, her whole body thrust forward provocatively by the height of her sandals. And she couldn't help wishing that there were three or four or five men to enjoy her, teams of them, a whole audience.

Ben smiled at her. He looked like a boy confronted by his first electric train and too impatient to read the instruction manual. Marion noticed the erection pushing out through his tweed slacks and she stepped over to unbutton his shirt. He stood there with his arms at his sides while she unbuckled his belt, pulled out his tie, unzipped his slacks. And then he shuffled off his clothes, pulled off his shoes, and stood before her in his boxer briefs and socks.

Marion sat on the edge of the bed and slipped off her sandals, quite aware of the classic curve of her knee and arch of her foot as she unbuckled each one. She unhooked her bra and lay back on the pillows. And then she raised her arms behind her head and waited for Ben to join her, to begin the age-old ritual of illicit pleasure played out in hotel rooms, in dark offices, in every time and place of human habitation.

Afterwards, they lay there in silence, staring at the shadows on the ceiling, listening to the start of the rush hour traffic far below. Neither wished to talk. They couldn't even look at each other now that they had turned themselves inside out.

Ben sat up first and stared down at Marion. She smiled and he pulled her up to him, kissing her hard.

"We must go," she said.

"I wish I could stay all night."

"Wouldn't that be lovely?" She unwound her legs and stood up. Ben nodded, watching her with wide eyes as she dashed off to the bathroom and then emerged again to dress. She picked up her clothes and shook them out, pulled on her panties, put on her bra and then her dress. All the time Ben watched her without moving.

"Would you zip me up?" she asked. Obediently, he stood up to help her, kissing her neck and shoulders before he did. "Ben," she said, buckling one sandal. "Are you going to leave here like the emperor?"

"Emperor?"

"With no clothes."

He laughed and began to dress, but slowly, never taking his eyes off Marion. "Marion—"

"Mmm."

"I've never—I've never had an experience like that."

Marion stopped brushing her hair and looked at him in the mirror. "Ben, I'm going to tell you something you probably won't believe."

"What?"

"Neither have I."

She came to him as he sat on the edge of the bed to tie his shoes. She laid her hands on his shoulders. "I have never made love so wonderfully. I have never been so satisfied."

"Oh, Marion!" He clasped her around her waist and pressed the side of his head against her stomach. She stood there, staring at the rumpled bedspread and the awful picture on the wall behind, and she began to understand the fragility of men, their vulnerability in the face of women's inscrutable satisfactions. She saw the disguises in their posturings, their techniques, their faithfulness or promiscuity. Marion saw now, as she stood before Ben circling his head with her arms, that the power she had felt was as nothing to the power she really possessed.

They crawled in silence through the traffic, back to the clinic. Every now and then he reached over and squeezed her hand. She turned the radio on to commuter baroque and closed her eyes.

"We're here," said Ben.

Marion sat up. "Oh, that was quick."

"Too quick by far."

She reached for her purse.

"Marion, when will I see you?"

"Friday."

"It seems years away."

"Ben—Phone me."

"Tomorrow."

She squeezed his hand and jumped out of the car. Her car stood alone in the clinic parking lot. Everyone had gone. Marion climbed in quickly and started the engine. She wanted to get home before Jonathan, to smuggle in her purchases before he could question her. Sarah would be there watching, waiting, her defenses ready. And José would need an explanation tomorrow. Marion sighed. Nothing was simple. No one thing, no action, could be separated from the rest of her life. Everything she did now seemed to involve her in another lie.

11

Marion woke very early the next morning to the full realization that she had further complicated her life. She wondered in her sobriety at yesterday's excesses. She closed her eyes tight in embarrassment but only saw herself more clearly stepping out of her red dress and viewing herself in the hotel mirror as Ben sat and watched.

The room was very silent. It was six o'clock. Jonathan had been called out at about midnight and she didn't remember hearing him return. She looked over to his side of the bed and then leaned over the mound of covers to see whether he was awake. But he wasn't there. He must have stayed on at the hospital to do his early rounds. Marion lay back and relaxed. The mornings and evenings with Jonathan were becoming increasingly tense. He was sullen or vicious, seldom his old aggressive jocular self any more. And she really couldn't blame him for his foul moods, especially when she considered her own wildness and irritation. In fact, now that he was withdrawing from her as she had been from him over these past months, she was beginning to notice a softening in herself towards him. As she faced him across the table at night, as they both watched in silence as Sarah picked and pushed her food around her plate, she wanted to reach out to him, to compensate him somehow for her treachery and deceit. It was his innocence, she supposed, that called up her conscience and led her into a labyrinth of self-doubt.

And yet Marion knew that she could never have him back as her mate, her lover. She wanted him as nominal husband only, co-professional, as the father of her child. For the moment. Till she could find another way, a better way. But then, as she looked from Jonathan to Sarah and around the room at all the paraphernalia of their domestic bargain—china, pictures, clocks, brass, and crystal—she saw it was impossible. She didn't have the power to impose these limitations. Marriage had a history of its own, a cohesive force, a set of rules that allowed only the slightest warping. And Marion realized that sex, or the pretense of it, was its informing core.

Lying in bed alone at six in the morning, Marion felt, with a shudder, the misery of the two people closest to her. She had watched their lives jolt and sputter as her own changed direction, and she alternated between anger and compassion, locked in as she was to her liability for their happiness.

The room was damp and cold and smelled of old shoes. Marion flung off the covers, wrapped her robe around her, and opened the drapes. It was going to be a lovely day. She opened the window to let in the fresh air and then, suddenly, walked out of the room and across the hall to Sarah's door. Sarah, until recently, would have been up at this hour, waiting for signs of life so that she could start practicing. But she had been silent in the mornings lately, and Marion turned the handle of her door with a slight misgiving.

"Mother?"

Sarah, at her desk, quickly shuffled away what she had been doing when Marion entered the room.

"Hello, darling," Marion said, sitting down on the edge of the bed. Sarah turned around in her chair. Her hair was once again rolled into curlers, but she had large gray circles under her eyes and her skin was streaked with yellow. "Aren't you going to practice this morning?"

"No."

Marion shifted to the middle of the bed and rested back on her elbows, looking soberly at Sarah. "Sarah, what's happening with your cello playing?"

"Why?"

"Oh, come on! You've cut your practicing down to a fraction of what it was. Every morning I listen for you and there's nothing. What's up?"

Sarah said nothing. She straightened a pad and a few pencils on her desk while Marion watched her in silence. This room had always made her feel like a stranger, not simply because she was unwelcome, but because the room itself seemed to hold its own shape and tone, different from the rest of the house. Bed, desk, chair, drapes, and carpet, all seemed to have been chosen impersonally, to offer no offense, or charm, to anyone who might live in it. Marion noticed Sarah's attempts to make the room her own—wind chimes hanging from the light fitting, prints of medieval icons, and music manuscripts stuck around the walls with slashes of yellowing Scotch tape, a bulletin board, the books on her bookshelves. But she could not shake off the conviction she always had while in this room that neither she nor Sarah belonged here. It was as if they were meeting half way, on the neutral ground of a motel room, without even the passion of lovers to carry them above the indifference of their surroundings.

Sarah turned in her chair to look at Marion. "Mother, I'd like to give up the cello. Just for a while."

Marion sat up and stared. But Sarah went on before she could speak. "You gave up the clinic—almost. So I don't see how you can object." Sarah's eyes were red and probing. She looked as if she hadn't slept for weeks.

"It's not a question simply of objecting," Marion said. "It's just that you were so dedicated to it. And you were—are—so good. Why? What do you hope to gain?"

Sarah shrugged and continued to stare at Marion.

"Have you told Grandpa?" Marion asked.

"No."

"He'll be very disappointed."

Silence.

"Sarah, has anything happened at school or with Sumiko to upset you like this?"

"I'm not upset."

"OK. But first the hair and the face, then the dieting, then that 'incident' at Beth and Alex's, and now this with the cello. It all adds up to a mystery. I admit that I don't understand it. I do understand your decision to take your appearance in hand. That's fine and healthy. But it will have the reverse effect if you starve yourself into ill health."

"I've still got a lot to lose."

"So you've said before. And I've told you I disagree. But that's not the point. The way you're going about all this is not healthy, darling." Marion shifted to the edge of the bed and crossed her legs and arms. "Now we haven't yet discussed that incident last Thursday night to my full satisfaction, but it is going to be discussed fully now, and explained. There is a full explanation due, not only to me, but to Beth and Alex too." As Marion spoke she felt herself move from benign concern to mild irritation. "Do you have an explanation ready or am I going to have to cross-examine you like a child or a criminal?"

Sarah was not prepared for this rapid shift of tone. She almost rose in her place, then she sat down again, like a frightened child confronted by a gang of bullies. She began to thread the sash of her robe through her fingers until she had wound her hand up to her waist. Then she pulled out the sash and started again.

Marion sat facing Sarah, watching her contort to avoid her gaze. She waited, breathing lightly, until Sarah looked up to check on her continued attention. Once their eyes met, Sarah was caught and frozen in place as if she were looking into a gun pointed by a maniac. She opened her mouth to speak but simply closed it again, never moving her eyes from Marion's. Marion remained silent.

"Mother, I—I apologized to Beth." Sarah tore her eyes away and stared down into her lap where her hands lay swollen from the tightness of the sash.

"I'm aware of that, Sarah. Apologies, however, are cheap and count for very little in a case like this, without the backing of an explanation."

Sarah looked up again at Marion. She was shivering despite the warmth of the room. Color had risen to her cheeks, combining with the hollows around her eyes to make her look ill.

Marion waited, watching Sarah in silence while the girl tried to find words, and searched for the voice to put them in. Finally Sarah began, faltering, swallowing, to give her the explanation she wanted.

"We were dancing, you see. Marlene and I. She was teaching me really. But I couldn't, sort of, get it. I couldn't relax. So she suggested a sherry or something. But they only had whiskey and gin and that sort of thing. So we had gin instead." Sarah tried to smile, but the smile collapsed even before the edges of her mouth could curl. She shrugged instead. "That's what happened," she said.

Marion looked at Sarah dispassionately. She took note of the girl's discomfort, her inability to find the right tone for this encounter, and she was suddenly flushed through with impatience and anger. She was beginning to find Sarah's silly attempt at a smile, her stiff shrug, her skinny explanation more enraging than the extraordinary event itself. "And what about the dresses and scarves?" she asked, her voice rising.

Sarah's face was now purple and her chest heaving under the chenille robe.

"Well?" Marion persisted.

"We were—we were dressing up . . ."

"In *Beth's* best evening clothes?"

Sarah stared at her mother in a dumb show of tortured guilt. "We were just playing. Sort of—"

"Why, Sarah?"

"I don't know. It was Marlene's idea."

"Sarah," said Marion standing up at last. "A lot of what has been happening to you lately seems to have been Marlene's idea. At first, as you know, I was very pleased that you had a friend—after all these years. I had never thought that your total dedication to the cello and your schoolwork, to the exclusion of every other interest, was healthy." Marion stopped and waited for a few seconds until Sarah looked up. Then she went on. "When you brought her home that first day, I was very pleased. I admit that I thought your choice—what shall I say—odd. Something about that girl is jarring."

Sarah stiffened.

"I'm aware that she is more sophisticated than you are. That she has a string of boys and so forth."

Sarah gripped the arms of her chair. "Where did you hear that?"

"Oh, I don't know. And it doesn't matter. But, Sarah, she's cheap. And I think she's dangerous."

"Dangerous!"

Marion sat down again on the bed. "Just think for a moment, please. Apart from the debauch that you conducted in Beth's house, think of what could have happened to Alfred."

"*Alfred?*"

"Yes, remember him? The retarded child for whom you were hired to baby-sit? What if there had been a fire while you lay stupefied in a pool of vomit, deserted by your so-called friend when things got a bit hot."

"I don't know."

"No!" shouted Marion. "You don't know, do you? Neither do you know what you're doing when you lose—what?—thirty pounds of weight in a few months? Or give up a promising cello career after ten years of obsessive practicing and performing. Do you know what you're doing?" she shouted. "Or are you so bent on self-destruction that you don't care whom you carry along with you?"

Marion noticed a slight smile cross Sarah's face, like invisible armor given to the gods. They were shifting positions and Marion realized too late that she would have done better to have maintained her silence.

Sarah looked across at her mother and waited. They both knew that it was time for Sarah to dress for school and make her lunch. But she sat back in her chair, showing no signs of hurry.

"Well?" Marion said at last.

Sarah folded her hands gently in her lap and bent her head down to stare at her slippers. As she did, Marion noticed the roots of hair pulled taut in row after row of pink plastic cylinders and she was mystified by the discomfort that this child was inflicting on herself. Minutes passed before Sarah finally began to speak in a low steady voice, so soft at times that Marion had to bend forward to hear her.

"If I am destroying myself by dieting and making a new friend and taking some risks, it is better, Mother, than what I did before. Don't pretend that I'm so talented. I know what you think of my abilities. I always knew. And your opinion, you see, was the same as mine. Except that I had nothing else to hang on to. The girls at school seemed to have different kinds of lives. I mean something to go home to, parents and family. I had only myself and the cello. It seemed to be my link to Grandpa and Grandma in a way. I don't know whether you can understand this, but when I played, I could sort of switch off. I imagined myself on stage, with Grandpa and Grandma in the first row. I wanted to please them so badly—" Sarah looked up. Her eyes were red.

"What happened then?" Marion asked softly.

"Then—I don't know. Suddenly nothing seemed worth it. I always knew I wouldn't be great, but I still hoped. Then suddenly I stopped hoping."

"Before or after you met Marlene?"

"It had nothing to do with Marlene."

Marion now stared down into her lap, holding her breath for Sarah to go on. Sarah raised her voice slightly.

"When Marlene came to school, I avoided her. I thought she was a loudmouth. And she didn't fit in. The girls all laughed at her because she didn't fit in. She was sort of loud and sassy. Well, then we got talking during rehearsal one day and she was criticizing all those debs with their asinine airs and graces and saying how much she hated them. And then I thought, well, I hate them too. I've always hated them. And I told her. So we started out by laughing at them. And then she told me about her life and her mom and I began to understand why she was so loud and *jarring* as you said. In fact, I liked her for it. I envied her. She really didn't care what anyone thought of her."

Sarah looked up at last. It was the longest speech she had ever made, and it didn't seem finished. Marion waited silently, watching Sarah shift and turn in the chair.

"She was honest with me, you see. She told me I should cut my hair and that I should diet—" Sarah suddenly broke off, looked at Marion for a minute, and then plunged on. "I know you always told me that. I mean you were always going on about my hair and my clothes and my posture, but it seemed to me that you wanted me shaped up for *your* benefit, not mine. And nothing I could ever do would measure up to what you wanted from me anyway. I could never be what you were yourself. Nothing I do will ever satisfy you."

"Sarah—"

"But Marlene likes *me*. I don't know. I felt sort of hopeful, that maybe I could look normal and be normal. Not a freak behind a cello. She showed me how to diet."

"*Showed you?*"

"She gave me tips and things. She diets all the time. But I don't do the things she does."

"Like what?"

"Oh, laxatives, stuffing myself and then throwing up. I can't."

"Oh, my God, Sarah!"

Sarah laughed a metallic cold cartoon of a laugh. "I know you think I have anorexia nervosa. Daddy told me. But I don't, you know. I even got a book out of the library on it. I'm nothing like those loonies."

For the first time ever, Marion heard Jonathan in Sarah. She felt the familiar repugnance at the jaunty assurance, the self-congratulation.

"And neither does Marlene," Sarah went on. "She's hardly a skeleton. She's just more radical than I am, about most things. Anyway," she said, adjusting her robe so that it covered her knee as she crossed her leg, "she's given me what no one else—except Grandpa and Grandma—has ever given me."

"What?"

"Confidence."

Marion thought of the girl sprawled across the rug. She thought of Sarah sliding behind the doorway as she and Jonathan argued, of Sarah slashing out with her bow, and she knew that this child was further away from the confidence she spoke of than she had ever been. Marion wanted to reach over to her and stop the pretense. She wanted to tell her that she knew it wasn't working. She wanted her to take comfort in the time she had, in the years and years ahead of her. Marion wanted to tell her of the bounds and fetters of achievement and success. She wanted Sarah to know the frailty of social accomplishment. But she looked at the girl sitting there staring at her out of sunken eyes, groping for some indication of the direction she was taking, and she felt defeated. She knew that nothing she could say had the power to reach across the space between them.

"So you see, Mother," Sarah said, standing up to end the interview. "When you gave up an unpromising career, I thought, 'Why can't I?' I'll always have the skills. So will you. I just want to try something else."

Marion slumped down where she was, dismissed. All she could do now was to reenter her role as mother. She saw that she needed it if she were not to lose Sarah entirely.

"Well," she said, standing up too. "It's a quarter of eight and you'll never be at school on time unless I run you over. Hurry up and get dressed and I'll make your lunch."

Sarah stood still, holding her robe closed waiting for Marion to leave the room so that she could dress. Marion turned as she reached the door and hesitated.

"Sarah, isn't it time I bought you some new clothes, now that you've lost all this weight?"

"Mother—" Sarah looked at Marion and then down. She shifted her weight. "I'd rather choose my own clothes if you don't mind."

"Well, of course you'd choose them."

"I mean without you."

"You mean with that girl?"

"Yes, with Marlene."

Marion paused. "I will allow that. On one condition. That I have veto power over anything you buy." She crossed her arms and cocked her head on one side, staring straight into Sarah's eyes. "I don't want you going around looking like a hooker."

Sarah walked over to her closet and stood there, her back straight, her head erect, taking out her uniform. "In that case, Mother, thank you, but I'd rather not have any."

They drove in silence to school. It should have seemed so normal to be racing through the park with all the other mothers in station wagons, weaving in and out of the morning traffic. But Marion was a novice to this world of service. She felt fatigued before the day had even begun. There were mothers drawing up outside the school, ready for tennis or shopping, wide awake and dressed up. They kissed their daughters, smiling, and the daughters kissed them back. It was a scene played over and over, every morning, a ritual of duty cheerfully observed in the course of their undramatic lives.

Marion stopped the car and Sarah quickly opened the door to get out.

"Sarah!"

"Yes?"

"I've been thinking. You're right, about the clothes. You're old enough to choose for yourself. I'll simply have to trust your judgement."

"Mother, I have to go. The bell's about to ring."

"Wait a minute. Did you hear what I said? I said you may go out and choose what you wish."

"Yes. Thank you."

"Up to, say— Well, I leave that up to you too."

"That's fine." Sarah turned to leave.

"And Sarah—"

"Yes?"

"What about Sumiko?"

"What about her?"

"Aren't you going to tell her that you're quitting?"

"I told her."

"When?"

"Last week. Friday."

"Why didn't she—"

"Mother, sorry, I have to go. Thanks for the ride."

Sarah broke into a run up the driveway of the school as the bell rang. Marion watched her. She seemed so sad struggling up that hill alone, amongst the groups of pushing and laughing girls, calling at each other by their schoolgirl nicknames. No one called to Sarah. She was invisible to everyone but Marion and even Marion found herself watching the others, picking out the leaders.

Marion sat back in her seat and closed her eyes. Despite her eight hours of sleep, she wanted to sleep again. She thought she might just go home and climb into bed before her lesson. She would cancel her lesson, in fact. Something was worrying her, something that seemed to have no solution. Marion sat for a moment, questioning the surfaces of her consciousness. Nothing came up. She needed to chase it down, catch it, and dig it out into the light for observation. But she was tired and shaky, as if she hadn't slept for weeks or had worked all night or was coming down again with the flu. She opened her eyes and shook her head, hoping that a few hours of sleep would rescue her from this mysterious desolation.

There were cars gliding up around her, unloading and then turning away. And then a shadow, differentiated from the cars and schoolgirls by the directness of its intent, moved across her window and stopped. She turned as if she had known who it was, as she did know, and looked up into José's unsmiling face. Quickly she rolled down the window.

"Where were you?" he asked.

"When?"

José rolled his eyes and looked over the top of the car towards the school.

"Do you mean yesterday?" she asked.

The muscles of his cheeks flexed and his nostrils flared. Marion wondered, racing over yesterday's movements, whether he could have followed her.

"I had lunch with Ben."

"Why?"

"To discuss Sarah."

Girls passed the car, late for school. They waved at José and he waved back, smiling.

"Hi, Mr. López!"

"Hi, Jane! Hi, Amy!"

Then his smile shrank again to a thin menace as he looked down into Marion's face. "Why lunch?"

"Because it was lunchtime. And we didn't want to be disturbed. For God's sake, José—"

"And afterwards?"

"I went shopping."

"With him?"

"Of course not. Don't be ridiculous."

"Where did he go?"

"Back to the clinic, I guess. How should I know?"

"He did not."

"What?"

"He did not go back to that clinic."

"How do you know?"

"I know."

"So? Am I supposed to account to you for his movements as well as for mine?"

"Only for yours—with him."

"José!"

"Where did you have lunch?"

"The St. Francis."

"Did you drive down there in your car?"

"No, we went in his. And then he dropped me on Sacramento Street to shop. I left my car in the clinic parking lot and walked back to get it."

"What time?"

"Oh Lord, I don't remember. I guess it must've been about five."

"All that time shopping?"

"Yes. All that time shopping. Do you want to come home with me to inspect my purchases and measure how much time each item would take to buy?"

He crossed his arms and frowned, as if in thought.

"José?"

He looked at her and seemed suddenly so helpless that she wanted to stretch her arm out of the car and touch him. She wanted to drive immediately to Sausalito, to close herself with him in their room, to forget about Ben and Sarah and Jonathan and Marta and all the other people who diminished their happiness. She looked up at him and he unfolded his arms and laid his hands on her elbow.

"I thought I had lost you," he said.

"To Ben?"

"Yes."

Marion sank her head and tried to control the tears which were falling in a few large drops onto her blue jeans. She watched them with a clinical interest as they spread into the threadbare fabric and joined each other at the edges.

"Why are you here this morning?" he asked.

"To drop Sarah. She and that Marlene behaved abominably at Beth's on Thursday night. It's going from bad to worse. That's why she saw Ben yesterday. And why she was late this morning. She's giving up her cello lessons, you know."

"I know. She told me."

"When?"

"Friday. She wants to continue in the orchestra though." José looked over the car and up towards the school. "I must go," he said. "I'm late already."

Marion glanced up at him and wondered if she would ever learn to keep Sarah out. She was only now beginning to understand the rule: he could discuss Sarah, she could not. None of her concern or anger or disappointment with Sarah could ever find a place to rest between them. He wanted her fresh, with no life of her own away from him.

"I must go too," she said. "Will I see you later?"

"Of course. I'll leave here at three."

"Only six more weeks."

"Five and a half."

"Five and three-sevenths."

"Good-bye, my love."

"Bye."

Marion started the car and turned it around slowly to drive home. But as she passed the school gate again, she saw Sandy Van Wyck walking briskly down the driveway and waving at her.

"Hi, Marion! How's the piano doing?"

Marion raised one hand in a small wave. The tears had stiffened her cheeks and she felt them restrain her smile. Sandy walked quickly across the road to the car.

"Why are you here so early?" asked Marion, trying to fend off any further questions.

"Oh, next year's scholarships, that kind of stuff. Hey, Marion, now that you're a lady of leisure, want to help us on the Pleasure Faire? We've got loads of slots that need filling and we sure could use some help."

"Oh—uh—Sandy, I'm still going into the clinic some days. And I take night call—nights. Why don't I call you when my schedule straightens out?"

Sandy smiled in triumph. She stood beside the car in the collegiate uniform of the fifties: loafers, wraparound skirt, and Peter Pan collar. Her short blond hair was parted at the side and caught neatly in a tortoiseshell barrette. She wore no makeup, no nail polish on her smooth girlish hands. Her breasts were flattened behind flowered cotton and her hips defeminized by flat shoes and feet kept slightly apart. Even her voice seemed calculated to remove any hint of sexuality. It was the nasal monotone of her class and breed. Marion could not imagine any man desiring such a woman and yet this one had a gorgeous husband and several children. And she seemed happy.

"I'll expect to hear from you," Sandy said, tapping the roof of Marion's car. "We're not going to let you get away this time!" She turned and marched across the road to her Mercedes. Marion lurched through the stop sign and drove home.

The phone was ringing as she closed the garage door, and she ran up the stairs to answer it.

"Hello?"

"Marion?"

"Yes, Ben."

"This is the third time I've tried you. Where have you been?" His voice was thin and cracked.

Marion sat down at the kitchen table and rested her forehead on the palm of her left hand.

"Marion?"

"Ben, I took Sarah to school. She was late."

"Oh."

Her breath was coming in shallow heaves. She was trying not to scream, but the scream was in her throat and wouldn't let the words rise above it.

"Marion, are you OK?"

"Mmm."

"I want to see you. Please!"

Marion pressed two fingers into her eyelids. Her chest subsided and she sat up. "Ben, not today. Perhaps—later in the week. I have to think. Everything is just crashing in on me."

"I know. I understand."

"Maybe."

"Maybe what?"

"Maybe you understand."

"Thank you."

"Ben?"

"Yes."

"Thank you for yesterday. It was wonderful."

"*Thank* me! Marion! Oh, Marion, I love you too much for these games. Don't make it sound as if it's over. Look, I've been thinking. I know you're going to the meeting in Puerto Vallarta. Would it be OK if I went too?"

Marion sat up straight. She was awake now, completely awake, every muscle, every faculty. "No, Ben, that's impossible. And anyway, what about Betty's family?"

"Impossible? Nothing could be more explainable. Why not?"

"Please, Ben. It's just impossible."

"Oh."

"What oh?"

"He's going with you, isn't he?"

Marion licked her dry lips.

"OK, Marion. That's OK. It's hard, but—well, I guess I can try to understand. What I'm saying is, well, I'll accept you on any terms. Beggars can't be choosers you know."

"Oh, Ben!" Marion wept again, smiling and sniffing. "You are so wonderful. So ridiculously wonderful."

"Marion! Marion, can you hear me?" Marion nodded. "Well, anyway, let me know when I can see you. Please. Just *see* you if that's—Anything. Will you call me? Or should I call you?"

"I'll call before three."

"I'll be waiting. I love you Marion."

The kitchen was silent now, except for the refrigerator and the clock and the blowing of the trees. It was woman's time of day, the closing and locking of a bathroom door. Marion climbed the stairs slowly, like an old woman in great pain. She opened her door and stepped out of her clogs in the doorway. Then she pushed back the covers of the bed and climbed in under them just as she was with the spring sun filling the room and six hours to fill before three.

Chapter 12

As Marion stepped out of the plane and into the hot, damp air of Puerto Vallarta, all her doubts, all her calculations and plots and plans for her five days with another man resolved themselves into euphoric suspension. She felt very far from home, much farther than the fourteen hundred or so aeronautical miles which separated this place from San Francisco. It was a strange place, a place with palm trees and hot breezes bearing traces of the sour-sweet foulness of inadequate plumbing. It was a place where she and most of those behind her, climbing carefully down the metal stairway to the ground, did not belong. They bore all the hallmarks, with their sunhats and phrase books and bags of medication, of fragile invaders, unadapted to local conditions. And the dark men on the ground seemed to enjoy this as they stood around in khaki uniforms watching the uneven line of tourists struggle through the heat towards the airport building, laughing to each other in their foreign tongue.

Marion was walking alone, ahead of José. They had arranged to meet at the hotel registration desk where José would order adjacent rooms. She kept herself from looking back to check that he was there and walked ahead, swinging her briefcase like a diplomat's pouch, to set her apart from the tourists.

The airport building was hot and close. Marion set down her

briefcase and shuffled it in front of her as she edged up towards the official stamping passports. Hers was ready, her tourist card typed and folded inside it as it had been for weeks now. She had taken to checking it every now and then, reading it through, folding it neatly and replacing it in her file under *P*. She allowed herself the satisfaction of such a small neurosis, the comfort of its foregone conclusion. It was unimaginable to her that anyone could forget a passport, or a visa, traveler's checks or airline tickets.

The line moved slowly through the immigration barrier and then out to the baggage claim room. There were a few physicians that she recognized among the crowd waiting for baggage, but no one whom she could name or place and certainly no one who would have a vested interest in her domestic arrangements. It was even hotter inside than out. People fanned themselves with their passports or hats or ticket jackets, waiting for the slow unloading of the luggage, piece by piece. Marion risked turning to look for José. She scanned the room quickly but found him nowhere. For a moment she panicked, standing there alone amongst the pairs of tourists, wives giving orders, husbands pulling suitcases off the rack; young city girls standing together in tight pants and high-heeled sandals, baring their teeth as they smiled and looked around to be noticed.

"Your bag is outside." José's voice was in her ear. Marion jumped and turned round, noticing as she did that the young girls were staring at him with unmasked interest.

"José! I was looking for you," she said in a low voice.

He had the oversolemn look of one entrusted with the crown jewels, of a schoolboy chosen to bear the flag. This was his country, it said. Here he was host, protector, diplomat, and interpreter.

"I will order a taxi for you. Follow me."

Marion looked up at the continuing stares of the girls and decided to do as he commanded. Several people seemed to notice as she followed him out. She even thought she saw a few smile, or sneer, but she couldn't be sure. She had no choice, in fact, but to obey, and she walked through the airport hall and out to the taxi with what she hoped would pass for nonchalance or, at least, professional fatigue. But José, standing there holding open the door of the cab, was almost obscured by a bunch of five or six dozen red roses which he thrust out at her as she approached. There were people standing around on the curb, tourists and Mexicans, who turned to watch Marion accept his flowers. They smiled. The Mexicans clucked and laughed.

"José!"

"Get in and I will give them to you." He handed her the flowers and then slammed the door shut, leaning in through the window to gabble at the driver in Spanish. Finally, he turned to her. "I'll see you at the hotel. I told him to wait until my cab passes him."

Marion nodded. The cab was hot and foul smelling. The driver smoked a cheap cigar and listened to some raucous crackling music on a portable radio. Everyone around her seemed to be loading cabs and buses and moving on, but her cab remained where it was, waiting, she presumed, for José's cab to pass. She looked at her watch. She had been sitting captive for five minutes while the driver stared at her through a long expanse of rearview mirror. It was becoming intolerable.

"*Qué pasa*?" she asked.

The driver turned in his seat and answered her at length over his shoulder. She nodded. It was ridiculous, she realized, to ask a question when one couldn't hope to understand the answer. She was just about to rest her head back on the seat and close her eyes when he started the car. José was now alongside them in another cab, his body all exaggerated attention lest her driver miss his cue. It was farcical, she thought, bad fiction, all this cloak and dagger in the face of his six dozen roses and attention to her baggage. What was he up to? Marion was stiff with irritation. If Jonathan had been there they would have fought. They always fought on vacation, especially on the mechanics of going and coming. But now she was obliged to behave, and, more than that, to be grateful. She began to wonder how she would put up with five days of it.

Marion relaxed slightly once she stood at the registration desk of the hotel signing her form. José stood beside her smiling at the clerk, arranging the room situation so smoothly that she didn't even realize it had been done until they were ushered up in the elevator by the bellhop and then shown into their rooms. Marion walked over to the window of her room and slid open the door so that she could stand on the verandah. The ocean was beautiful, the beach, the sun, the white of the waves, all as she had imagined they would be. A light breeze just lifted her hair and her skirt. Boats flitted back and forth along the water, pulling parachutists behind them, the chutes billowing out in vivid reds and blues and yellows. It was a festive, whimsical scene, a celebration, and Marion felt her spirits lift with the contemplation of it.

Suddenly she felt herself grabbed from behind, held by strong arms, and a chin hooked over her shoulder. She could smell José and feel his cheek against hers.

"My God! You scared me!"

He nuzzled her neck.

"How did you get in here?" she asked, still held in his vise.

"Magic."

"Did they give you two keys?"

"Nope." He turned her around and kissed her long and hard, pressing her back against the wall of the verandah. Marion imagined then tumbling over backwards and somersaulting down to the beach below. She struggled free and edged behind him back into the room. He bounced in after her and pulled her down onto the bed. The air conditioning had added a chill to the room now. It was working at full force against the hot air which streamed in through the open door. José peeled off most of her clothes and his and began his ritual of arousal and release. Marion shivered as the thin layer of perspiration that covered her body chilled in the cool air of the room and he immediately accelerated his pace in mistaken response, leaving her far behind to contemplate the patterns of sun and shade on the ceiling and to notice the door, slightly ajar, that connected their two rooms.

Afterwards he lit a cigarette and looked over at her with uncomplicated satisfaction. He kissed her breast, her cheek, and then lay his head on her stomach, sure that she was his, never once imagining that his skills could lack where his intention was so generous.

"Welcome to Mexico." He smiled up at her chin.

"Thank you."

"What do you think?"

"Of what?"

"Of Mexico? Of this place? Of my country!"

Marion propped herself up to look down at him and smiled. "It's lovely," she said. "I love what I've seen."

"You'll see more. I'll show you everything. You can meet my friends. Everything. I'll do it." He caressed her legs, her feet, like a landlord checking the extent of his holdings. Then he sat up cross-legged, smoothing both hands over her belly. "Mariana, I have never asked you something . . ."

"What?"

"What kind of anticonceptive do you use?"

Marion laughed. "Contraceptive."

"Yes. Whatever."

"I have an IUD."

José turned away from her and blew out a cloud of smoke with a sigh. He said nothing. Marion ran her nails lightly down his back and out towards the edges where she knew he was sensitive.

"What's wrong?" she asked, kissing his shoulder. He shrugged her off.

"José, what in hell is the matter?"

"I don't like it."

"Why? You don't even know it's there."

He swung round to face her. "Because I want you to bear my child." He lay his hands on her stomach. "Our child. I want us to create a child from our love."

Sudden uncontrollable nausea rose in Marion's throat. She leapt off the bed and darted for the bathroom, flipped up the toilet seat with its sterile strip of paper intact, and retched violently into the bowl. A livid yellow stream of half-digested airplane food and drink sprayed out of her mouth leaving her gasping for breath, snorting the foulness out of her nose and throat. She sank her head over the bowl, resting her forehead against the far rim, waiting for her heartbeat to return to normal. She felt José's hand on her back, but it didn't help. Her head alternately spun and arched. She knelt back on her haunches and bent her forehead to the bathroom floor, locked her hands behind her head and then pressed up against them to prevent herself from fainting. It worked. She sat up slowly, flushed the toilet and then rinsed her mouth out in the basin. Her toilet bag was still in her case and she turned to get it. But José blocked the way.

"José, please—"

"You didn't tell me you felt sick."

"I didn't. It came on suddenly. I just need to get my toilet stuff."

"You must have caught it already. Did you drink any water?"

"No, of course not. I'm fine. Really. It's just the sudden heat—and the excitement." She tried to smile, and he stood aside in response, touching her cheek as she passed.

"Have you got medicines for this?" he persisted, as she returned with her toilet bag.

Marion laid the bag down on the counter in silence and then looked up at him. He had draped himself in a towel and stood in the doorway with his hair sticking out at angles around his beautiful face, like a model for one of the old Brylcreem ads. She smiled.

"You feeling better?" he asked.

"Much better." She scrubbed away at her teeth, rinsed her mouth out, then ran herself a bath and trotted out past him to unpack her new clothes. José followed her.

"José, look, it's five o'clock. I'll have a bath and get dressed then let's go out."

"Together?"

"Why not? If I see anyone I know, I can say we met here and you happen to have the room next to mine. I just have to register for the meeting before I do anything. I can do that on my way out."

"You're going to go to this meeting?"

"I'll have to put in an appearance. Just for a few hours."

He glowered at her. "What will I do then?"

"Go to the beach. Anything you like. Surely you can occupy yourself for a few hours here and there?"

"Yes. Don't worry about me!"

"José, please!" She closed her eyes. When she opened them, he had gone, and she sat on the edge of the bed, staring at herself in the mirror, trying to get used to the idea of José's new and strange demand. Actually, it was logical. She wondered how she could not have seen it coming long ago. He had been going on about creation and the immortal power of love to create. But she had simply grown deaf to those kind of pronouncements, putting them down to Latin effulgence. In fact, she found herself less open now to José's vaguely stated credo of purity in art and the power of feelings than she had been when she first met him. She suspected him of stopping short, of making a virtue out of a convenience. And she suspected above all that he was half in love with the very tightness and common sense in her that he claimed to disdain, that she was now trying so hard to loosen.

And now this. A child. Marion clicked her tongue in irritation. First Jonathan and now José. Next, she supposed, Ben would be wanting to mingle his genes with hers. And all of them dreaming of some New World Madonna, juggling home and sex and career around the cherubic angel that lay in her lap, reaffirming for them all sorts of ancient rites of passage and God-given dominance. She stood up, sideways, to admire her flat, muscular stomach, and then strolled through to the bathroom to wash the airplane out of her skin and hair.

It was one of the new restaurants that had sprung up over the last ten years all over Puerto Vallarta but particularly along the ocean road. José evidently knew it well and was greeted effusively by the owner. He ushered them to the premier table on the open patio overlooking the bay. He smiled and bowed and pulled out first her chair and then José's. And suddenly, sitting down, watching José as he smiled and nodded and shook hands—suddenly, Marion was happy. She felt cared for, protected, sheltered, an object of love and pride and possession—all the silly things that she knew trapped women into wanting and finding husbands. But here, under the setting sun with all the foolishness about babies and anticonceptives left behind, she watched José leaning back in his chair and laughing in Spanish, beautiful, immaculate in his light linen suit and starched shirt, and she recognized with a familiar flutter the thrill of an intimacy dressed and disguised to face the world.

"This," said José, "is Señorita Roth. Mariana, Mr. Morales."

Marion smiled demurely as the owner kissed her hand. He and José exchanged a few more pleasantries in Spanish and then José flagged a waiter. A few minutes later a pot of yoghurt was delivered to Marion's place.

"For your stomach," said José. "You must be careful. Eat it!"

She ate the yoghurt obediently, like a child.

"What do you want to eat?" he asked.

"I don't know. I haven't seen the menu."

He handed her his menu and watched carefully as she read it. Suddenly it struck Marion as she glanced down the English side with the prices marked in pesos and their dollar equivalents that she had never, in all her planning and worrying about hotel rooms and airports and taxicabs, considered how they would handle the payment of meals. It was awkward. She had never paid for a man in her life, never even paid for herself when with a man. She had never had to consider a man's budget or her own expenditures. It had simply never come up. But she had noticed that he was careful with money. He counted his change, left small tips. And the only extravagances she ever saw him commit were for himself, tangibles, things he could wear, especially. She stared at the menu and then up at him.

"I'll have the barbecued spareribs please. And a salad."

"Wine?" he asked.

Marion smiled in assent. Jonathan would never have asked whether she wanted wine and, if he had, his voice would not have been as tight as José's was just then. She began to feel her own stomach tighten. It is strange, she thought, how sensitive I am to questions of generosity. It's not the money, really. I know that. It's the impulse behind the money that affects me. I have money, Jonathan has money, maybe José doesn't. So what? I'll pay. I'll play rich older woman to his impoverished lover. She looked over at him and he smiled at her, a flashy cosmetic smile. No, she thought, it's not the money. I'd pay anything to be rid of this burden of discontent, to be rid of this feeling of being used.

She looked out over the bay, ignoring José. For the first time she found herself comparing Jonathan favorably with him. The question of generosity had never come up with Jonathan. Somehow Jonathan was never gauche with money or about the spending of money. He never chose his entrée or dessert or cognac with regard to the price. Quite the contrary, in fact. And he never, of course, ordered the house wine which was right now being set before Marion and poured into her glass.

The wine was awful, but she drank it anyway, the whole glass, feeling its benign effect on her mood almost immediately. José smiled at her across the table as she drank.

"Good wine, hey?"

"Mmm. Yes, thanks."

The food was laid before them and José immediately began to eat, seldom looking up, never talking, but smiling occasionally at Marion with proprietary pleasure. She ate in silence. The vegetables were overcooked and starchy, and the meat tough. When they had finished, the waiter came over to ask about dessert. He addressed only José, however, in Spanish. Marion heard him list a few things. José shook his head, and then looked over at Marion.

"Would you want a dessert? I'm not having one."

Marion was full, but she looked up at the waiter. "What do you have?"

"We have flan, Mexican pastry, cakes, crépes suzette—"

"I'll have the flan," she said. "That sounds lovely."

José smiled nervously and pointed out the moon. She smiled too. "It's lovely," she said.

"Like you. Always."

He reached over for her hand but the flan was delivered just then and he withdrew it. Marion remembered those phrases well.

It was Marta and José on the piano stool. She picked up her spoon in silence and began on the flan.

When she had eaten about half of it, she looked up at José. He was observing her intently, seriously, as if he were trying to make a diagnosis. "What is bothering you?" he asked.

"Nothing. Why?"

"Because you are bothered by something, that's all."

"Would you like some of this flan?"

"Don't you like it?"

"I do. But I've had enough."

He took the dish and ate the flan quickly, scraping the spoon around the bowl. "Coffee?" he asked.

"Yes, please. Mexican style."

The coffee came and they sipped it slowly. Marion was thinking of the bill and she was sure that he was too. But no bill came. They had more coffee and then more. Marion shifted in her seat in irritation.

"Tired?" he asked.

"Very."

"Well, we'll go. I'll order the bill," he said significantly.

"José, let me pay for this meal." She didn't smile.

José bit his lip as if deep in thought and then waved a hand for the bill. As he waited he pretended to look for someone in the crowd. She saw him avoid her eyes, take the last sip of cold coffee, smack the cup back down on the saucer. Finally, the bill came and was placed in front of him. He flipped it over casually, glanced down at the tally, and then looked at her.

"You sure?"

"Quite sure," she said, reaching for her purse. He handed her the bill she took out her wallet and handed both back to him. As he riffled through her wad of pesos, pulling out what he needed, he giggled. And then he handed the notes and the bill over to the waiter, waved off the change, and gave her back her wallet. Marion put it away without a word and they left the restaurant in silence.

All the way back to the hotel in the cab, José was in high spirits. He pulled her over to him and ran his hands up the inside of her legs. He hummed. He sang. He murmured in her ear about breakfast in bed. But Marion was stiff and brittle. She had moved away from him, a hundred and eighty degrees away, and could only think of herself signing the breakfast bill, facing the crisis of her own irritation at every meal for the next five days. But why, she asked herself, why was this small thing now setting her so relentlessly against him? How had she allowed so trivial a nonsense to irritate her so extremely? She reminded herself over and over of the discrepancy in their incomes, of his generosity of spirit, of his little presents to her, the flowers, the gift of his love. And yet, despite her own voice in his defense, she could not eliminate from consciousness his silly nervous smile as she handed him her wallet, the sight of him fishing out her money and handing it to the waiter. And now this euphoric relief of his in the face of her obvious discomfort and irritation. He was, she decided, self-serving in his analysis of her moods and attitudes. This one, this remove of hers, far from disturbing him, seemed to drive him into a frenzy of adoration.

They arrived at the hotel and Marion hopped out of the taxi leaving José to pay. She stood on the hotel steps watching him count the change, and she suddenly wished that Jonathan were there to stand between her and this dollar-and-cents aspect of an affair. Then she would be able to suspend practicalities and lie with her lover in the afternoons exchanging only looks and words and desires, leaving the rest—the plane tickets and the train tickets, food, clothing and shelter—safely within the marriage contract.

Marion woke the next morning and the next to the smell of fresh coffee and a tray of breakfast for two on the table near the window. José had ordered it, but she couldn't find a way to ask him whose room the bill had been signed to. She had paid again for their dinner the second night. And they seemed to be skipping lunch, largely because she preferred to starve than to face her own quite predictable irritation. But now, when he seemed so pleased and proud, when he had gone to such pains to carry the tray in on cat's feet, now she felt ashamed for even caring.

The first day had been divided between lying in the sun and making love, except for the few dull hours that Marion had felt obliged to spend at the convention meetings. José had sulked for hours the first afternoon when she left him for a meeting, and after the second day's meeting, he was nowhere to be found when she eventually emerged hot and irritated by the complacency of the physicians inside. She had placed herself at the back of the room to make her escape easy. She had even tried to concentrate on the monotonous droning of the speakers on the platform, but her mind kept winding away from their small findings masquerading as breakthroughs and from the abstruse illnesses she had never seen and never hoped to see. She remembered the days when she had taken notes at every meeting, books and books of them. She could see them now, yellow and dusty, on the shelves of her study. What had she hoped to gain from them? she wondered. Or had it simply been her attempt to reaffirm her own involvement in the choice she had made for herself and for her future? If so, the fact that she had long since ceased opening those books to read over their contents and now only glanced occasionally at the shelf with the small satisfaction of knowing that they were there if she needed them should have warned her that someday the whole world from which they had emerged would diminish in importance to her to a point beyond significance.

When the lights dimmed for a presentation of slides, Marion slipped out quickly. She emerged blinking into the sunlight and walked directly to the pool. There she stood on a step and looked down at the bodies strewn around on chaise lounges and towels, but José was nowhere. He stood out among the Americans and Europeans like a panther among lions. He seemed to be a species apart from the pack, a different shape and color, solitary and nonconforming against the background of twos and threes and fours grouped around the water.

Marion walked back into the lobby and rang his room and then hers. There was no answer. She stood for a moment looking around at the guests wandering through the lobby in pairs. They looked, most of them, like comfortable shoes, mirroring each other in color, shape, and style, showing equivalent wear, marching together in the same direction. It seemed so simple to settle for less. So comfortable. And yet here she was, trying to turn her back on all that, searching for her lover, straining to make the most of what was turning out to be a trying experiment. She flung her bag back over her shoulder and walked out again into the sunshine.

It was four o'clock. He must have slept already and be somewhere avoiding her, punishing her with his absence. Marion wished she had her book with her but found a chair in the sun instead and stripped down to the bikini she wore under her sundress. A waiter came over immediately and she ordered a sandwich and a mai tai. She was starving and took some satisfaction in eating her sandwich alone. The sun and the mai tai made her head whirl. Everything looked incandescent. It was the time of day when even the moisture in the air seemed to absorb the light and then throw it back out a hundredfold.

Soon, the doctors emerged from the meeting and spilled down to the pool. They took up the chairs around Marion and ordered drinks, called over their wives. The speakers were being discussed, the findings, cases, X rays, new drugs. Marion lay listening with the sun beating through her light head until she thought she would faint, there, in their midst. So she sat up slowly and then bent her head down, pretending to look for something under the chair, so that the blood could fill her brain and allow her to leave without any drama. She stood up slowly, put on her sunglasses, and walked away, down to the beach.

It was fresher on the beach with the breezes coming up off the ocean. Marion walked down to the water's edge and then along to the end of the hotel's beach. There she turned and, on an impulse, walked over to the first row of palapas, winding between them up and back towards the pool.

He was sitting with a girl a few yards ahead of her, under a palapa, the third row back from the ocean. He could have seen Marion walking along the edge, turning, coming up towards him, but she knew he hadn't. He was sitting on the sand, one leg crooked under his arms, facing the girl who sat back in a chair and smiled at him. And he was talking, never taking his eyes from hers, earnestly, just as he had done with Marion so long ago now on the lawn of the Mary Ellis hockey field. Marion saw the girl lean forward to give him her full attention. She saw her throw back her head and laugh. José smiled. He picked up a book from the sand and asked the girl something about it. Then he paged seriously through it, nodding as she talked.

Not trusting herself to move, Marion stood where she was. Everything else on the beach was moving. People talked or swam or walked. Donkeys, gathered in groups at the shore, stamped and twisted as they waited for riders to release them from their bondage. Boats and parachutists buzzed back and forth along the water. Only Marion stood there in the sun, motionless, watching in horror as her lover and an almost naked girl channeled their desire for one another through a book, touching fingers as they passed it between them.

Marion lurched forward and crossed at an angle before José. She was walking fast, but she saw him stiffen as she passed. She heard him say "good-bye" and "see you" quickly and then she felt his hand on her shoulder, like an old friend, a past lover, not the man who woke in the middle of the night to watch her as she slept.

"Leave me alone, please."

"Why? What's wrong?" He had the same silly singsong pleading voice that teenage girls used with each other. Marion felt him turn to look behind him, and then look quickly again at her.

"Are you worried about the girl?"

"I am worried about nothing."

"I was just walking on the beach, Mariana. You were with your doctors. She waved at me." He cleared his throat. "Her hat flew away. That is what happened. And I caught it. She waved to show me where she was. Do you believe me now?"

Marion walked on. This was ridiculous. Whatever she said would make it more ridiculous. And there had been no hat. She was sure of that.

"You are jealous for nothing this time. Come on! Let's go up to the room?"

He was looking up into her face for a response as they climbed the steps to the pool. We must look, Marion thought, like a woman and her discarded lover, not a fool and her gigolo. She looked around for her chair and her things. People had moved the chairs around and hers was pushed up against the wall. Her bag and her towel were still on it, claiming it as hers. Marion walked across the cement with José close behind her, wondering how she would tolerate his lies in bed. They had been making love now for two days, over and over, this way and that, so that Marion was beginning to feel as if she were in training for some event. And she couldn't help suspecting that even José didn't desire her to this extent. She had, on a few occasions, noticed him surreptitiously pulling at himself when he thought she wasn't looking so that he could face her with his needs and desires in obvious array. But now there was no getting away from it. He was clearly convinced, despite the absurd illogicality of it, that by making love to her he would clear himself of her suspicion of his desire for another woman.

Marion picked up her bag and turned to leave. It was a lovely time of day. The sun was beginning to sink and the heat was less fierce. People had woken from their siestas and sat refreshed in the open air, drinking and laughing for the few hours before dinner. Marion wished that they could sit too, even in silence, instead of withdrawing to repeat what they had already done once today. But José was behind her, offering to carry things, urgent now in his desire to remove her from the public view.

"Marion!"

Marion stopped, and José, who held her elbow, stopped too. She looked around quickly, but saw no one and turned again to leave.

"Marion! Here!"

This time she saw him sitting in a group near the bar, waving to her. He looked hot and red faced in his blue and white seersucker suit and red bow tie, as if he had just arrived and had not had time to change. There was a briefcase, in fact, at this side and she saw a room key on the table in front of his drink. For a moment, Marion stared at him dumb. Then she took a step towards him. "Ben!" she cried.

13

José had left the hotel before Marion reached her room. She noticed that the adjoining door was ajar when she came in and peeped through carefully, as if she were about to enter the cage of a sleeping carnivore. She knew that she would have to face his raging and sulking, but somehow the presence of Ben in this unlikely place had fortified her against José's madness. They had only been together, she and Ben, for about ten minutes out there before she remembered José and excused herself reluctantly to join him. But now, as she entered his empty room and looked around at all the vestiges of his presence there—the towels on the floor, the dead cigarette butts, the strong smell of his cologne in the bathroom—she was sorry he had left without confronting her. Marion hated unresolved conflict. And she knew, even though it seemed like months away, that her return in four days to a San Francisco without José would leave her feeling dispossessed, barren, without the comfort of her secret afternoons.

Marion returned to her own room, closing the door behind her, and dialed reception.

"This is Dr. Roth. Has Mr. López checked out of the hotel?"

"Mr. López? López." She heard the man murmuring names to himself as he ran his finger down a list.

"Mr. José López," she said.

"Mr. José López. Yes, madam." She heard him speaking to someone in Spanish. "Mr. López is just checking out now. You would like to speak with him?"

"No, thank you. I'm coming down."

Marion replaced the receiver, grabbed her purse and key, and ran out to the elevator. She pumped the button, attacked it, held it down, cursed, until finally the elevator arrived and the door rolled back to admit her.

When she arrived in the lobby, José was gone. She ran past the desk and out to the driveway just in time to see him climb into a taxi and close the door.

"José!" She ran towards the cab, but José leaned forward and said something to the driver who crunched the car into gear and drove away laughing. She stood on the curb watching them disappear down the driveway.

The message light was blinking on her telephone when she returned to her room. She dialed quickly, hoping that José had changed his mind.

"Dr. McCarthy. Extension 836."

Marion dialed. "Ben, it's me."

"Hey, that was quick.... Can you talk?"

"Oh, all I want to. He left."

"Left! What do you mean?"

"Left. Checked out."

"When?"

"Now, while we were outside. I just saw him fleeing in a taxi."

"Don't you think he'll come back?" Ben couldn't mask his delight.

Marion smiled at herself in the mirror. "I doubt it. You seem to have a devastating effect on him."

"I can't pretend to be crushed. Marion, will you have dinner with me tonight?"

"Of course. Where shall we go?"

"Let's go away from the hotel. There are too many people here—"

"I know. OK. Come down in an hour and I'll get some suggestions from the front desk guy."

"See ya!"

Marion dropped the receiver into its cradle. "Oh, Ben," she murmured to herself in the mirror. "You're just as damned predictable as he is."

Ben's paper was to be given the next day. Actually, it was not strictly his paper. It was the blossoming of some work he had done years back with Rick Trillby, a pediatrician at the clinic. Rick had left soon after Marion joined the clinic, but she had met him several times subsequently when he returned to confer with Ben on their various clinical research projects. Rick had always struck Marion as pushy and ambitious. It was always he who presented the research at the meetings. And so, when he broke his leg skiing two days before and rang Ben asking for his help, Ben had felt smiled upon by a benign god. He had managed everything in a few hours, reservations from his in-laws' home in Milwaukee, having a copy of the paper delivered to him at the airport, everything. And now even José was out of the way. Ben raised his glass to Marion.

"To us!" he said, and sipped reverently, as if taking communion. She smiled back and sipped her own wine. It was a good French cabernet, the best offered on the limited wine list.

"You look dazzling."

"Thank you." Marion spooned around in the hot sauce.

"Well, this is an unexpected turn of events."

"Every cloud has a silver lining?"

They were in a corner, away from the noise of a mariachi band and some raucous people around the bar. And they were, like teenagers, making conversation.

"Do you know anything about the food here?" he asked.

"Very little. But this side is all in English."

"Oh, yes." He laughed. "That's for the *gringos* like me." He surveyed the list quickly and then looked up. "I think I'll settle for the lamb. It seems to promise the least harm."

"Don't bank on that. And, by the way, be sure to eat yoghurt every meal. That's what they say anyway."

"'They'?"

"José said so." She smiled. "It's supposed to replace the flora I guess."

"Fascinating!"

"Ben! Is that sarcasm I detect?"

"It's for the *they*. For you I have only White Anglo-Saxon Protestant devotion."

"And I, a heathen!"

"A lovely heathen." He leaned across to kiss her.

"You're being very reckless. This town is swarming with our kind."

"Marion, I have something to tell you," he said ignoring the platter of lamb and vegetables that had been placed in front of him. "I don't care. I don't give a damn. Not one. In a way I wish Betty would find out so that it could all come to a head."

Marion put her fork down and stared at him. "Ben! For God's sake! *What* could come to a head?"

"Us. You and I, Marion. I want to marry you. Don't shake your head like that. I've been thinking about it day and night. I want it so much I would do anything, whatever you want me to do."

"Ben! I don't believe this. A few months ago you were advising me to go to a marriage counselor. You sat opposite me cautioning me, giving me sound advice."

"I know. I know all that. But that was before—I've been thinking a lot. Your marriage is over and so is mine. We've betrayed our trust in a way—"

"Trust! Ben—"

"Wait. We can never go back, you know. I can never settle for Betty again. I can't bear the thought of going on as I've been going all these years. I've got to the point where I don't care. Even if you won't—Well, I don't know. I can't bear the guilt, I guess. Not just about what we did but of wanting you, wishing that she were you every time I climb into bed."

He looked up at Marion and she tried to say something, anything, to catch him on his way down, to stop him falling beyond her reach. "Ben, you're overwrought, tired from the trip—"

"I couldn't be more serious."

"Well, then it's my turn to tell you to cool it. This is absurd. How many years? At least twenty years in a perfectly working marriage, four children, everything neat and tidy and suddenly you're behaving like a teenager. It's absurd. It's not you."

He poured himself some more wine and sat back in his chair to observe her. Small streams of sweat began to fill the creases of his forehead and then to overflow into his eyebrows. They coursed around his eyes and down his face to the rim of his damp collar. Every now and then he wiped a folded handkerchief across his forehead and dabbed at his neck, but it was hopeless. The heat of the restaurant combined with the spicy food and the wine and his own agitation to transform him into a vision of discomfort. Damp semicircles appeared under each arm of his suit jacket. His hair, normally immaculate, hung around his ears limp and sodden.

"Why don't you take off your jacket and tie?" Marion asked in the voice of a nurse, a mother.

He obediently slipped out of his jacket and loosened his tie. Marion noticed that he was wearing a thick undershirt with sleeves, and that his chest was as soaked through as the rest of him.

"Ben, are you feeling OK?"

"You're in love with that guy, aren't you, Marion?"

Marion rested her forehead on her palms and stared down at her plate of food. "No. I'm not 'in love' with him. I don't think I've ever been. It's not that easy, Ben. It's not an either/or, you know."

"What is it then? What is it with you and him?"

Marion looked up and smiled. "I don't know." She shrugged. "It's not so much me and him, anyway, or even him. It's his world, I guess, and me in it."

"*What* world?"

"The music, the attention I get, the drama. The romance of it all. And his apartment, Ben. That is the most wonderful of all."

"His apartment! Marion!"

"I am quite serious. Going there is like being on vacation from my own life. And yet I feel more at home there than I have ever felt anywhere. Isn't that funny? I feel free. That's it! I've never *been* as free as I feel there. Never." She lowered her voice and leaned towards Ben. "But it's his world, you see, and if I want it I have to have him along with it, and on his terms. Which seem to change daily, or hourly, depending on what suits him."

Ben gazed at her, trying to understand.

"You see Ben, I don't want to live my life on anyone else's terms. I've even thought that the life I have, however inadequate, is at least partly mine. My choice, my bargain, my terms. If I want to change them, I can. In fact I'll have to. For everyone's sake."

"Do they include me, Marion?"

"What?"

"Your changes."

Marion could not bear to look at him. His distress confronted her like an accusation or a threat. It demanded the truth, and yet she couldn't utter it. She couldn't look at him, face to face, and say, I haven't given you a thought for weeks. To marry you would be an act of destruction, as unimaginable as the thought of making love to you in your sweaty undershirt and boxer shorts.

But she looked up at him and smiled feebly. "I can't. I can't ever do that to you or Betty. You'd be miserable with me anyway, beside yourself with misery. How many women have you ever slept with?"

He jerked upright and blinked at her, dabbing at his neck and chest. "Why?"

"How many?"

"Two."

"Betty and me."

He smiled sheepishly and ate a few mouthfuls of rice while she sat back and looked at him.

"Do you know something? You are ridiculous! More ridiculous even than I am," she said.

"You're not ridiculous."

"Oh but I am. 'Full of sound and fury, signifying nothing.'"

"This is a new mode, Marion. Self-contempt."

"It's not contempt; it's amusement."

"Well, I'm not amused."

"That's because you're convinced that you're in love. Years of safe and sensible infatuation and then one fatal afternoon of sex and you're ready to dive into the deep beyond. For God's sake, Ben, see this in your old perspective."

Sometime before Marion reached the end of her sentence, Ben scraped his chair back and was leaving the table.

"Ben?"

He gestured her to stay and half-staggered, half-ran toward the *Caballeros* sign above the picture of a Mexican sombrero. His food had only been picked at, but hers was half eaten. The waiter came over and offered to take her plate. She nodded.

"Speak English?" she asked.

He nodded, not too forcefully.

"The gentleman here—this man"—she gestured—"in toilet there. You check he not sick? OK?"

The waiter nodded again and she saw him put down her plate and disappear into the men's room. A few minutes later he emerged looking grave, like a surgeon whose patient had just died under the knife. He came over to the table.

"He sick." The waiter made retching motions. "Very, very sick."

"Thank you. *Gracias*. Please bring check, OK?"

When Marion had signed the American Express form, figured the tip, and put away her card, she stood up, gathered up Ben's jacket and tie and asked the maître d' to have a cab ready. Ben was just then steadying himself at the door of the men's room, judging the distance to the table. Marion met him half way, slipped her arm through his, and supported him out to the waiting cab.

They had to stop twice on the way back to the hotel so that Ben could get rid of what was left of his lunch and dinner. As he crouched behind the car, next to the road, heaving and retching, Marion closed her eyes to feel the warm sea breezes that came in through the open car door. Then she looked out at the black ink of the bay and the scatterings of light from the houses and hotels along its edges. It is a magic place, she thought, and I am passing it by. I am squandering my time here in amateur histrionics. Ben climbed back in and sank down beside her, mumbling apologies, and she leaned across him to close the car door. He sank his head between his knees and held his damp handkerchief across his mouth until they reached the hotel.

His room was pristine. While he was closed in the bathroom, Marion looked around at his arrangements. There was an alarm clock poised next to his bed on top of a *Time* magazine and a copy of the paper he had to give tomorrow. His clothes hung neatly in the closet, in descending order of formality. Evidently he had worn his best suit this evening as next in line was a sports jacket and then the seersucker he had worn for traveling. He had his underwear ironed and folded in one drawer, and his socks, all dark and woolly, in neat pairs in another. His shirts were hung out on hangers in the closet. There was no hint in this room, no clue, no intimation of the man who occupied it. No one thing betrayed a special preference except that for order, and, even then, the order was more social than personal. Marion thought of Jonathan's chaotic array of mismatched clothing, his excess luggage on trips, the dozens of books he always took along and never read. No one could mistake his room for another's, she thought.

Marion heard the shower start over the flushing of the toilet. For a moment she panicked and thought of fleeing before Ben could emerge recovered and refreshed. But she knew this was impossible. He had been too ill. And it was just like him to shower off all that bodily secretion, sick or not, before he climbed in between clean sheets. She waited, half expecting to hear a thud as he collapsed in the shower. But he seemed to be moving around, picking up the soap, putting it down again. Marion opened the curtains and the door to the verandah. She stepped out into the darkness and breathed deeply. It really was lovely. She wished that somehow she could have started again here with José. Somehow now her own vehemence with him, her irritation about something as trivial as money, her wildness over the girl, all seemed overblown and melodramatic. She should have had the sophistication to see the week through with her lover as lover, not as husband or mate or anything more rooted than what it was. She had spoiled it. Even Ben's arrival could have been handled with more finesse. She could have taken José with her to introduce him instead of turning her back on him and his offer of lovemaking. Oh well, she thought, as she stepped back into the room, I too am unsophisticated.

Marion stopped on the threshold of the room and stared at Ben. He was tying up the cord of his blue cotton pajama bottoms as he stood there, white faced and red eyed, looking at her.

"Marion—"

"How're you feeling?" she asked, closing the door behind her and then the curtains. He sat down on the bed.

"Marion, I've got this danged Montezuma's revenge."

"Have you got Lomotil?"

"I've got everything and I've taken it. But I'm just not up to—"

"Oh, for God's sake, Ben! Please don't be ridiculous. It would be like necrophilia!"

He smiled weakly. "No, this time you've got it wrong. I mean I'm not up to giving my paper tomorrow. I mean I don't know if I'll be able to see it through. It's at eight A.M. Would you do it for me, Marion? Please."

Marion blushed. Embarrassment acted on her like a tether on a wild horse. She bucked and twisted and turned herself upside down to be free of it.

"You're lovely when you're embarrassed, you know?" he said.

She stared at him coldly. "No, I can't. I know nothing about the work. How can I possibly answer any questions? Call in sick."

Ben lay back on the pillow and drew up his knees. Marion saw him swallowing down his nausea in his attempt to talk and she softened. "Are there questions?" she asked.

"No."

"Slides?"

"No. It's just a case study really."

"How long?"

"Ten minutes max."

"*Max!*"

"Please, Marion. I've got all the research data here, all the backup stuff."

"OK. But, Jesus, it's one o'clock and I've still got to read it through." She bent down to kiss his forehead, took the papers he was handing her, and switched off the lights. "Go to sleep. Call me if you need me. I mean that."

"Thanks. Thanks, Marion. Oh, and something else. Did you pay for the dinner?"

"Yes. Of course."

"I'd like to pay you back, please. I insist."

"Don't be ridiculous, Ben," she said, closing the door behind her. She stood for a moment on the other side in the quiet hall and then walked over to the elevator. To hear me, she thought, as she punched the elevator button repeatedly, one would think everyone ridiculous but me. She smiled to herself, a thin vestige of her recent embarrassment. The elevator arrived and Marion stepped in. Her smile had tightened into a stiff line by the time she reached her room. She switched on her light and her air conditioning and went to stand at the window, still and sober, so that the confusion in her head could settle into some sort of order.

Finally, she turned back into the room and began to undress. It had worked. She had a solution, at least for the problem of Ben. She would tell him that she had decided to make a go of her marriage. He would never tamper with the healing process. And anyway, it could easily be true, might be true for all she knew of her heart and its strange rattles and knocks. She looked at herself in the mirror with satisfaction. Marion liked neat solutions. She washed and creamed her suntanned face and then settled down at the table to examine the topic for presentation.

By 8 A.M. Marion had read through the data several times and substantially rewritten Rick's paper. It had been poorly written, full of scientific clichés, non sequiturs and unsubstantiated claims. She tightened it, tied it up, and smoothed out the surfaces to her satisfaction, and then slept fitfully for the two hours before she was called at seven.

Ben had apparently explained the situation to the meeting coordinator, as he seemed ready for Marion's appearance. He held out a chair for her behind her place at the table, a look of forbearance on his blotchy, sunburned face. Possibly he was irritated by all the substitutions, the messiness, by the fact that she, a casual in the midst of professionals, was being elevated above her station. Marion ignored him and paged through her talk, alert and quite composed, still buoyed up by her night of hard work. About twenty-five physicians straggled in with Styrofoam cups of coffee and sheaves of papers. Marion watched them from the platform, saw them look at her, consult the program, and look again. A few seemed to ask each other about her and then she saw them shrug and settle back, like Romans at the Colosseum.

When Marion stepped up to the podium, she felt the hush and the curious eyes. She smelled the coffee and the stale breath, the cleaning fluid, the closeness of the room, like school again after the summer. Her hand shook slightly as she opened the notebook, and her voice wandered through the first few phrases until it found its pitch. Then she heard it booming out through the speakers like the voice of a stranger, a ghost. A few people shuffled and sat forward to hear. Some took notes. She kept her sentences short and simple, with no equivocation, or glossing over of hazy findings. The paper had a beginning, a middle and an end, like a model English composition. It described the effects of a regimen involving a new drug on a child with congenital heart disease. And there was something to learn, namely that the drug was ineffectual. It was what is known in the medical world as 'a nice piece of work.'

The challenge that had filled the room when Marion first stepped up to speak had vanished. There was to be no killing today. Marion approached the end of her talk feeling competent, like a craftsman holding the right tool, confident, almost powerful again.

As she began on her conclusions, she noticed a door at the back of the room open a few inches and a head pop through. It stayed there for about a minute and then a man came in and moved stealthily along the back row to about the middle. His demeanor did not seem to fit that of the rest of the audience. There was something in his presence there, in fact, that seemed peculiarly aimed at her. But Marion was not secure enough in the text to give him more than a glance, and a glance in this dim light was not sufficient to identify him.

The talk was over. Marion returned to her place. The coordinator leaned across to her and smiled. "That was a nice piece of work," he said.

"Thanks. But it wasn't mine, you know."

"I know. Who wrote it up, Ben or Rick?"

"Rick did, and then I rewrote it last night, very quickly!"

"It was well done." He smiled again.

The audience and the speakers were moving out towards the patio for breakfast. She gathered up her papers and purse and then remembered the man in the back row. He was still there, sitting and staring at her, half smiling. It was José.

"Marion," said the coordinator, "would you join us for breakfast?"

"Yes, thanks. I'd love to. But, look—uh—there's someone I have to see first. Would you save me a place and I'll join you in, say, five minutes."

"Sure."

She walked around the chairs to the back of the hall and stood unsmiling at the end of the row in which José sat. He patted the seat next to him for her to sit down, but she stood where she was, observing him with impatience.

"Hi!" he said.

"José, what are you doing here?"

"I came to hear you do your thing."

He was posturing like a teenager with his mother, refusing to acknowledge the cause of her irritation. Marion waited, looked at her watch, and began to turn away.

"Hey, hey!" he said. "Where are you going?"

"I have to meet them in there for breakfast." She nodded in the direction of the patio.

"Can't you skip that and have breakfast with me, upstairs?" He smiled and winked. Marion put her papers down and folder her arms, cocking her head to emphasize her resistance.

"José, I haven't the time to go into the full absurdity of this situation, but I'm sure you can figure out the main points. Isn't it time we called off this farce?"

José leapt up and held her tightly by the shoulders. He tried to kiss her, but she bent her head away, feeling even then as she did so, against all reason, the impulse to soften and draw him to her.

"Mariana, don't act out of spite. I was angry and jealous, I admit it. You know how I felt. But today I'm back, so let's forget the whole thing, OK, and finish the vacation together? I can't live without you." He looked up at her slyly, softly, while he held her captive with his strong arms. Marion heard the breakfast dishes clinking, the masculine murmur of the doctors eating and laughing. She knew where she belonged right now, where she wanted to be. But José clung onto her like a determined child, compelling her to give in or to flee.

"Well?" he asked. "Shall we go up?"

Marion again looked away. The room was close and smelled of stale air, old coffee, and José's cologne.

"You were wonderful up there," he went on. "You didn't tell me about a talk."

"I didn't know. Ben stepped in at the last minute for someone else who broke a leg. And then last night Ben got *turista* and so I had to do it for him."

José smiled. "He's sick now?"

"I guess so." She picked up her books again and backed away. "How did you know I was here?"

"I asked at the desk," he said, following her. "They told me they woke you for the meeting. So I came to look." He was talking quickly. "What was it all about?"

"What was what all about?"

"The talk you made."

"It's complicated. I'll explain it to you another time. José, I really must go. They're expecting me. I'll see you later, in about an hour or so."

Just then a bellhop walked through the room and out toward the patio with a slate and a bell. "Dr. Roth" was written on the slate and the boy was intoning as he walked and jingled the bell, "*Dottaraw! Dottaraw!*"

Marion looked at the slate as it was presented to her and stepped up to the boy. "That's me, she said. "I'm Dr. Roth."

"Telephone," he said and beckoned her to follow him. Marion walked quickly behind him out towards the lobby. José was bounding along beside her, trying to catch her hand or elbow. When she reached the reception desk, the boy disappeared and left her to wait in line for the attention of the bored-looking girl checking out the departing guests.

"Excuse me, there's a message for me. Dr. Roth. Can you give it to me, please?"

The girl ignored Marion while she searched for an account and then handed it to the couple first in line. Then she looked up at the next pair without acknowledging Marion's presence or request.

Marion stepped up closer and raised her voice. "I have been told I have a message which I assume to be urgent. Will you kindly give it to me immediately?"

The girl laid down her pen and turned to look at Marion. "Madam, can you see all these people ahead of you? You will have to wait your turn."

Just then José stepped in front of Marion and addressed the girl. A spray of Spanish like the stuttering of a muffled machine gun filled the lobby so that everyone stopped to listen. But he was smiling as he spoke, a smile Marion knew well. It was the superior bloodless smile he used on his students or on waiters or taxidrivers or the boys on the beach who rented deck chairs. Marion saw the girl freeze, then bow her head slightly, and then turn and scan the pigeonholes that held the room keys. She pulled a piece of paper out of Marion's and handed it to José with a mumble of something that Marion assumed to be an apology. He handed the paper to Marion. It said only: "Sara. Urgent. 731-7894."

"What is it?" José asked.

"I don't know. It's urgent. But it's not my phone number. I'm going up to the room to phone."

"I'll come too."

In the room, Marion threw her papers onto the bed and grabbed the phone. She gave the number and then waited while the various operators passed her along towards Sarah. She was hot, on fire, thinking of the awful possibilities behind *urgent* and the unknown telephone number. Finally, a voice answered, a woman.

"Hello?"

"Hello. This is Marion Roth. I have an urgent message to phone Sarah Roth."

"Oh, yeah! Hi, Marion! I'm Loretta, Marlene's mother. Your little doll is right here waiting for your call."

"Hello, Mother?"

"Sarah! Are you all right? What's wrong?"

There was a small silence. Marion could only imagine Loretta and Marlene waiting at Sarah's elbow while she uttered her news across the continent.

"Mother, Daddy left."

"What?"

"Daddy left. He moved into an apartment with Beth. He wanted me to go too, but I came here instead. Mommy? Do you—Can you please come home?"

Marion sat down on the bed. She changed ears. She tried to push out her voice, to pull it up into words, any words, but speech seemed to have dried up in the face of Sarah's words, the news marked *urgent*.

"Mommy?"

"Sarah—"

"Will you come?"

"Today—" And then the words rushed out. Marion shouted into the phone, trying to embrace Sarah through the wires. "Sarah, darling, go home. Wait for me there. I'll be on the next plane. Don't worry, I'll sort everything out. Have you got a key? I'll be there as soon—Oh, Sarah!"

But they had been cut off, or Sarah had hung up. The line crackled and sang aimlessly. As Marion put the phone down, it rang again immediately.

"Sarah?"

"Marion?"

"Yes. Oh, Ben."

"Did you expect Sarah to call?"
"Oh, no. Well, yes. What's up?"
"How did it go?"
"What?"
"The paper."
"What?"
"Marion, are you OK?"
"Oh, yes, Ben, I'm fine. Fine. Wonderful." She cackled and rasped, leaning back against the headboard as she did so. José stood at the window observing her, like an intern on his first visit to the psychiatric ward.
"What happened, Marion?"
"With the paper? Nothing. Well, not really nothing. It was a success. Reentry level success." She cackled again.
"I don't understand. Why are you laughing like that? What are you doing now?"
"Packing."
"What?"
"PACKING! I'm going home. Today."
"But Marion—Why?"
"Well, I've just had some bad news. News? Maybe it's not so new. Maybe it's as old as Methuselah. Anyway, Benjamin dear, I must go, you see, because I have become a victim of the oldest cliché in history. My husband has run off with my best friend, my Beth. And my child has fled, and needs me." She whooped and snorted. "And here I stand, the jilted innocent, talking to one lover while the other at this very moment realizes that his worst fears were true, true, true."
"He's back?"
"Large as life, standing before me. And now I bid you both adieu," she said gesturing José towards the door, "so that I can pack and leave this paradise forever." She replaced the receiver with a bang.
José jerked towards her as if he would hit her. Then he stopped, stared into her silly grin for a moment, and ran out of the room with a cry or a curse or both, slamming the door behind him.

Marion heard him stamp towards the elevator muttering. She heard the elevator arrive, the burble of guests emerging, the clank of the elevator doors, the fading of voices down the hall, and silence. She walked out onto the verandah and looked down at the boats and parachutes and donkeys and people laughing in the sun. She felt the space that filled the gap from her to them, the frailty of the cement beneath her feet, the pull of the earth, and she turned back quickly into her room. She pulled her clothes roughly off their hangers, scooped them out of drawers, and bundled them into her suitcase. She looked around her, in the closet, under the beds. Only the paper and the notes from this morning's talk remained. Marion stood for a minute at the table glancing over her first paragraph, and then the second, until she had reread the whole paper. Then she gathered the pages up neatly, arranged them in order, tapped them onto the table to align the edges, and slipped them carefully into her briefcase.

14

It was after midnight when the taxi drew up in front of the house. There were no lights on, not even the front porch light. The house stood there, a looming shadow in grays and blacks, given only a hint of profile by the night lights of the other houses on the street.

Marion paid the driver and struggled up the steps with her bag. She had never done this before, carried her own bags up the steps. There had always been Jonathan there, even at one or two in the morning, to carry them, bitching about the weight, the hour, anything for a word or two of thanks. But now he was with Beth somewhere, lying in a strange bed asleep, or God knows what. Marion put down the bag and hung her head. For the hundredth time that day she felt panic rise in her chest and flutter there, making her head light, her breath short. She couldn't even cry. Marion fumbled in her purse for the keys and then struggled up the remaining steps to the front door. The house smelled stale. The air was damp and cold, unwelcoming after the warm sea breezes. She buttoned her sweater and flipped on the hall lights, upstairs and downstairs. It worked a magic on the place.

All the objects around her were snapped back into existence. But, once familiar, they were now seen again, for those first few seconds, as strangers, like the fleeting sight of oneself unrecognized in a distant mirror, from a new perspective. Marion stood in their midst, the object of their silence, of the sarcasm that linked them there, mute, as they had always been while she struggled to adjust her own perspective.

She shut her eyes for a moment and then opened them again to recapture the strangeness, to reaffirm the existence of the pain. But it had gone. The hall chest was just what it was, what it had always been. There was evidence of polish, though, and the magazines and bills that usually filled the large brass tray were neatly stacked, unopened. Carmelita must have been in. Marion wondered whether Jonathan had remembered to pay her. She walked over to the coat closet and looked inside. They were all there, coats, ponchos, rainshoes. Only Jonathan's parka was gone and his sailing togs.

Marion turned on the heat and walked through to the kitchen. A mug half full of cold chocolate stood on the table and under it a note. Marion snatched it up.

Dear Mother,
I've gone to sleep. Wake me if you like when you come in.
Love,
Sarah.

She smiled. How typical of Sarah's notes. No stamp of Sarah, no teenage flourishes or those ghastly happy faces or cupid hearts. Just the old Sarah, closed up, like a lily in the dark. Marion filled the kettle and sat down to wait for it to boil.

There was a shuffling at the door and she turned in her seat quickly, surprising herself as she did so by her hope that it would be Jonathan, not Sarah, wanting to see her. But Sarah stood there, blinking in the bright light. Her hair hung around her face in uneven strands and clumps, no hint of curl in it. And her face itself looked gaunt, gray, the flesh around the eyes swollen and red, the mouth pale and pouting. Marion pushed the chair back and stepped over to Sarah with her arms wide. Sarah did not move. She allowed Marion to fold her in her arms. She sank her head onto Marion's shoulder and left it there while Marion patted her back rhythmically with both hands. Then Sarah began to shake, at first only slightly, but building up until her whole long body convulsed in spasms as she sobbed onto Marion's shoulder.

"Don't cry, Sarah. Don't cry," Marion said softly. But her own words, impotent with Sarah, worked perversely on herself and she heard her voice tail off into a thin moan. She laid her head against Sarah's and wept loudly with her, heaving and snorting, their misery twisted and bound into one lament, so congruous that the grief itself was something close to a celebration.

The shriek and hiss of the kettle brought them both to a halt. Marion unwound herself and switched off the gas, sniffing and shuddering as she reached for the instant chocolate in the cupboard and then two mugs. Sarah slumped down in a chair and watched Marion measure and pour, as if she were observing a strange ceremony for the first time. She followed each movement of Marion's, twisting herself to look around Marion's back at the way she tapped the spoons on the edge of the mugs and wiped the drops of chocolate from the counter with a sponge. Marion pulled off two paper towels and gave one to Sarah. She blew her nose hard on the other, wiped her eyes, and came to sit down with the two mugs of chocolate.

"Now tell me, darling, what happened. Let's start at the beginning. I am in total ignorance."

Sarah stared down into her steaming mug. She had not quite recovered her voice, as Marion had, and needed some time to calm down. They both sat in silence, blowing on the chocolate.

"Mother—" she began, and then stopped, closing her eyes for a moment. "Mommy. I thought you knew about it. I mean I just assumed that you were seeing what I was seeing. And that you had reached the same conclusions."

"I didn't, Sarah. I didn't see anything to make conclusions about. Go on."

"Well, it's been months really since I first thought there was something funny with Daddy and Beth. Since that day they went sailing together alone, without you or Alex, I guess. It was the day that—" She looked away from Marion, and then swung her head back, looking Marion in the face with determination. "It was the day that I cut your cheek with the bow." Her face flushed slightly and then returned to its gray pallor.

"Mommy, that was so unfair," she said, beginning to sob again. "It was after that argument, and I blamed you. I blamed you for everything when all the time—" Sarah slouched over the table and wept into her arms. Marion's own voice had vanished again and her breath came slowly through long heaves. She stretched across the table to pat Sarah's head, distracted, staring out into the night as if something there would light up to deliver her from this moral impasse.

"Go on, Sarah, please."

Sarah sniffed and blew her nose again on the paper towel. "There was something after that about the way they were together. And then I overheard him talking to her, calling her disgusting names."

"What names?"

"*Baby*, *sexpot*, things like that. And I sort of put two and two together, but also I didn't. I didn't want to believe it and so I ignored it. I thought you knew anyway. You seemed so oblivious to everything, off in your own world. And, I don't know, you seemed happier than you had been. I thought maybe you were glad to be free of Daddy or something. Especially after that argument. So I thought, well, since neither of you seemed to give a damn about each other or about me, I should try to concentrate on myself, on what I wanted." She looked at Marion quickly. "And that sort of ended up in a mess too."

"You mean that night at Beth's?"

Sarah nodded.

"Then what?"

"Well, then you went off to your meeting and Daddy seemed all pleased to be left here with me. I thought maybe I'd been wrong."

Marion stared at Sarah, unblinking, willing her to go on.

"And then," Sarah said, "he said he wanted to take me out to dinner."

"When was that?"

"Last night."

"Go on."

"He said to dress up, we were going to La Bellecour."

Marion raised an eyebrow and cocked her head to one side.

"I asked why, but he just smiled, as if he were doing it for me. So I went along with it, the mystery and all. I wore my new skirt and did my hair. I honestly thought he had done his usual and mixed up my birthday or something."

Marion smiled, a lean, spare smile of recognition.

"Then he came home early and showered and dressed. And we left at about six-thirty. But we didn't go straight to the restaurant. We went by the office. He left me in the car and ran up. He was gone for, like, fifteen minutes, and then came back down again with Beth. All dressed up and smiling at me in a funny way. Well, she was about to climb into the back of the car, but Daddy said no, she should get in the front with him and I could sit in the front or back, whichever I liked. He seemed to have forgotten about me in a way, to be paying all his attention to Beth. I got into the back and we drove to La Bellecour. All the way there Beth tried to make conversation with me, but in a funny way, sort of forced. And Daddy would check my responses in the rearview mirror. He seemed nervous, like he was worried I was going to say the wrong thing. So I mostly kept quiet. Their strangeness was making me nervous.

"We parked and went into the restaurant. Daddy ordered me a sherry. He's never done that before. And the waiter just went and got it. Then he gave me some wine. Oh—when they brought the wine, Daddy and Beth toasted each other, clinking their glasses together and smiling. I'm sure they would have kissed if I hadn't been there. So then I thought, well, this is crazy. They'd said nothing about why I was there or what the occasion was or anything, so I asked Beth, when we got to the entrée, where Alex was. They sort of looked at each other and then at me, and then Daddy said to Beth, 'You tell her.' So she started to tell me all this bullshit about how she and Daddy had grown together or something over the years, how they'd worked together for so long, how much she admired him, how full of life he was, how they loved the same things, worked so well together, that sort of thing. And then she went on about how their admiration had turned into love, and how her marriage with Alex and Daddy's with you were really dying—" Sarah began breathing faster. Tears started in her eyes again and she let them roll down her cheeks unchecked. Red blotches of anger began to appear on her neck and face.

"She actually said that to me, Mommy. And all the time she was smiling at me in that dumb way, like Mary Poppins in the loony bin."

Marion laughed, slapping both hands onto the table. "Oh, Sarah! That's perfect!"

"It wasn't funny actually. I just sat there staring. I think they expected me to smile back or something. I don't know what they expected. She said that she and Daddy had rented an apartment and were moving in tomorrow—today, that is. Just like that. And that they wanted Alfred and me to move in too. Can you imagine that? Me and Alfred!

"I said nothing. I was just shocked. I mean even though I'd suspected something, I'd never sort of imagined anything like this. I never thought it would involve me."

Marion smiled again, and shook her head. "We never do, do we?"

"No. Well, anyway, when she got to the part about you I stood up."

"Me?"

"She said you were going through 'changes,' an 'identity crisis,' and out came the clichés one on top of the other. She had the nerve to say she thought I'd be better off with *her*, that you were 'in an unstable phase,' and that 'Jonathan and I' had discussed it fully. I stood up and almost threw my wine in her face, in both their faces. I just ran out of the restaurant and onto California. Daddy ran after me, of course, and tried to stop me. He said when I thought about it, I'd see that it wasn't so bad, and that it was a good thing for all of us, and that sort of thing. I didn't cry. I just stood there wondering what to do, and then he asked me what I wanted to do. I said I wanted to phone Marlene and he said OK. So we went back into the restaurant and I phoned Marlene and told her more or less what had happened and asked if I could stay until you got back."

Marion was silent, thinking of her own night the night before, the restaurant, Ben, his retching and heaving behind the car in that balmy tropical place.

"I had nowhere else to go, Mother!" Sarah cried. "He wouldn't let me stay in the house alone."

"Of course, Sarah. I understand completely."

Sarah slumped down into her shoulders, thrusting her chin forward as she used to do in the face of Marion's wrath.

"They took me home to get my clothes and stuff and then they dropped me off at Marlene's. Daddy didn't even come in with me."

"He was probably embarrassed."

"I guess so. Well, I was embarrassed too, you know. Marlene's mother thought I came from this wonderful, perfect family. She was always asking me things about the way we live, the boat, you and Daddy."

"But Marlene knew you'd had problems with me. I don't think you left her with any illusions."

Sarah blushed and jerked upright in her seat. She couldn't look at Marion, but she spoke to her, facing away at the wall. "I know I told her things. I'm sorry now. I was wrong. I didn't realize I'd misjudged things, you—"

"Sarah, you were not all that wrong. There are a lot of things— Some of what you said, a lot of what you said is true."

"You don't need to say that, Mother. I appreciate it, but you don't need to let me off the hook." She tossed her head back in a futile attempt to get the hair out of her eyes. "Anyway, Mrs. Mancini didn't know any of it. And she was shocked. I guess she didn't realize those kinds of things happen up and down the scale. Marlene's father abandoned her when she was pregnant with Marlene and she's never seen him since."

"Poor woman."

Sarah searched Marion's face for signs of sarcasm but seeing none, went on. "I stayed with them last night. Originally I thought I'd just stay on there till you came back on Saturday without bothering you. But Marlene was getting on my nerves. I don't know how to explain it. She seemed to be enjoying the fact that something bad had happened to me. She kept nagging me to tell her about Beth, every detail. Mother, I felt sort of desperate. And so I called you—"

"Good God, Sarah! Of course you should have called. 'Bother me'! How could you?" Marion jumped up and took Sarah's head in both arms, cradling it against her stomach, rocking her back and forth. "Sarah, my love, when this whole thing's over, we are going to go to France together, just you and I, or to Spain, or to Greece. We're going to take a long, long trip, just us, you and me. It's been too long that we've been like strangers, sharing a house and a dinner table but nothing else. It's been my fault. No, don't shake your head. It has been my fault, ninety-nine percent of it has been my fault. I've made no attempt to know you."

"Why did you have me, Mommy? Why didn't you just have an abortion?"

Marion looked down into Sarah's face and saw there the child's terror, her dread of the reply. "It never crossed my mind," she said. "I wanted you. I wanted *you*, I wanted a daughter. That much I knew. I thought I was happy, and that I could just go on collecting the things that meant happiness—academic distinction, a career, a lover, and then marriage and a child. I was convinced that I could handle everything. And you see, with babies you never know, Sarah. They adjust to whatever they have. And you, thank God, had Grandma."

Marion paused and looked down at Sarah leaning against her, snuggling into her arms. She pulled her chair close to Sarah's and sat down.

"Please go on, Mother," Sarah mumbled.

"Well, after medical school, somehow there were gaps, voids, I don't know how else to explain it. There was no one to blame. Daddy and you seemed perfectly happy. And I was ready for my internship. But I couldn't get rid of the feeling that something was missing. Everyone around me seemed happy to settle for what they had, but it was always less than what I wanted.

"Finally, I picked on New York—the grayness, the craziness—and decided that that was the problem. It was easy, you see. We could move somewhere else. We could start again. I was convinced that if we moved from New York, we'd be happy."

Only the low buzz of the refrigerator and the night crickets filled the silence. Sarah said nothing. She stared at Marion, adjusting to this new mode of communication. Marion grasped one of Sarah's hands across the table.

"I remember sitting there, with Grandma, in her living room, trying to tell her we'd decided to move to San Francisco. And I remember her face. She stayed absolutely silent, only reaching out every now and then to touch your cheek or to kiss your hand. You thought it was a game to run and hide every time she reached out. And she pretended to run after you, all the time ignoring me and what I was saying. Or so I thought.

"Grandpa asked her to sit down. And she did. She sat down and looked at me blankly, which was worse really than if she'd argued or begged me not to go or something. I couldn't stand it. I couldn't stand not having her blessing. So I pushed on. I asked her if she understood, if she realized that we wanted a change.

"'Yes,' she said, 'I understand. It's not a new idea.' And then she just took you onto her lap and began to cry. I'd never seen her cry before. She made absolutely no sound, just held you as you wriggled and pulled at her earring, and wept silently."

Marion stopped. Sarah was saying something, whispering into her lap. "What was that, darling?"

"Poor Grandma," Sarah whispered. "She lost us both."

"No, Sarah, she never lost you. I see her face when she gets off the plane. You must see it every day you're with her. I see there, you know, what I've never allowed on my own face, what I've never, I guess, allowed in my own heart." Marion looked up at Sarah and then out of the window into the night. "What I want you to know now, in the middle of this awful mess," she said, "is that you should never try to do what I did. Never ignore the hollow in your own heart."

Marion ran her hand across her forehead and rubbed her eyes on both palms. She looked across at Sarah and then sat up. Sarah was staring at her with a strange half-smile on her face. Marion smiled too.

"I know you're probably amused at my talk of heart and so forth, but Sarah, I have no less—what can I say?—I have no other way of saying what I mean. I'm trying to explain something that is so close to corniness—"

"I know. I'm not smiling at that. It's just funny in a way to hear you talking like Mr. López."

"Mr. López?"

Sarah smiled. It was almost the smile of a lover, private, unwelcoming to any but the object of the smile.

"What do you mean, Sarah?"

"Oh, only that he talks like that—the hollow in your heart, that kind of thing."

"To you, or to the class as a whole?"

Sarah attempted a friendly laugh, but it came out forced and silly. "It seems specially to me, as a matter of fact. But he does come out with it regularly in rehearsal too."

"When? I mean, privately?"

"Oh, just sometimes."

Marion closed her eyes as if she were tired, and then opened them again and looked at Sarah, unsmiling. "Sarah, I must say something on the score of Mr. López. I know that he is an attractive man, a very attractive man, and that he is talented and sensitive and—"

"But you think he's sneaky, right?" She was still smiling.

"Sneaky? Whatever gave you that idea?"

"You said so the day of the picnic last year."

"Oh, then. Did I really? Well, I probably didn't mean it. That's not it. No. What I want to warn you about is what you know already. He must be at least twenty-five—"

"Thirty, actually."

"OK, thirty. And he has been married. He has a child. He's from another culture, Sarah, and above all, he's your teacher." Why? she thought. Why couldn't she just dump the truth between them? What cowardice kept diverting her words onto neutral ground?

"Mother, you're back in your lecture mode. What are you trying to tell me? I know all that."

"I'm trying to warn you, Sarah, not to fall in love with him. It's the easiest thing for a girl of your age to develop a crush on a teacher like him. Guard against it, darling. Please."

Sarah stood up and looked down at Marion. Marion thought she saw something between pity and disdain on her face. But there was also a dignity in her composure, in the way she kept her secret behind that smile.

"Don't worry, Mother," she said, bending down to kiss Marion's forehead. "I can look after myself."

"Oh, Sarah!" Marion threw her arms around the girl's waist. And Sarah stood passively, her arms hanging loosely on either side of Marion's. Then she laid her hands gently on Marion's arms and eased them away from her body. She smiled down at her and seemed about to say something, but she didn't. She just whispered "Good night" and left the room.

Marion's head began to swim and dip. She had slept for only two hours in the last forty and didn't trust her own responses. She knew she had to stand up, switch off the lights, and go upstairs to bed. But she sat there staring blankly at the dark window ahead of her, the edges fuzzed and hazy under her unblinking gaze. Nothing that she dragged into consciousness could eliminate the vision that she had there, suddenly, of Sarah kneeling at José's feet, receiving benediction. She saw him bend to raise her face to his, lifting her chin in his exquisite hands. And Sarah's face, beatific, gazing up into his smile, waiting for his next command. Marion closed her eyes, shivered. So there it was, plain and clear. How could she not have seen it before? And how could she now tell Sarah the truth? How could she possibly break her own child's heart?

Sarah was fast asleep, breathing softly when Marion finally dragged her bag upstairs. And in Marion's room the drapes were drawn and the bed made with fresh sheets. Marion looked around as if she were in a hotel somewhere and needed to locate the closet and the bathroom. She walked through to her closet. All Jonathan's clothes were gone. In one day he had moved everything, even his shoehorn and his Exercycle. He hadn't even bothered to spread her clothes out in the space he had left behind. They had remained where they were, neatly hung in their plastic boxes and jackets, the shoes on a rack under them. Marion was fascinated. She checked his drawers. They were all empty. She looked at his bedside table. He had taken all his books, his decongestants, even his lubricating jelly. She smiled. Somehow, in his absence, in the absence of all his objects and paraphernalia, he had ceased to irritate her. He had gone.

She stumbled out of the room and downstairs to his study. The door was closed, and she opened it carefully, as if he might have sprung a joke on her, a bucket of water from above or a broom. She switched on the light. The desk had been cleared, and the bookshelves, but he had obviously had no time or no room to take the books. They were stacked neatly in moving boxes, boxes and boxes and boxes. Marion seldom came into this room. It had been full of Jonathan's trophies, arty sailing photographs, certificates from his wine courses, a few cups he had won racing. They were all gone. Only his books had been dispensable, apparently. Marion wondered when he planned to return for them, when she would see him again, how they would proceed through this jungle of separation.

She sat down on his desk chair and kicked it into a twirl with her knees up and her eyes closed. When it stopped spinning, she leaned over and grabbed a journal, flipping through it without seeing. One of the pages came away in her hand. It was nothing really. Just drug ads and a few announcements. The binding was cheap—glue—and she found that all the pages were coming loose. They needed only the slightest tug, in fact, to pull away. Marion pulled out a few and threw them onto the carpet where they fell like leaves in early fall. Then she covered them with more and more until she had pulled out all the pages and flung the cover across the room. She reached over for another journal, and then another. It was easy. Remarkably easy really, once you got the hang of it. In just under an hour she had worked through four boxes of journals and was ready to move onto the books.

But the books were tougher. They were sewn, not glued, and Marion found she had to pull harder, do fewer pages at a time. And sometimes she managed to leave half the pages behind in the binding. But it worked almost as well really. It just wasn't as neat.

By five, Marion had worked through every box, every book. She was exhausted and her legs could barely move. Her tearing arm was weak and aching. She stood up slowly and opened the study door. The sun was just rising. The whole house seemed to be on fire.

Marion stumbled across the hall and down into the garage. She groped for the light pull and a thin cold light spread through the garage and the basement behind. She struggled past her car and back to where the tools were kept. Jonathan had left those alone apparently. She looked along a shelf of cans and finally selected one labeled "Roof Black." She took a new brush, bit into its plastic cover, and then peeled it away. Then she made her way again back through the garage and up to Jonathan's study. She stood in the middle of all the mounds of paper and she smiled. Quickly she pried open the can with Jonathan's silver letter opener. The paint had settled out. A thick skin covered the surface. Marion plucked it off and dropped it onto the desk. Then she stirred vigorously with the brush. Flecks of paint flew onto the desk, the drapes, and onto her. But she was in a hurry. She had to finish soon, before Sarah woke up.

Marion stood in the center of the room holding the can of paint and the brush, her head cocked to one side, looking around like a decorator sizing up the potential. She stepped over to the wall nearest the kitchen, dipped the brush and began.

"BETH LOVES JONATHAN," she painted in bold capitals.

And then she mixed capitals and lower case letters in the fashion of a semiliterate. "BeThs a FuCkinG WhoRe," she painted.

"Jonathan fucks Beth."

"JONATHAN LOVES BETH."

"BeThs mY BeSt fRienD."

Over the filing cabinet she drew a crude approximation of a penis and a vagina. Using arrows, she labeled, textbook style, the labia minora and the labia majora. When she had circled the room, she stood again in the middle to admire her work.

She had been too liberal with the paint. It dripped down the walls towards the carpet like blood from gaping wounds. But it didn't matter really. It sort of added to the effect.

Marion tipped the can and dribbled what was left over the piles of shredded paper. Then she threw the can and brush into a corner, took off all her clothes, including her underwear and shoes, and left them where they fell.

There was a key in the door. Jonathan's study was the only room in the house, in fact, that had its own key. Marion slipped it out carefully and stepped out into the child golden light of the hall. She closed the door behind her and locked it quietly from the hall, carefully removing the key. Then she padded upstairs, wrapping her arms around her shivering body, closed her bedroom door, and ran herself a hot bath. Steam filled the small bathroom and warmed her skin. It hazed the bubbled glass of the window, filtering the gold sunlight through the bathroom.

Marion breathed in deeply, stretching out her arms and hands to expand her chest. Just then, something clunked out of her hand onto the back of the toilet and plopped into the bowl. She peered in. It was the key. She had forgotten it. And there it was now, innocent, under the water, settling into the porcelain depression, almost out of sight. Marion stood over the bowl, smiling as she depressed the lever. She laughed into the swirling rush of water as the key sank out of sight and then grinned as the water rose again, smooth and clear, like the sea after a night of wind and storm.

15

It was already dark when Marion woke. During the heat of the day she had kicked off the covers and, now that the chill had settled in, she lay curled up and very still. Her head throbbed and her jaw and gums ached after her long sleep. She hooked the covers back up with her foot and stretched out under them. Outside, people were getting into cars, talking quite loudly. She calculated that it must be Friday, probably about eight or so. Her clock showed two-thirty. Someone must have unplugged it. And Jonathan's was gone. She uncurled her left arm to look at her watch. But there was only a strip of clear skin where her watch had been. The rest of her wrist and her hand were speckled with small black dots and slashes. She switched on the lamp and sat up, looking down at both arms, turning them to the light to observe more closely.

When she looked in the bathroom mirror, she saw that her face too was speckled with black dots. She brushed her teeth and then washed her face vigorously. But they came up bright and shining like freckles after the sun.

"Oh what the hell," she said to herself, walking through to her closet and pulling on an old pair of jeans and a turtleneck. She ran the brush through her hair, opened the drapes and the windows and then trotted downstairs to find some paint remover. The lights were on in the hall and the kitchen. Marion tried to sidle past the open kitchen door down to the basement, but Sarah was waiting for her in the doorway, welcoming her down. Her hair had been washed and curled. Her eyes were clear, her cheeks flushed. And she still had last night's half-smile on her face.

"Hi! Did you sleep well?"

"Yes, thank you, darling." Marion averted her face. "I'm just running down to the basement. I'll be up in a minute."

Sarah stepped forward and peered at Marion through her thick spectacles. "Mommy! What are all those black things on your face? And all over your hands?" She stepped back quickly, as if she could catch the disease.

"Paint."

"Paint? When were you painting"

"Oh, last night. Just touching up here and there." Marion opened the door to the garage.

"Black?" Sarah followed her to the top of the stairs. "Where did you touch up with black paint? Why last night?"

"I couldn't sleep," Marion called up. She was clanging around amongst the cans.

"Where did you paint?" Sarah persisted.

"The trim outside my bathroom window. It's been leaking."

"But it hasn't rained for months!"

"Oh, for God's sake, Sarah! It *did* leak, during the winter. And I couldn't sleep. And I wanted to do something to take my mind off things."

"Oh."

Marion was back up with the can. She unscrewed the top and poured some out onto a Handiwipe. As she dabbed and wiped, she looked up at Sarah and smiled. "You look much better today, darling."

"So do you—except for the paint."

"Well, it's nearly off. There." She threw away the Handiwipe and washed her hands and face thoroughly at the sink. "Anyone call today? Anything happen? I seem to remember sleeping through a few phone calls."

"Daddy called."

"Oh?"

"And I told him you were back and sleeping. He said he was sending someone round for his books and to tell you that he'd phone tomorrow."

"Did anyone come for the books?"

"Yes. A man, about an hour ago. But they couldn't get in. The door was locked and I didn't know where the key was."

"Mmm." Marion busied herself checking the refrigerator and the freezer, peering under the shelves to see whether anything had been forgotten at the back. She unscrewed a few jars and sniffed at the contents, checked the date on the milk and cream cartons, pulled open the vegetable and fruit drawers and threw out some slimy celery and a few furry carrots.

"Anything else?" she asked.

"Mr. López called for you."

Marion stood up. "When?"

"About lunchtime. He said to call him when you woke up."

"Where?"

"He didn't say. At his home, I guess."

"I'll call him later."

"He said as soon as you woke up. Do you want me to look up the number?" Sarah's cheeks were scarlet, and she had to swallow several times as she spoke.

"No, no. Let's have some dinner first. I'll call later. It didn't sound urgent, did it?"

"He didn't actually say urgent."

"Then it couldn't have been. What would you like to eat?"

It was hours before Sarah decided to go to bed. She seemed to be staving off separation from Marion with talk, as if her customary silence would banish her from Marion's presence. She wanted to continue their talk of last night, but calmly, cozily, as if they were friends sharing a passionate interest in the same subject. She asked Marion dozens of questions about things in which she had never shown the slightest signs of curiosity before. About Marion's childhood, her school, whether she had been happy as a child, who her friends had been. She even asked about Beth, how they had met, about Alex and Alfred. And then she moved on to her own infancy in New York and the days she had spent with Gertrude while Marion was a student.

As Marion recounted what she knew, the small details, the smells and sounds of Gertrude's apartment, the portable crib she kept there, her special "Sarah" apron, and the smile that filled her face when the elevator doors opened, Sarah lay back on the couch in a swoon of delight. "And then?" she asked, like a small child. "Who bought my clothes? Where did we go on the weekends? Did Grandma and Grandpa come too? Tell me again about that summer in Europe."

Marion glanced at the clock. It was almost midnight. She had been sitting there under Sarah's cross-examination for over three hours, forced to smother her own impatience for fear that it would destroy their newfound intimacy. But her restlessness was almost tangible. It seemed impossible that Sarah had not picked it up, and yet she reclined there now, smiling up at Marion, as if her pleasure in this new friendship were shared equally, as if Marion took as much joy in the telling of these tales as Sarah did in the listening.

"Sarah, it's midnight. Let's go to bed."

"But you only just got up."

"I'm still tired."

"I'm not."

"Well, would you mind if I went up? I need some strength to talk to your father tomorrow."

"Oh." Sarah turned to face the back of the couch.

"You know, you asked me about everyone, but not about Daddy, Sarah."

"I don't want to know."

"And I don't believe that."

"I hate him."

"No, you don't, and neither do I. Anyway, hate, you know, is not far from love."

"There you go again," Sarah said, sitting up and glowering at her.

Marion sat down on the edge of a chair and smiled at her daughter. "Me and Mr. López you mean?" And, as she said it, she wondered at her own fascination with danger, her need to hover around the edges of pain, to bite on the aching tooth. "Sarah—"

Sarah smiled quickly. "Mother, I'd rather not discuss Daddy if you don't mind. I don't want to see him either. He asked me if I'd changed my mind about moving in with them. And then whether I'd go to dinner with them tonight."

"You said no?"

"I put the phone down."

"Oh Sarah! That's so—"

"So what? So childish?"

"Yes."

"Well, Mother, I feel childish and betrayed and deserted and all those other things you're supposed to feel when your father leaves you and runs off with another woman. How come you're so calm? How come you're not flying around the house screaming and swearing?"

Marion closed her eyes. Her lips quivered slightly, but she pressed them close together into a straight line. Sarah stood up and walked towards her. Then she stopped and knelt in front of Marion, laying a hand on each knee and looking straight into her face.

"I'm sorry. I know how bad it must be. I know you're probably suffering more than I am. I'm sorry. Mr. López says that the one thing you must always guard against is assuming you understand the suffering of others. He's so right."

Marion opened her eyes and looked at Sarah. The girl had assumed a look of Understanding and Forbearance. She was an apt pupil. Sarah rose slowly to her feet and touched Marion lightly on the shoulder. "Get some sleep, Mother. You look tired again. Don't worry," she said, bending over softly. "You still have me."

There was a question in her voice and Marion answered with a smile. "Yes," she said. "Thank God for that."

"And perhaps Daddy will get tired of Beth and come back. Do you think he might? I mean, are you going to ask him to?"

"Don't hope too hard for that."

"I'm not!" she shouted, suddenly in tears again.

"Sarah, I'll see you in the morning. Good-night, darling."

Sarah left the room quickly and Marion waited until she heard her finish in her bathroom and close her bedroom door. Then she crept halfway up the stairs to check. Sarah's light was still on, but Marion heard the bed creak and knew she must be reading. She crept past Sarah's room and into her own. She closed the door and flipped the bolt that Jonathan had installed so that they could make love in the afternoons. The room was freezing. The windows flapped and strained on their hinges in the strong wind, and the drapes billowed into the room like spinnakers on a windy day. Marion struggled with the first window, the one at the side, and then tackled the two front ones.

There was a strange haze over the street, however, that held her still. One of the street lamps had been blown over by the wind and the street, for about twenty yards around the pole, was left in a gloomy pool of gray half-light. The wisps and snakes of light winter fog were blowing in between the houses, lit here and there by a pale white moon. Marion stood at the open window looking out into the cold night, feeling only the wind cutting through to the bones and hollows of her chest. She could feel nothing else, not even the panic that had been fluttering around her heart since she had woken up. It had hovered there, only rising to her throat when she thought beyond the moment and into the next hour and the days and years ahead. She breathed in deeply and then stretched out to grasp the handles of the windows. But as she drew them in towards her she stopped dead.

She had not noticed the car parked opposite or the man inside until he hissed at her. He had climbed out of the car when she reached for the window and stood there now, below her, looking up, his hair wild in the wind, like a mortal spitting fury at the gods.

"José!"

"I want to come in."
"You can't. Sarah—"
"Why did you not call me back?"
"I couldn't. I woke at eight and Sarah has only now gone to bed."
"You have been talking to her for hours. Why could you not have called?"
"José! Shh!" Marion hissed. "Please believe me! I couldn't. I came up now to call you."
She stared at his contorted face for a minute and then folded her arms. "Anyway, if you've been watching us for hours, how could I have called?"
"One hour."
A car cruised by slowly and stopped at a house farther down the street. Marion leaned out of the window and dropped her voice.
"Please, José, believe me. It is impossible for you to come in now. How can you think of it? Do you know what we are—what Sarah is going through?"
He said nothing, but Marion saw his neck flexing and she knew already the portent in his clenched fists.
"I will wait for you tomorrow," he said. "Eight o'clock. We have many things to discuss." He wheeled around, stamped back to his car, and then roared off down the street and out of sight. Marion pulled the windows closed and sank to her knees beneath them, leaning her forehead against the windowsill.
"Dear God," she mumbled, "see me through all this without destroying Sarah."

The fog was still thick when Marion drove across the bridge at a quarter of eight. She had left a note for Sarah saying she would try to be back by lunch time, and a p.s. list of groceries they needed and two twenty-dollar bills. But she could not shake off the burden of a new discomfort that had plagued her through the night and that sat now like a pile of bricks on her chest. Its presence, in fact, camouflaged all her other distress, even the anxious leap in her pulse every time she thought of her meeting with José. Driving across the bridge that morning, Marion Roth understood that she was suffering her first attack of real guilt.

On the other side of the bridge the fog was already lifting, revealing the quiet of the bay. Only a few boats were out and very few cars. Marion covered the distance to José's place more quickly than she had thought she would, and she parked in her usual spot just after eight. The door to his apartment was ajar. Marion could hear him playing her Chopin prelude as she descended and she stopped half way down, reluctant to give him the satisfaction of her arrival at the right time. She sat down on the stair and waited, unmoved, thinking of Sarah. No plan came to mind, no scheme, no solution for Sarah. Only a determination to compensate her for the pain of the last few days, for the pain, in fact, of all her years in that unnatural household. And now, to do anything, everything, to prevent her discovering the truth about José.

The prelude was over, and Marion stood up. She heard José mutter something, and then oddly, begin again, the same prelude. There was clearly no point in waiting any longer. And it was five past eight. Marion climbed down the remaining steps and walked into the room.

José looked up solemnly and nodded. "Wait a minute," he said. "Let me finish."

"You finished once already," she said loudly. "Do you mind if I make the coffee? Carry on. Finish again."

She went into the kitchen and began on the coffee. He had bought some Danish pastries which she laid out on a plate. José stopped abruptly in the middle of a phrase and came to stand at the kitchen door, looking sheepish.

"You were listening out there?"

"Yes." She poured the water into the coffee and sugar as he had taught her, stirring while she poured.

"I was playing it for you. Why didn't you come in?"

"I don't like to be manipulated," she said. "I thought I'd wait until it was over. But that could have been lunchtime."

He came into the kitchen and stopped her hand, took the kettle from her, led her out into the apartment. "Sit down," he said.

Marion pursed her lips and sat.

"I will bring the tray," he said. "Wait there, please."

She heard him setting out the cups quickly, and the coffeepot, and then he appeared with the tray and set it down in front of her. She sat forward to pour, but again he stopped her hand to do it himself. Marion turned to look out over the bay as he served the breakfast, but she could see nothing out there. She could see nothing but him, his arm muscles flexed through his T-shirt as he poured the coffee, his thighs and hips shaping the tight denim fabric to their own perfect contours, the wonderful mound, like a dancer's, pushing provocatively against the buttoned fly. She could smell his cologne, and the traces of his own pungent masculine odor, and she closed her eyes, as if by so doing she could prevent the effect he was having, had always had, on her own resolve. Poor Sarah, she thought. How much worse it must be for her.

"What are you thinking of?" he asked, handing her her coffee.

"Sarah."

"Oh."

"I can't stay long. I've left her a note without an explanation."

José faced her now with his legs crossed. He put down his cup and leaned towards her. "Mariana, I have not asked you here to talk of Sarah."

"Somehow I guessed that."

"It is you and me we must discuss. Our future."

Marion looked up at him. "José, I cannot discuss myself without reference to Sarah, I'm afraid, and certainly not my future. If there's one thing I've realized in the past two days, it is that."

"Well, then, her later," he said impatiently. "But first us."

"No!" she shouted over the crack in her voice. "No! NO! NO!"

"Drink your coffee," he said softly. "Here, take one of these pastries." She shook her head. "*Take* one!"

Marion reached out obediently and took one, but left it on her plate untouched.

"It was a bad time we had in Vallarta," he said, chewing at his Danish. "We had too many misunderstandings, too many problems. I too, I know. I was very uptight. And you could not relax.

You were always worried, always watching me. I think that situation made you feel very insecure, very guilty, right?"

Marion shook her head, no.

"You are always talking about the truth," he said, waving his arms in the air as if truth were a subject so irrelevant as to be frivolous. "Well, I have always been truthful with you, haven't I? Hey?"

Marion stared at him mournfully and shrugged.

"You won't say yes, but you know I have. *I* have not cheated you."

"Cheated *on* me."

"Whatever. But you—" he said, raising his voice to a menacing pitch. "You cheated me! You didn't tell the truth, did you? In fact, you lied! You lied to me each time I asked you about—that man."

"I lied only once. It happened only once."

"When?"

"The afternoon that I said I went shopping."

José jumped to his feet and began to pace around the room, weaving in and out of the pillows. He grasped an elbow in each hand and rocked as he walked. Marion watched him silently.

"I knew that it was then," he said. "I knew by instinct. And even then I hoped that I was wrong. I wanted to believe you when you lied to me. Why? Why did you lie?"

"Because I didn't want to lose you."

"Why did you do it, Marion?" He had come to stand in front of her. "Why did you do that to me?"

Marion turned away from him, but he stepped up closer, standing over her. She could see his thighs quivering as he spoke. "You were so pure and fresh when you first came here. New. Uncorrupted."

"José, for God's sake. I'd been married fifteen years!"

"That's not what I mean. You were not calculating. You were natural, frightened—"

"You mean it was my first affair."

He stared down into her eyes, but she could not play along. She had been too schooled against melodrama to be able to suspend her disbelief.

"Perhaps that was all it was," he went on. "And yet I cannot believe that was all. I fell in love with you, Marion, deeply in love."

He seemed about to cry. Marion was desperate to stop the scene, but she could think of nothing to say that would not turn his drama into fury. At least she no longer felt the tug in her groin at his presence. At least she was free of that in the face of these histrionics.

"You were just beginning to discover yourself," he said. "You began to unfold, like a rose or a lily. I saw what was happening to you and I loved you more."

"But it didn't work, José. What did I discover beyond my own dissatisfaction? Only a lot of people around me whom I'd succeeded in making miserable."

"No! You discovered how to love, how to open your heart. How can you say you discovered only dissatisfaction?"

"Yes, you're right. Loving you was wonderful."

"And even the pain you caused them. How do you know it was pain? It is a great danger to assume you understand the suffering of others." He stopped and looked at Marion. "Why do you laugh? What's so funny?"

"Oh, it's just that Sarah was quoting you on that very subject last night. It's like the prelude this morning—" She laughed, doubling over and resting her forehead on the rug in front of her. "I'm just beginning to find it all so funny."

"To me," he said with dignity, "it is not funny. And I do not see the connection with the prelude. But anyway, you can laugh if it makes you feel better. Let me know when you are finished." He sat at the piano and fiddled through a few exercises.

"I'm not laughing anymore, José. Please go on." Marion stifled a few giggles.

"I have a question to ask you, Marion, a very serious question."

"Ask away."

"But first, I must finish with this other man. Did you tell me the truth about the reason for his visiting Vallarta?"

"Yes."

"What happened that night before you talked to the doctors?"

"I told you. He got sick. During dinner."

"If he had been well, you would have spent the night with him?"

"I doubt it."

"Doubt? Doubt? Only doubt?"

"How can I be definite about an hypothesis?"

José came back again and settled down opposite her. "Well, that, at least, is the truth. What will you say to him when he returns from Vallarta? Or have you spoken to him already?"

"I shall never go to bed with him again. That's what you want to know, isn't it? And I don't love him, although I think that he truly loves me in his own way. I cannot risk his breaking up his marriage for no good reason. I've said that to him already and I'll say it again and again until he believes it. And I haven't spoken to anyone since my return except you and Sarah. And the cab driver. And myself, quite a bit. Not even to my husband."

Marion uttered the statements in a monotone, like a litany of confession.

"Well, he's left hasn't he?" José's voice rose as he leaned towards her. "Your husband has left?"

Suddenly Marion's head spun and dipped. The laughter of a few minutes before had dissolved as quickly as it had come and she found herself close to tears again. She closed her eyes tightly and dropped her head onto her chest. "Oh José, Jesus Christ, how will I face it all?"

He was beside her in a second, kissing her neck, stroking her hair, whispering words in Spanish into her ear. Finally, she heard him through all the words and the kisses repeating and repeating the same question, urging her to respond.

"Mariana, Mariana, my question. I have not yet asked my question. Marry me, Mariana. Marry me and everything will work out. Marry me. I will take care of you. Marry me and we will never be sad again."

She looked up through her tears into his face. He was smiling at her, and then laughing. He jumped up and darted off, and then came back with some champagne and two glasses. While he untwisted the wires and eased the cork out of the neck, he talked on quickly, mixing Spanish phrases in with his English, laughing, kissing the bottle and the glass in which he handed her the frothy pink liquid.

"Mariana, we will be so happy, happy, happy. *Mi encantadora!* I knew, I decided when you were up on that stage, talking about all those drugs and diseases. Then I decided to marry you. You were like a queen there, like a Madonna. Perfect! You were powerful, a queen on a throne! My queen!" He raised his glass, emptied it, and refilled it. "Then I decided. She must be my wife. We will have children, perfect children. Our love will blossom and grow into such beauty. Wait here." He darted off again leaving Marion to look into her own untouched champagne. He was back in a minute, holding a small box in his hand. He thrust it at her. "Open it. Open. Open."

Marion set down her glass and peeled off the card. She knew what she was doing, her hand was steady. But her movements seemed irrelevant, a forced exercise, a mere politeness. She pulled the little card out of its envelope and read it silently.

To my Mariana,
Please accept this ring as a sign of my true devotion.
It is a pledge to our future. May it blossom with our
love into true fulfillment.

Con mi amor,
José

She unwrapped the gift and opened the box. A tiny antique ring with emeralds and diamonds was nestled in yellowing cotton. Marion stared at it there as if it were a dead bird in a nest, a thing not to be touched.

"Take it out," he said. "Put it on."

But Marion did not move. Nothing moved in her, no thought, no fleeting image beyond the bird and the nest.

"Mariana! Don't you like it? It was my grandmother's ring. My mother gave it to me last year when my grandmother died. Marion?"

Marion put the box down on the rug in front of her and tucked the card into the pocket of her blouse. She looked up slowly at José and then untucked her legs and stood up. He stood up too, half afraid to touch her. She walked over to the window and then back to the piano. He watched her, waiting silently while she sat down on the bench.

"José, it is beautiful. It is one of the most beautiful rings I have ever seen. But you never waited. You asked me about Ben and about Jonathan, and as soon as you had satisfied yourself on those scores, you asked me to marry you. But you never waited for my reply. You were so sure, so sure that what you wanted was what I wanted, that this little scene you had so carefully prepared was going to run according to your plan, that you never once stopped to hear my answer. You ask for the truth from me but you want only so much, only what it suits you to hear. Well, I'm going to tell you the truth now, and it is that I will never, I can never marry you."

She paused for a minute, and then went on.

"You talk of blossoming and fulfillment but those are just empty phrases, clichés, outworn, overblown, nothing metaphors. What have we got, you and I, that could blossom? What's there to fulfill? Oh, yes, in the beginning I grant you, it was wonderful. You did open some doors for me, doors in myself that had long since been closed off. I realized that what was missing from my life was partly what I'd left behind when I opted for the career and the man I chose. I grew up with music, after all, with all the reverence and the respect for things other than the power of money and position.

"But love? No. This is not the love that could propel me into another marriage. Never. There are huge gaps between us, José, that can never be filled. We don't discuss anything of interest any more. That lasted about a week. I don't even know what you're interested in really, beyond yourself that is, and the effect that you have on people. And, by the way, you have some strange effects on me that you didn't calculate on. You make me uptight about things I never thought about before. Like paying for your dinners and breakfasts. Oh, yes," she said, waving her head in response to the shock that jerked him upright as if he had been hit from behind. "I have found that relic in my soul. It goes together with the vestigial tail. Nevertheless, it is there, and I have come to terms with it.

"But, apart from all this, you boggle my generally balanced judgement with your platitudes and euphemisms. At first I found myself rejecting them. Then I would persuade myself to believe them, only to find that you had used them largely in self-service. Like that business with Marta. No, don't protest. Listen to *me* for once!

"Have you examined what it is that you think you want from me? Have you ever examined your own needs and desires?" Marion stood up and walked around the piano. "So, you decided when I was giving my paper that you wanted to marry me? Did it ever cross your mind to ask yourself why? Queen! Madonna! It was because I was beyond your reach, independent, triumphant, as I was when we first met. What you wanted was to control me, to get a hold of that independence and bend it to your own needs. And what are those needs, José? What is it in yourself that you want to see reflected in my strength?"

Marion paused as if she expected an answer. But she received none and went on. "Well anyway, when you realized that you couldn't control me by impregnating me, you were going to do it by marrying me first.

"Well, I don't want to marry. I've had enough of marriage. And I don't want any more children, not yours or anyone's. I've got one pathetically sad child to account for as it is, to pay back for all the misery I've caused. Why on earth would I want to have another?"

Marion looked up into José's face and immediately stepped back up against the piano. He was facing her like a wild man, his eyes wide and staring, one cheek twitching out of control. His right fist was pulled back as if he was going to hit her, but he stayed where he was, stretched to his limit and about to snap. Then suddenly he saw the ring, lying where she had left it, and he snatched it up and flung it at her hard. It bounced it off the piano and onto the rug at her feet. She watched him cross his arms and turn away, a fist under each armpit, his muscles stretching out the cotton of his T-shirt.

"I'm leaving," she said.

He nodded.

Marion stared for a moment at the volume of Chopin preludes perched on the music stand. She swayed a little and clutched the wood under the keys to steady herself. She wanted to run to him and take it all back. She wanted to reclaim the ring, to accept it, put it on, wear it forever as her payment to him for being allowed to come here, to go on belonging where she already belonged, an exchange for this refuge to which she would now no longer have any claim. But she didn't. She focused her gaze on the music stand, the wood on either side, a small white envelope lying on the side nearest to her. She stared at it. It was addressed to José in a large unformed hand. Marion snatched it up and turned it over. There was no return address.

"José, who sent you this?"

"What? Oh, that. I don't know."

"But it's opened."

"Read it. Go on, read it. But why should you care? It's nothing to you now." He stared at her belligerently.

Marion drew the folded paper out of its envelope. She sniffed it. It was heavily scented with a familiar perfume. She saw the translucent splotches of perfume scattered over the page as she unfolded the letter. Inside, three sentences had been carefully written in purple ink.

"My darling José,
I have loved you always. I will love you forever. You are the stuff that dreams are made of."

It was signed with a lipstick imprint of a kiss. Marion took a step towards José holding out the paper, and then she stopped. She read the note again.

"José, do you know who wrote this?"

"I told you no. I get a few every year. This one was in the mailbox when I came back. It's one of the girls, I guess. Marion, why do you taunt me?"

"It's from Sarah. It's her writing."

José looked up quickly to assure himself that she wasn't joking. When he saw her standing there staring at the letter, her hand shaking, he threw back his head and laughed.

"Ha! Ha-ha-ha! Hee-hee! Oh-ho!" He leaned back against the window roaring out his delight. "That's funny! Ho-ho! Poor Sarah! Ha! Ha! Poor, poor Sarah!"

José's laughter followed Marion as she ran up the stairs. She heard it as she started the car and crunched it into gear. She heard it follow her down the hill and back across the bridge. It echoed with the purring of the traffic as she edged through the tollbooth. And, finally, when she drove up to the house and saw Jonathan's car parked outside, it subsided into a demonic cackle. Marion folded Sarah's note carefully and slipped it into her blouse pocket. Then she drove into the garage and climbed the stairs to confront Jonathan and Beth.

16

They had heard the garage door and were expecting her. She heard their voices drop as she approached and then, as she opened the door through to the house, they were silent. They stood at the open study door staring at her. Marion stopped on the threshold for a moment and then walked past them and into the kitchen.

"Anyone want coffee? A sandwich?" She put the kettle on and opened the refrigerator. They had followed her to the kitchen door and stood again, waiting, keeping their distance.

"Aha!" she said into the empty refrigerator. "Some brie, a half a tomato. Now all I need is a loaf of bread and—" Suddenly she looked up at them and smiled. "What is it to be?" she asked.

"Oh, nothing for me—" Beth said, shooting a glance at Jonathan.

"I'm not talking about *food*, little Elizabeth, sweet, innocent Beth. I mean performances, roles. Which do you want? Ophelia? Camille? Medea? Name it. Name it and I'll do it."

Sarah snickered and the sound soothed Marion's hot head more than the chill, damp air that blew gently over her from the fridge.

Jonathan stepped forward to take command. "Marion, we would like to talk to you. Would you please close the refrigerator and let's all sit down somewhere?"

"Oh, lets!" she said, falling into a chair.

Jonathan grasped Beth's elbow and steered her towards the table. But before she could sit down, Marion had edged her own chair away, closer to Sarah, and averted her head as if Beth had a communicable disease. Sarah giggled again.

"Stop it, Marion!" he snapped. "For God's sake, let's get this thing over."

"Thing?" Marion asked. "What thing?"

Beth opened her mouth to speak, but Marion, her timing finely tuned to the occasion, slapped her hands onto the table with revelatory zeal. She looked up at Beth and smiled through her at Jonathan.

"Oh!" she said, tossing her head in Beth's direction. "*That* thing! Yes, indeed. Do sit down. We must most certainly get it over."

The kitchen was hot. It caught the morning sun from two sides and by one o'clock, if the fog had burned off as it had today, it was like an oven. Marion wiped a dishcloth across her forehead and then fixed her eyes on Beth.

"Marion?" Jonathan said.

"Mmm." Marion never took her eyes off Beth.

"I'm prepared to forget about the books. I'm not going to be angry." It was his delivery-room voice. He was taking control.

Beth tried to look away, but Marion held her prisoner while she received Jonathan's speeches on her left cheek.

"I've called McDermott," he went on. "He's coming in on Monday to repaint. And he said he'd see what he could do with the carpet. I think we can count on him to be discreet."

"Fascinating!" Marion said. A slow blush was filtering out through the layers of Beth's blue-white skin. It ran purple and scarlet through a craze of channels below the surface and then erupted into splotches and streaks across her face and neck.

"I have engaged a lawyer," he said. "And I would advise you to do the same. I didn't use Grant. I thought it would be putting him in an awkward position."

"Undoubtedly."

"So I'm using Justin Collier."

"An apt name."

"What?"

"Apt. *A-P-T.* Justin. An editorial comment."

Sarah snickered again. She was pulling at the hem of the abandoned dishcloth and had managed so far to unpick one side.

"Marion! Please!" he said. "This is bad enough. Can't you look at me while I'm talking?"

"I can." She didn't move.

"Oh, fuck it! What's the use," he said, taking Beth's hand. "Let's go."

Beth half rose in her seat and then sat down again. Her face was now purple. "No, Jon," she said. "I want to speak to Marion."

"Ah!" said Marion. "The vision has a voice."

"Marion, do you mind if we speak privately?" Beth's voice was stronger than she looked. She had always had this ability to take Marion by surprise.

"Private from what, or whom?"

"I don't think Sarah should be subjected to this."

"Willy-nilly, willy-nilly," sang Marion.

"Yes, but—"

"Beth's right," Jonathan interrupted. "This is not for Sarah."

Marion turned away at last and faced Sarah. She stretched out a hand to touch her lightly on the shoulder, hearing as she did the light rustle of paper in her own blouse pocket.

"Sarah, they don't want you to be hurt. Would you rather go or stay?"

Sarah blushed. She looked down into the dishcloth. "I think I'll go if you don't mind."

"No, I don't mind," Marion said softly. "Go ahead, darling."

Sarah pushed her chair back and then flattened herself to ease behind Jonathan's chair. He leaned back to grab her hand as she passed, but she pulled it away and lurched free, out of the room.

Marion listened for Sarah's heavy tread up the stairs, but she heard nothing and hopped up lightly to close both doors. They watched her, turning their heads in unison as she darted across the kitchen and then came to sit down again opposite them.

"I have one request to make," Marion said, back in her chair, with the dignity of a prisoner before the execution. "And that's that you spare me any histories or explanations. There is nothing about the two of you that I care to hear about and no explanation that could possibly interest me."

Jonathan and Beth looked at each other again in one of those silent flashes that serve, between members of a well-trained team, to change a strategy midaction. Jonathan leaned back in his chair to give Beth the floor.

"Marion, it's mainly Sarah that needs to be discussed then," she said.

"By you, or by Jonathan and me?"

"By all of us, my dear." Beth's voice was without a trace of sarcasm. Marion wondered irrelevantly what on earth she would be like in bed.

"You see," Beth continued, "Jonathan and I really feel it would be in her best interests to live with us. For a few years anyway."

"Why?"

The glance was exchanged again, and Jonathan sat forward. It really was a masterful performance.

"It would be better for her in every way," he said. "If she stayed on with you, there would be no father figure in her life. For the meantime anyway. On a day-to-day basis, that is." His small eyes flitted around the room avoiding Marion's steady glare.

"Say what you really mean," she said.

Jonathan sat up, impatient. It was Saturday and already getting late. The wind was up. He had probably thought they would accomplish all this before twelve and then take Sarah out on the bay to celebrate.

"You're in an unstable phase, Marion. I—we think it's not a healthy environment for her. Especially after all these traumas she's had. The drinking, the dieting, giving up the cello."

"Oh! OH! But I thought all those things were within the normal bounds of adolescent experimentation? Ha!" Marion folded her arms and sank down into her shoulders.

Another glance was passed between them. "Well, I've changed my mind," he said. "It's a free country. A person is entitled to change his mind."

"*I* changed his mind," Beth said. "Marion, you know I've been concerned about Sarah. And about you . . ."

"Thank you!" Marion bowed. "But tell me this, Beth. What about Alfred?"

The blush which had been fading from Beth's face returned instantly. "He'll live with us, of course."

"*Of course!* Does Alex object?"

"No. He's been very sensible."

"Sensible!" Marion snorted.

"For God's sake, Marion," Jonathan barked, sitting up. "Stop repeating every word Beth says!"

"Well, what I want to know from you both now, now that we're talking of sense and healthy environments is how healthy, how sensible you consider it for my fourteen-year-old daughter, half starved and confused out of her mind, to live with her father and his paramour and the paramour's idiot child? Answer that!" she shouted, standing up. "But before you do, allow me to bring Sarah back. Let's hear her answer to this proposition. No? I wonder why? I wonder whether it's because you know her answer already? Because she's rejected you before and you know she'll reject you again. Just listen to me, both of you. Before I abandon my daughter to a fool, a traitor, and an idiot, I will need to be convinced, point by point in every damned detail that what you offer her has a higher value for her health and future than the love of a mother."

"Mother! You call yourself a mother!" Jonathan had leapt to his feet and shrieked at Marion, shaking off Beth's restraining hand. "I have sat here in silence while you called Beth foul names—a *paramour*, for God's sake! But to call yourself a mother—"

"I do! I do! I do! She is my daughter and I love her. I have a right to love her. I have a mother's right to repent and start again."

"You sound like a God damn preacher, Marion! You've gone nuts. Loony! What in hell are you trying to say?"

"I'm *trying* to say nothing, Jonathan." Marion lowered her voice and grasped the back of the chair to control her trembling. "I'm telling you that I love Sarah and that I will never release her to the likes of the two of you unless she begs me to go."

"Then go get her," he said through thick lips, drained of their color, dried and cracking. "Let's give her another chance to decide. Maybe we can talk some sense into her. Tell her nothing's final. She can try it out with us. She's a free agent. Tell her that."

"I'll tell her the truth," Marion said. "That should be more than enough." And she left the kitchen to find Sarah.

Something restrained Marion from calling out to Sarah in the hall. There was something familiar, a smell, a sound she couldn't place, that kept her there silent, eyes closed, trying to find its source. Marion cocked her head to one side and then, as if filtered through layers of silence, she heard the floating notes of Sarah's cello. It was the Bach, the sarabande, slow and beautiful. Marion sat down on the third step and closed her eyes again to listen.

Sarah had not lost her touch. In fact the phrases seemed to flow more easily, to be less labored, more like her grandfather's playing. He was there too now, behind his study door, running up and down his morning scales, waiting for a late student. And Marion, nineteen, was stretched out on the couch with a book, waiting for the phone to ring. New York. Easter vacation. Plans for the summer. Gertrude humming the "Ode to Joy" as she carried a tray of tea and strudel to Herbert. Then one to Marion.

"Marion! Your shoes! On the couch! Off, please!"

It was her cue. She flipped them off with a laugh so that Gertrude shook her head and smiled in that way, loving her more, it seemed, for her thoughtlessness. Thoughtless.

Thoughtless. Marion lifted her head. Could she, Marion, ever love in that way? She listened to the last few measures of the piece. Everything about it was perfect—the tone, the notes, everything. I've never given her a chance, she thought. I have, without ever knowing why or how, left her feeling deficient, even when there was no discernible difference between what she was and what I could possibly expect her to be. I've affected her as men affect women, making her feel deficient by simply being herself. Oh, God!

Marion pressed her face into her knees and struggled with her impulse to grab Sarah by the wrist and run. Anywhere. Anywhere

where they could start again. Where Sarah could be flushed through, cleansed of Marion's neglect, be made to forget. Anything to preclude the long and painful years of healing ahead and, God knows, the questionable cure.

"Marion? Marion!" Jonathan and Beth shouted together. "Sarah? Sarah, come down sweetheart."

Marion stood up to greet them as they came to the foot of the stairs. "She's not upstairs. She was playing. I thought that the least I could do was to give her a chance to finish."

"Did you call me?" Sarah stood at the breakfast room door, blinking into the dark hall.

"Will you—"

"Come—"

Marion and Jonathan spoke together. Then Jonathan stepped towards Sarah with a smile. "Come into the kitchen, honey. We have something to ask you."

Marion and Sarah were left in a sudden hush after Jonathan retreated with Beth. The discussion had been brief and Marion had said nothing. She had let them hang themselves by extending to them the short rope of her own dignified silence. And when they saw that Sarah remained hostile, despite their careful words and tone, they simply stood up, as if on some silent cue, and left.

Sarah mumbled something to herself with a small smile.

"What was that, darling?"

"I said 'good riddance.'"

"Sarah," Marion said softly. "Don't retreat into hostility."

"It's not a retreat, Mother. It's revenge."

Marion looked at Sarah in surprise. "I don't understand."

"For trusting him and not you all those years. I gave him every reason to believe that I loved him and hated you. And he never resisted that. So I'm enjoying it in a sort of perverse way. You really can't object to that, after all, can you? I mean your position is almost worse than mine."

Sarah had leaned back in her chair. She seemed quite happy to sit this way, chatting about hostility and revenge, until the subject petered out and they found another to replace it. Marion had never seen her so relaxed.

"You were playing the Bach quite beautifully you know. Is this the first time since you gave it up?"

"Yes. And it just came so easily, even the prelude. I was wishing I had the tape recorder on to record it for Grandpa."

"I heard it. I'll never forget it."

Sarah blushed. She reached for the sugar, but abandoned the impulse and folded her arms.

"Do you think I should take it up again?"

"I think you know what I think." Marion smiled. But her chest heaved and her pulse was racing. There was something demonic in the happiness of these minutes. And in their passing she felt herself the mortal object of the laughter of the gods, doomed to destroy her own child in a ritual of revelation as old as literature. But she was denied the remove of art. She was as feeble as a toothless old hag, as impotent to resist the role she had created for herself as she was to resist the pull of gravity.

Marion cleared her throat. "Sarah, there is something I must talk to you about before we can go on like this."

"What is it, Mother?" Sarah looked interested. She smiled.

"It's about Mr. López. About José."

Sarah closed her eyes suddenly and tightened her jaw in forbearance. "What now, Mother?"

"Sarah—Oh, god, how can I say this?"

"Say *what*?"

Marion's courage failed. "I know about your crush on him, Sarah. I know you wrote him a love note."

Sarah stared, at first in disbelief, and then in fear. She pushed herself away from the table, stood up, upset her chair, and stumbled backwards to the sink opposite. "You're a liar! Why do you have to lie like that?" Tears had filled her eyes and were overflowing down her cheeks and around her nose.

"I wish I were a liar, Sarah. But I'm telling you the truth. Ask me how I know. Ask me!"

"How do you know?"

"I know because I also loved him, Sarah. I've been in love with him since the school picnic last year." Marion's own tears were choking her now, blocking her throat, making her repeat the beginnings of her statements two or three times. "I've had an affair with him, Sarah. I've been to his apartment, sometimes every afternoon, at least three or four times a week, for months and months. He came with me to Mexico. We had planned it. Sarah, I—I am sure that I loved José before Daddy ever looked at Beth."

Sarah had turned to the sink and hung over it now, heaving, retching into it. She was crying at the same time in wheezes and moans. Her whole body rejected at once the poison Marion had poured into her ears.

"Sarah! You have to listen," Marion shouted over the noise of Sarah's weeping. She stood up, afraid to approach Sarah too closely, not unaware still of the faint scar on her cheek.

"I saw him this morning, Sarah, for the last time. I went out there because he was here last night, outside, after you went to bed. He wanted to come in, but I wouldn't let him. He wanted to ask me something and I said I'd come this morning. So I went. What he wanted was for me to marry him, Sarah. And I said no. Not only because of—because it's impossible. But because I no longer love him. I ended it before I ever saw your note, Sarah. It's over."

Sarah turned slowly and stared at Marion. Her head shook slightly before the words came out. "No. No, I don't believe you. I don't believe a word you're saying. You're a liar, a stupid liar!" Her voice had risen into a high shriek. "Why are you trying to hurt me? He would never love *you*! He would never even *look* at you! You're too old! It's ridiculous! *You're* ridiculous! How could he love you! Ha!" She tried a laugh, but it only released the next outpouring of tears and gasps.

Marion sank her forehead onto the palms of her hands and stared down at the table. "You are quite right," she said. "It was ridiculous. But it's the truth, Sarah. Why would I lie? Just when we're coming together? I thought of it. I thought of trying to hide it from you. But then I was afraid you'd find out. How could I live with it, knowing you could find out at any time from someone here, someone there, even from José himself?"

She looked at Sarah for some response. But there was none. Sarah stared at her in silence, waiting.

"There's one thing I can say in my defense," Marion went on. "I had no idea, no inkling, of your feeling for José before the night I came home. If course, now it's so obvious." She closed her eyes and shook her head. "And then I found your note this morning..."

"Where? Where was it?"

"On his piano. I recognized the writing, the paper, the ink, immediately. He didn't. He had no idea. I'm afraid I told him in my shock, Sarah. Oh God, I'm sorry."

Marion fumbled in her pocket and drew out the paper. "Here it is," she said. "Take it."

Sarah snatched the note and, as she did, José's card fluttered to the ground. In a second Sarah had grabbed it. She stood quite still, almost without breath, holding it close to her face, moving her lips as she read his words.

They stood in the warm kitchen, silent, both staring at the card while Sarah read. There was no cure Marion knew of for what Sarah was suffering now. And the silence of the place served only to emphasize her impotence. She had no words to convince Sarah of what she was now so convinced of herself, that José deserved neither of them, that the bond between them, between mother and daughter, which now seemed so frail as to be nonexistent, was stronger by a thousandfold than anything that could unite either of them to such a man.

"There's something more I want to say, Sarah."

Sarah looked up at Marion slowly. Nothing in her face or eyes or the stoop of her shoulders showed anything but her hatred for Marion. José had been reduced for her to the small vellum card she held between her fingers: all her grief had been spent in reading it, leaving her dry-eyed and empty of everything but this wordless loathing.

Marion sat down again at the table and rested her forehead on the palms of her hands. "You may now want to reconsider your decision against living with Daddy and Beth. I don't have to give you permission. But I want you to know that I'll understand if you change your mind."

Marion looked up. Sarah had not moved. She continued to stare at Marion with wide dry eyes.

"Sarah, whatever your feelings are for me now, whatever they are, I want you to understand something, or to hear it and try to understand it when you hate me a little less. Someday, you too will be twenty and then thirty, and then thirty-six. You may have children. From your perspective, the perspective of a fourteen-year-old virgin, I am old, ridiculous, unmotherly, beyond the point of losing my heart and my common sense. But from my perspective, you see, life stretches out ahead of me. I have hopes for myself. I have never reached the plateau on which you've placed me and I hope I never do."

Marion slumped farther down into the kitchen chair and threw her head right back, arching her bare neck, stretching the skin so that she could stare at the ceiling, the leafy shadows and the shades of white. Her voice changed tone, softened, like the voice of a patient on a couch with the psychiatrist out of sight. She seemed to be speaking to herself.

"I've spent my whole life, Sarah, looking away from myself. And I still have to fight the impulse to explain a lousy marriage, an unhappy child, and a mediocre career as a formula for success. Or at least rationalize them as inevitable. But none of them was inevitable. And now I'm going to have to accept the blame."

Marion looked up to check that Sarah was still there. She was. She stood like marble, listening, Marion presumed.

"So where am I now, Sarah, with you standing there hating me, a husband who thinks I'm a loony, a lover, out right now, you can be sure, trying to replace me with another heroine? Where am I?"

Marion's voice had risen to fill the kitchen. She dipped the spoon into the sugar and then carried it to her mouth. The sugar dissolved between her teeth and on her tongue leaving its sweetness there like manna.

"I want to start again with you, Sara. Not from the beginning.

That's impossible. But from where we left off before the shock about José. There is nothing I can say or do, I know, to change that. It happened, and you *have* to accept it, Sarah, even if you can't understand it. All I want now is to have you back."

Sarah remained where she was, still holding José's card, while Marion stood up, steadied herself against the table, and then left the room. As she climbed the stairs to her room, she heard Sarah open the door to the basement. She stopped to listen. The basement stairs creaked under Sarah's heavy tread and then she heard the clatter, far below, of tools or cans. It flashed through Marion's head that Sarah might be setting the house on fire, but then she heard her climb the stairs again and walk across the hall to the breakfast room. Whatever Sarah had wanted, she must have found because she closed the breakfast room door softly and began to tap lightly, bang, twang, on the cello. Marion was relieved. She continued the climb up to her room, closed the door, and sat on the bed thinking of what she would say to her mother.

But her mind was blank and gray. She had spent all her words on Sarah and had nothing left for her parents. She picked up the phone and dialed the old number quickly.

"Yes?"

"Mother, it's me."

"Ah Marion. Back already? How was Mexico?"

"I came home early, Mother. Jonathan has left us. He left while I was out of town and so I came back to Sarah."

"Left? What do you mean *left*?"

"He's gone off with another woman, with Beth, in fact. We will be getting a divorce. Fairly soon I should imagine."

There was a pause punctuated only by the scratchings and singing of the long-distance line. Marion could see Gertrude braiding the fingers of her left hand into her pearls.

"Marion, what is to become of my Sarah?"

"That's the point, Mother. She's very—Well, she's distraught. For all the obvious reasons. Can you come out please? I think it would really help."

"Is she with you? Where is she?"

"Here, with me. Playing the cello actually, downstairs."

"Thank God for that! I will come tomorrow. Alone. I don't think your father should be with me, do you? And anyway, it's impossible."

"No. Absolutely not. It's mostly you that she needs."

"I'll phone you from the airport to tell you which plane. Marion, go to that child. Do not leave her for one minute."

"I'll go now, Mother."

"Good-bye."

Marion ran to the door and down the stairs. The conversation had acted on her like the lifting of weights. She felt expansive, able to breathe again. She wanted to tell Sarah now that Gertrude would be with them tomorrow. She herself wanted to give Sarah that comfort.

At the breakfast room door she stopped, waiting to hear whether she could enter. But the room was silent. Marion peered through the glass and the curtain on the other side. Sarah was there, sitting, she thought, on her chair in the middle, but she wasn't playing. There was no familiar scroll protruding over her shoulder or the broad expanse of Sarah's legs around the base, giving her, Marion had always thought, the look of a pear. She just seemed to be sitting motionless, doing nothing. Marion knocked lightly and then, receiving no response, went in.

It could only have been five minutes, no more than ten, since Marion had gone upstairs to phone, and yet it had taken no more than that for Sarah to destroy the cello almost beyond recognition. She had obviously snapped off the fingerboard first, standing on the body and pulling with both hands. Then she had hacked at it with the hammer and the saw. The strings lay snapped and curled around the fragmented wood. But the wood of the body itself, the strength of the instrument, the deep rich wood so lovingly bent and molded to give resonance and tone, had been vandalized as if by gangs. She must have jumped on it first and then pounded it with the hammer for it to have split and fractured into so many uneven parts. And then she must have flung the parts around the room. There was wood everywhere. Even the bow had been snapped in two and the music stand bent. The music itself, some of it anyway, had been roughly torn and scattered over the debris.

In the middle sat Sarah on her practice chair, the saw and hammer laid neatly in her lap. Her nostrils flared and her eyes were wild as she smiled up into Marion's face, a grim lunatic smile that made Marion step back towards the door. She smiled on as Marion stood there sweeping her eyes across the wreckage and moving her head around. Finally her gaze stopped on Sarah.

"Sarah, I just spoke to Grandma. She's flying out to us tomorrow."

A scream echoed around the room. Sarah flung away the saw and hammer and fell forward onto her knees and into the wreckage. She stretched out her arms over the shredded music, buried her face in her arms and wept.

Marion closed the door softly and walked through to the kitchen. She took down two mugs and some chocolate, and then set the pan on the stove to heat the milk. She heard Sarah's wailing and crying build up to a crescendo of misery and then fade out, slowly, into the whistling of the wind. And after a while there was silence. Marion heard the breakfast room door open and she heard Sarah come to stand at the kitchen door. The pan was ticking slightly as it heated up the milk. Marion dipped her finger in to test the heat and then measured out the instant chocolate and stirred.

"Mother."

Marion looked over at Sarah, the wooden spoon poised in her hand.

"Mommy, I want to stay here with you. I want to start again like you said."

Sarah hung her head and twisted her hands into the fabric of her skirt. Marion could see they were torn and bleeding. Her skirt was smeared with blood, and rust from the tools she had used, and so was her blouse.

The milk was boiling now. Marion switched off the stove and laid the spoon down on the counter. The sun had moved to the other side of the house, leaving the kitchen in shadow. She watched the steam rise and curl off the surface of the milk, filling the kitchen with the rich smell of chocolate. She wanted to sing, loudly, in a group of thousands. She wanted to celebrate. But she turned to Sarah and stretched out her arms. She folded Sarah into them, hugging her gently as if she were an infant, feeling the warmth across her chest and the head of soft curls resting lightly on her shoulder.

Epilogue

Indian summer had lasted only four days this year and then the chill had returned. There was even some question as to whether they would have to postpone the picnic because of rain. But they had held on and, in fact, the day turned out to be cool but bright. Marion and Sarah were among the first on the hockey field. They set their basket down next to the hedge and then laid out the rug in front of it so that they would be protected from the wind. Marion kept her poncho on and sat with her knees up under it. She was watching for Jonathan. He had insisted on coming today, on laying his claim to Sarah publicly, even though both she and Sarah had suggested to him that it might be awkward for them all.

Sarah fished a book out of the basket and stretched out on her stomach to read. There was a new ease in her stretching, a fleshy resilience, as if her joints were oiled and working for the first time. Over the summer her body had plumped and curved back into womanhood. Her hips had filled out again, and also her breasts, her cheeks. Even the curve of her head and shoulders seemed less angular, less apologetic. Marion smiled at the sight of her. Sarah's legs were still bronze and her hair several shades lighter from the summer sun. She tanned evenly, as Marion had always done. But Marion had never had such hair. It was like cream now, the rich yellow cream they had eaten all summer with their fruit.

Marion lifted her own face to the cold fall sun. She too was tanned, but at her age a tan was a mixed blessing. Around her eyes and mouth, for instance, the skin looked evenly tanned as long as she smiled or spoke. But if she relaxed her smile it slackened into uneven stripes. The crevices around her eyes and around the edges of her mouth remained white while the skin that had taken the sun was, on closer inspection, coarse and dry like raw silk.

"Marion Roth! Is that you? Here already?"

"Hi, Dede."

"My!" she puffed, finally making it to the edge of the blanket. "Whew!"

Sarah looked up from her book and twisted around.

"Hi, Mrs. Benton."

"Why, Sarah! How tanned you are! *Both* of you! You two look *great*!"

"Thanks," they both said in unison. Sarah returned to her book. Dede dropped onto the blanket, folded her long stockinged legs to the side and shuffled closer to Marion.

"Well!" she said. "Long time, no see."

"We spent the summer in Greece, Dede, Sarah and I, that is. In fact, we only got back two days before school began."

"Greece!" Dede peeped. "How sup—perb! I think I'd just *love* to go to Greece. But we have our place on the lake, you know. And so many people count on coming up. I'm afraid we're stuck."

Marion smiled. "I can imagine. But even so, it must be lovely to have it, winter and summer."

"Oh, yes. It is. But sometimes you know I'd give anything for a change. Greece! You lucky thing!"

"I think so."

There was a silence. Marion smiled at Dede and up at the sun. She wondered how Dede would ask what she had come to find out.

"How're things going otherwise?" she asked, finally.

"Swimmingly," Marion said. "You know that I've left the clinic I've worked at all these years, don't you? No? Well, I've taken a fellowship, a clinical fellowship in internal medicine at U.C. for this year and possibly next too. And then I'll see. I think I'd like to stay on in hospital practice."

"Fas—cinating!" Dede was disappointed. She looked around the field for the new arrivals. "Are you still in Forest Hill?" she asked, looking towards the gate.

"Sarah and I have stayed on in the house. Jonathan and his new wife have not, of course."

Dede blushed. Marion heard Sarah stifle a giggle into a sniff and she looked across at her sharply, and then back to Dede.

"Dede, by the way, let me know if there's anything I can do for the Pleasure Faire next year. I can probably fit in something not too onerous around my schedule. Tell Sandy to put me at the bottom of her list."

They both laughed. Dede smoothed out her skirt and struggled to her feet. "That would be *neat*, Marion! Don't worry, we'll find something for you to do." She blew Marion a kiss and staggered off again across the field.

Sarah sat up. "Why on earth did you do that, Mother? What possessed you?"

"I was compensating her for your guffaw. Anyway, what the hell. They can use our garage as a repository for their auction junk or something. Why not?"

Sarah sank back into her book and Marion reached over for the wine. She unpeeled the lead foil and then wedged the bottle between her legs to get a grip on the cork.

"Want a swig before anyone sees?"

"No, thanks," Sarah mumbled. Then she rolled over onto her back, resting her hands behind her head. "Mother? Do you think Daddy will bring Beth?"

"I should hope not, darling. But knowing him, probably yes."

"It's going to be weird. I mean I haven't seen her since before we left. And now she's my stepmother."

"Weird for me too, I assure you. This whole episode is weird."

They were both silent. José had never been mentioned between them since the night of Sarah's cello. But Marion knew Sarah had seen him every day at school after that and she wondered what way the girl had found to protect herself from what he knew. She sipped at her wine while she looked around. The field was filling up. A few people waved, but most seemed not to see her there up against the hedge, and joined together in high-pitched clusters. Without the wind the sun was hot. Marion pulled her poncho off over her head, clasping the wineglass between her knees.

As she emerged from the woolly tent, she looked up quickly. She had felt someone move in front of the sun while she struggled with the poncho and she felt exposed there in the dark, airless. She threw the garment down and looked up quickly into José's face.

He smiled his public, cosmetic smile at her, and Marion smiled back, turning her head slightly and moving her eyes to check on Sarah. Sarah lay there, still, her eyes closed, pretending, Marion was sure, to be asleep.

"How are you?" she asked.

"Fine, thank you. Just fine. And how have you been?"

Marion smiled. She shaded her eyes with one hand, and leaned back on the other to look up at him. She could feel the wine surging like quicksilver behind her neck and around her chest and thighs. It had made her head giddy and her body light. She smiled at him, but she wanted to laugh, to sing, to kick up her legs in celebration. It was gone. The shiver across her heart, the pulsing in her groin—gone, gone, gone. She looked at him standing there before her in presentation, his thighs and the tight swelling between them just above her eyes, and she felt nothing but the tingle from the wine. Not even curiosity. She knew it all already, and the twist of her hips as she looked up at him, the way she ran her tongue across her lips, the tilt of her chin indicated nothing more than a pro forma response in kind. She felt nothing.

"Where have you been?" he asked, folding his arms and flexing his biceps.

"Sarah and I went to Greece for three months. To the islands, actually. It was quite wonderful."

"I went to Mexico," he said, still smiling with all his teeth showing. "Also two weeks in Paris. With Marta."

"How nice. What about your son?"

"He was there too, of course, but with the grandparents. I played in Paris. A few places. And with Marta, duets. It is a wonderful place, a city of the heart."

"Mmm." Marion looked down into her wine. "José, would you like some—"

"There they are! Come on!"

Jonathan was loping across the field pulling Beth behind him. She pitched and stumbled, trying to keep up and to avoid stepping on other people's blankets. They arrived in a rush. Beth was hot from the run and out of breath. Jonathan knelt down to embrace Sarah and Beth stood by awkwardly, panting, and smiling at José.

"Hello," she said. "I'm Beth."

"José." He bowed.

"Ah! The music teacher. I've heard all about you."

"Oh? From Sarah or from her parents?"

Beth blushed. "From the whole family."

Jonathan bounced onto the blanket on the other side of Sarah. He looked slyly at her and then at Marion. But they ignored him, and, to his evident satisfaction, stared only at Beth. Marion's wine, long forgotten, had tipped over on the rug. The purple liquid first quivered on the surface and then slowly seeped through to the grass beneath.

"Surprise, eh?" Jonathan asked. He reached into Marion's basket for the wine bottle, inspected the label, and then put it back quickly.

"Hey, Bethy! Where's the wine we brought? Bring it out."

Beth squatted in front of the string back she had dumped next to her. She scrabbled in it, taking out various plastic bags and square foil packages, and then the wine. Then she busied herself putting all the packages back again.

José squatted too, so that the fabric around his thighs and zipper pulled provocatively. He was watching Marion closely, waiting for a sign. But she looked past him, at the shape of Beth's smock. The color had gone from her face, leaving only the surface tan, like finely cracked porcelain.

"Five months today," Jonathan chortled. "A January baby."

Sarah swallowed and looked down into her lap. Marion tore her eyes away and looked at Jonathan squarely.

"Perhaps this kind of surprise could have been given earlier, a little more privately," she said softly.

"That's what Bethy wanted," he said, opening his bottle. "But I insisted. After all, you've only been back a week. We could keep it under wraps that long—so to speak!"

Marion looked up at José and then smiled past him at Beth. "That wasn't quite my point, but, anyway, here's to it." She drank Jonathan's wine down in one gulp.

José had been watching her carefully, listening, observing the others. He accepted a glass of wine and toasted Beth too, looking back at Marion as he did.

Only Sarah was silent. She sat there amongst them pulling up the grass around the blanket and shredding it into her glass of juice.

"When does the fellowship start, Marion?" Beth asked.

"It started last week. They day after we got back."

"How is it?"

"Fine, so far. Dick's a pleasure to work with. And it's a wonderful contrast to the clinic."

"Hey!" Jonathan leaned in towards Marion. "I heard Ben went into practice back in Milwaukee. Jeez! That's a change."

"*I* told you that before I left," Marion said, smiling with the forbearance of a wife. She looked over quickly at José and met his eyes on the way. "I think he'd had enough of the Bay Area," she said, turning back to Jonathan. "He fits in well in Milwaukee. And I think Betty will be happier there, surrounded by all that family."

"That's more their style anyway," said Jonathan. Ben had always given him a welcome sense of his own superiority. "Never could find anything to say to him." He lay back on the rug, next to Sarah, and she shuffled over to make room.

"No, stay here, baby," he said. "Don't move. I haven't seen you for months. Here, let me get a look at you."

Sarah stiffened and blushed.

"How was Greece? Hey? Super? And what about a sister? It's a girl, you know. Surprised?"

Sarah looked around desperately for Marion, but she was chatting to Beth, with José listening.

"It's nice," Sarah said.

"Yep!" Jonathan was up, pouring out more wine. But as he reached Marion, she looked over quickly and saw at a glance the tears filling Sarah's eyes. She saw her jerk her head aside in anger, wipe her face against her shoulder, and position herself at an angle away from the group. Marion covered her glass with her hand and shook her head.

"Oh, no, thanks," she said, standing up quickly and groaning as she did so. "Actually, we have to go. We're late already for the concert."

"Concert?" asked Jonathan. "What concert?"

"At the Herbst. The Juilliard, I think, or the Amadeus. One of them." She looked at her watch. "Hell, we're late. Come on, Sarah, we'll have the sandwiches in the car."

Sarah looked up at her like a child rescued from the lost and found. She scrambled to her feet and tugged the blanket out from under the basket. She flapped the grass out of it, away from the group, and then bundled it up roughly under her arm as if she had no time to fold it. Marion quickly corked the wine she had brought and laid it back in the basket. Then she picked up the basket in her right hand and slipped her left through Sarah's. They stood for a moment, smiling good-bye at the surprised trio on the ground, and then ran off across the field together, weaving between the blankets, smiling, nodding, shouting a few good-bye's and explain-later's until they reached the gate. And then, inexplicably, they dropped the basket and the blanket and clasped each other tightly, laughing, maybe crying too, it was hard to tell at a distance, like the photographs in the paper sometimes when the troopship docks or the gates of the prison open to let out one famous prisoner. It was like that. Something to remember.

About the Author

Lynn Freed is the author of *The Mirror*, *The Bungalow*, and *Home Ground*. *Friends of the Family* (formerly *Heart Change*) was her first novel. Ms. Freed's short stories and essays have appeared in *Harper's*, *The New Yorker*, *Atlantic Monthly*, *Story*, *The New York Times*, *The Washington Post* and elsewhere. She lives in California.